short**UNIVERSE**

10 Part Anthology

joshua**RADBURN**

ʃ

Short Universe

ISBN-13: 978-1-9997349-0-9

www.authorjoshuaradburn.com
Twitter: @AuthorJDRadburn
Instagram: @theblondjosh
Facebook: AuthorJoshuaRadburn

Edition 1.1

J D Radburn
United Kingdom

ʀ

*For my wife, my never fading
light in the darkness.*

CONTENTS

PREFACE

Have fun with this. That's the most important piece of advice I can give you going into Short Universe. Let it scare you, let it shock, let your mind run as the victims of its pages would, but please, just have fun. It was the MO I went into the project with, and the best lens under which to enjoy it.

Short Universe is my seminal work, a smorgasbord of experimentation designed to quickly expose this once fledgling author to as many different techniques and styles as possible. The results were unique... Given a technical once over as recently as 2021, it still retains all the intrinsic, flavoursome lumps and bumps of this author's genesis. But of course, Short Universe is much more than that.

Quite aptly, I suppose, when I wrote this anthology, I was in a bad place. I don't want to claim depression short of self-diagnosis, but suffice it to say my family, writing, and an obsession with imagined worlds were the few anchor points holding me together. As an escape from real life, and in order to put my own hardships into perspective, it made sense to tackle the largest horror I could imagine: all of time and space. An anthology was the most refreshing and economical way to establish several stand alone yet interlocking mythologies. So, what started as an exercise to develop and keep my pen hand fresh, quickly became a numbing agent against the real world's trials.

So, have fun with this. It's the best way to keep these imagined worlds alive, no matter how spooky. Keep them fed and watered and growing, for too little stock is placed in them already.

shortUNIVERSE

THE GREAT LIBRARY: PART 1

Hearing another's footsteps when you ought to be alone isn't inherently frightening. You can take fright of course, because those footsteps might belong to a thief, a murderer, or worse. At best, they might belong to one of unsound mind, frail and confused, wandering aimlessly into your home. Whatever the alternative, you can at least be sure those footsteps belong to someone, because the world is full of someones.

When, however, you're the last living person in the entire universe, and *then* you start to hear footsteps, that is the moment true fear becomes justified. Phillos was one such person.

He reacted as most Librarians would, by ignoring that which he just knew couldn't be true, and putting those faint, far off sounds on the top shelf at the back of his mind. And that's where they should have stayed. But, if people were raindrops, Phillos was a person who fell onto the very edge of the umbrella that defined what a person was. So late on in existence, the waters of the term were long muddied. It had been generations since he had out-evolved the labours of walking, which made the unfamiliar sound of feet against stone even more troublesome. Instead, his four-armed blob of a torso trolled itself about on a levitating circular platform. It was a necessary way of living that his species had adopted long before outliving every other. As a Librarian, he would no doubt have ground the souls of his feet to the bone.

The upkeep of the Great Library at the end of the universe was Phillos' number one priority, and no ghostly imaginings were going to deter him. It housed, or so claimed, every word of every language ever written, and it did not discriminate by format either. The guardianship of such endless texts was a sacred duty, the only one Phillos knew, and he would do it until age took him, as it had all the others. The collection of tales—both fiction and non, informative and instructive, drivel and rich—was so immense that the walls of the Great Library spanned half of the planet on which it was based, and its spires rose so high that once a year the tallest peaks scarred the surface of the planet's orbiting moon. It was a jade palace like no other, and even though the universe was at its end, ripped apart by war long ago, the Library remained glistening and untouched, held together by a series of continent sized shield generators and, of course, Phillos.

Phillos had floated about the construct alone for fifty years, fulfilling his administrative duties like clockwork despite no one benefiting from them. The stepping sounds that had appeared in recent weeks had certainly dirtied his gears, and they clunked along a little more strained than usual, but still he continued. How could he stop to investigate such things when it often took years to file just one book? Filing and recording the backlog of books stored in the Library's *In Tray*, a mountain of literature located in the Great Library's Southern Hemisphere, was not a task in which to dawdle. The teleportation system had died long ago, as had anyone with the knowledge to fix it. He could not let himself be distracted, he could not follow the inner aches within himself that longed for company, especially if they weren't real.

The Librarians had never been much for talking, or emoting, anyway. They were altogether seen as dull, even to themselves, so why the one behind those imagined steps would want to spend time with Phillos seemed beyond him. In their world duty was duty, and the written word of the universe the only cross worth bearing. Unlike his ancestors, however, Phillos had been doing a lot of thinking lately, a lot of worrying, and considering. These were dangerous actions, but a solitary existence often changes a person. He had developed subtle nuances compared to his stock ancestors. They could be found in the way he hummed along to the whirr of his transport, how he made explosive noises with his tongue whenever he successfully placed a book on the shelf, and how his underdeveloped feet dangled and danced above the cold, sparkling Library floor. It was an act that made you believe Phillos was actually enjoying himself, that he was in love with the books and his loneliness.

But the dancing stopped and his toes curled on the day he first heard those shadowy steps. Not as a distant tapping or dream-like vision as before, but something all too real to just tuck away on the same shelf as his earlier experiences. It was a cold day, even for a planet that sat in the light of a dying star, and he had just slipped a particularly difficult to place book into the section for "*Those Books That Bear More Genres Than Sense*", a section that was becoming increasingly full.

Once the rumble of his tongue had passed his teeth, he heard a sudden sprinting that turned a harsh corner to his right. Down the long corridor, glowing with a mismatch of download ports and audio cassettes, a blurry shadow flitted out of view. The steps faded with it.

Phillos shook his head and rubbed his beady eyes with his two front arms. The pair of arms growing from his back continued shuffling a folder of archaic papers as the rest of his body seized up.

He decided he must have been hearing things. This was a very old library after all. One of the arms protruding from his back craned awkwardly from behind his neck and wiped the sweat from his single brow. After gulping back into normality, he laughed at himself.

'Fool,' he said aloud. 'Don't start hearing things now. Only two-hundred and ninety-seven years until retirement, you can start hearing things then.'

Occasionally, he would have to talk to himself if only to hear a sound he hadn't heard in months. The rest of his day went as usual, if not slightly shakily. He spent it stamping any unstamped book covers stored by his more laid back predecessors, as he glided towards the next filing destination. It would take several days to reach the *"Tribal Government Records"* section, which was located in the next continent over. It was a relatively short distance for Phillos to travel but still afforded him enough time to collate a collection of ancient documents correctly before storing them. It also allowed him space of mind to concoct a lie that would discredit that running sound.

He was sure that by the time he reached that part of the Library that whatever dysfunctional pipes had caused those odd noises would be long behind him. As sure as sure could be. Except he wasn't so sure. As he shut down his hovercraft and readied his neatly packed pyjama shirt for a most uneventful night, he realised those footsteps had followed him.

It was all too apparent without the hum of his transport to drown it out, the slapping of skin on smooth stone floor. It ebbed in and out of hearing as Phillos tried to imagine what it could be. It couldn't be a person. It just couldn't.

All the textbooks were clear on the unfortunate events that brought about the apocalypse: Desperate acts of germ warfare, domino-like waves of exploding black holes, and the Tainted Atom Virus. They were not tragedies that mortals had a propensity for surviving. Unless the one playing hide and seek in the Library wasn't a mortal? *No,* Phillos thought. It didn't matter what you were, or how efficient your shelter, that final virus grew faster than existence could flee. Everything fell, except for the Librarians. Phillos' father had once joked—his only joke—that they had evolved beyond sickness. Instead, it was an obsession with work, and a comparable lack of interest in the opposite sex that had put an end to them.

Some called them more machine than people, or would have done had they been alive to say it, but machines didn't fear that which they knew couldn't be possible. That kind of irrationality was reserved for the living. And Phillos apparently.

In that moment, as shadows hopped in and out of his peripheral, Phillos ran through a series of terrifying circumstances that didn't make sense.

Below, above, to his left and right, behind but never in front. The gaping halls, receptions and stairways, which spanned like webs for thousands of miles, played host to the echoes. Phillos' imagination ran away with him. What if the Librarians weren't the only beings to survive the Tainted Atom Virus? The universe, although mostly destroyed, was still very large, and the Library at times felt larger. Could a creature have hidden away in its endless recesses? And if it hadn't, what was making those noises?

'No. Impossible,' Phillos said to himself. 'I'm the only designated member of faculty left, and the Library is closed.'

He dialled a small panel on the chassis of his hovercraft. It detailed the number of organisms within the Library: One. Phillos gasped as his stringy hair kicked up by way of a passing wind. He spun on his transport and nearly toppled out. Still nothing.

'He-hello?'

It had been over fifty years since he had said that word, and he hoped it would remain unanswered even longer. Then, after the stepping faded, a creaky voice replied.

'Hello.'

It was not a word as you may have expected it. It hung low in the air, more of a groan than actual speech, although Phillos' mind construed it that way. It was far away, which didn't set him at ease, and invisible, with no clear origin. And that's where the apparition ended.

His eyelids remained pinned to his forehead and cheeks, respectively, until daylight petered through the Library's open ceiling canopies hours later and caused them to flutter. His breathing had slowed so dramatically that he feared he may have slipped into a coma. All night he fixated on nothing, expecting it to move. A blur, a shadow, once just background shapes, now alive with potential ghouls. He was slow to return to the fold, but the day gave him new perspective. There was no time in his line of work to dwell on nightmares.

'That's all that was, surely,' Phillos said, into a rare empty shelf with a single odd book poking over its edge without a stamp.

He didn't know why he was down this particular corridor. The lack of sleep was no doubt to blame. Empty bookshelves were uncommon but not unheard of. He took the small book, withered, water stained, and blue, and stamped the spine. He then placed it into a satchel hanging from his transport, ready for replacement. He made a mental note to make a written note that when his mission was done he should do something about it.

His hovercraft teetered to the left as he continued the journey, the tiny blue book somehow enough to weigh down the technical advances of its thrusters. By most standards, this would have been alarming, but for Phillos the discomfort of constantly looking over his shoulder kept him distracted. Even he, a being of back-breakingly laborious work and literary guardianship, couldn't shake the previous night. With the day drawing to an end once more, he knew he wouldn't be able to sleep when it finally did.

It had been so long since he had to fear anything that he wasn't entirely convinced he was feeling the right emotions, the knot in his stomach more strangulating than he imagined fear being. It choked him over the next week as the days passed without another sound. Every time he attempted to sort through his files, they muddled themselves and tore at the edges, as though a veiled hand was ruffling his own. The dates and words on the pages had become blurred and jumbled into phrases he couldn't read. He lost his way through the Library more than once.

Hearing the evidence of another in his glistening fortress of solitude was no longer necessary, the prints of those feet had already left their mark, and that ghostly call through the dark echoed in his memory. *Hello.* He knew it couldn't have been real, but that didn't stop him waiting for it to surface again. Then, something worse did.

As Phillos made his way over a tall iron bridge that hung over a slow flow of green water, he saw a person standing at the other side. Or what he presumed was a person. Whatever it was kept low and in the dark, hidden in shade that hadn't been cast. It had a head like kneaded dough but wrought from metal and was breathing heavily. Phillos halted. He couldn't make out any of the creature's details aside from small scratches cut into its soft, meteorite-shaded skin. It was a human, albeit misshapen, but Phillos was shaking too much to focus and define beyond that. Someone really had spoken to him that other night, and he was looking right at them.

Humans had gone extinct aeons ago, but Phillos had seen them on the covers of books many times, their literature more invasive and numerous than any other. Was this a ghost, released by the books of its people? Occult sections were plentiful in the Great Library.

As it stood there panting silently, uncomfortable in its own skin, Phillos tried to gain control of his own breathing. He succumbed quickly to the fact that his whimpers could not be ironed out, and so the Librarian gulped and reverted back to the ways of *his* people.

'Excuse me. Th-There's no running or t-talking allowed in the Great Library.'

The figure didn't move.

'Did you hear wh-what I said?'

Its neck snapped. Phillos jumped. Another crack echoed behind him and he wheeled around. There was nothing. He whipped back to the dough-headed human. It was gone.

Phillos hovered on the bridge, unsure which way to run. The end of it looked darker than before, but to return would mean a wasted eight-month trip. The small analogue stick that propelled him slipped in his clammy palm. He couldn't commit one way or the other until a groan rumbled behind him. Suddenly his mind was made up.

Phillos shot forwards, at a blisteringly frustrating ten miles per hour, as the hollering followed. It chased him through the hallways, reverberating off the walls as he picked up speed. He decided then and there that he would simply place the documents on the shelf and immediately return to reception. No sense hanging around. Once he was back safe, he could launch a proper investigation as to what in the universe's supposed eighteen different hells was going on.

He charged on, for hours, humming a tune he had never heard in an attempt to blot out the groaning. To his left and right, at the end of corridors and in the corners of darkened rooms, the broken shape of the metallic, dough-headed man crept. Phillos refused to look directly. He had the documents ready in his front hands, as unmixed-up as possible, and prepared for their drive-by filing. He wasn't even going to stamp them.

His two back hands held each other, wagging in the air as his hovercraft fired on all cylinders.

He was in the *"Tribal Government Records" section* now, finally, and even though he doubted his own reasoning, he felt that when he placed the documents on the shelf his visions of the human would stop.

Phillos saw the shelf and a space between two heavily bound folders. This was it. He slam dunked the papers between them and breathed a sigh of relief. The groans ceased. Was this it? Was placing those tribal documents the key to regaining his sanity?

The steps returned.

So taken was Phillos by the sound that he re-entered that coma-like trance, he couldn't turn from the shelf. He would have preferred that existence, to face the wall and remain blind to the coming horror, but the gold fastenings of the binding folders yielded the distorted reflection of the metal human.

It was moving towards him, and the closer it got, the more rooted Phillos became. He wanted to scream but couldn't find the breath, so fit to burst with pent up cries that his eyes leaked. In the golden clips he watched as the human extended a hand, bulging in their reflection. Phillos felt its cold touch before it had even landed, and let out the faintest squeak before he realised it actually hadn't landed at all. Phillos didn't understand. He could see the human, it was very much real and so close they could be one person. And yet, apparently, it wasn't him the human wanted. He felt something slip out of the pack attached to his hovercraft and then, rather than disappear as it had before, the human doddered away.

When he felt brave enough, about six minutes later, Phillos pivoted. He was all but ready to seize up again as he saw the human waiting for him. Then it gave the Librarian a beckoning nod as it rounded a corner.

Why Phillos would give a ghost, or worse, the time of day was beyond him. And yet, without truly knowing why, he did. The icy grip on his soul that kept him locked in place had melted. After seeing what the human had stolen from his pack, he knew there would be no question. That old blue book, unstamped and weeks-forgotten, was nestled in the human's palm. Phillos deduced that a deep-seated instinct to put every book in its place had something to do with this sudden bout of bravery. Perhaps he had inherited the previously untapped adventurous nature of his parents. He was being communicated with for the first time in half a century after all, with someone who didn't look exactly like him. Even he had to admit, heart palpitations aside, this had been an interesting chain of events thus far.

Then there was another odd feeling, the unfamiliar twang of hope. Some instinctual yearning that convinced him maybe this wasn't the end of life as the universe knew it. It was a thought that had never occurred to him before. They headed to the underground levels of the Library together.

Phillos found himself in further unfamiliar territory. The smell of damp filled the air, the halls so unwalked for so long they were collapsing from disuse. There wasn't a single digital port for the downloading of stories to be seen. Instead, an assortment of physical books so numerous that they gathered in mounds on the floor beside shelves stuffed to the brim.

The architecture of the Great Library was different too. In a matter of hours, it had devolved from crystal green into something more akin to ancient white marble, veined with jade tinted gold. Broken pillars bore the overflowing shelves that bent beneath the weight of their books. One wrong vibration and the entire foundation could collapse.

Phillos couldn't begin to imagine how he would sort this mess, and why the section had been allowed to descend into such deuniformity in the first place. As he silently snarled over the dust caked environment, the human looked upon it in wonderment. Every now and then it would pluck another small book from the Library's collection and stuff it under its arm, holding them so tightly and so close that its coarse skin stained the covers.

These books were old, some far older than others, and it was a wonder how the inks on their pages were still legible. In fact, all of the books in that bizarre section wore the same scars. Weathered, loose in their binds, and no doubt once handled by the famous brutes of the universe. Phillos, if very rarely, had seen these kinds of books before. The dust coating them was thick with the powder of guns that did little to hide the red stains that would never wash out. He knew exactly what he would name the section if he ever got back to reception: *The Stories the Universe Would Rather Forget*. Most were stamped with a giant red *"CLASSIFIED"* symbol. For a Librarian, this was very much like wandering into the wrong part of town. Like a rebellious teen after that first exhilarating taste of anarchy, Phillos was eager to keep pace with the human. He would have blushed from embarrassment were there anyone left alive to see him.

The pair eventually turned into a room together, one the size you might attribute to a local library rather than a planet sized one. It had not aged well.

The once glamorous fittings and fixtures were hardly apparent through the decay. A flickering lamp sat on a small, lonely reading table, revealed the occasional golden detailing lost to time.

Despite the overwhelming number of books, emptiness filled the air, and the room felt dead. A dizziness overcame Phillos as he spun slowly on the spot, looking up, unable to believe the state of it, unable to fathom the endless pain emanating from the walls. He wanted answers, but the human had disappeared.

In its stead were the books it had plucked along their journey, laid neatly in a row from left to right beneath the table lamp. Phillos approached the table, checking nervously this way and that, and then slotted his craft and belly beneath its top. He thumbed the table edge.

All this time spent with books, he had never found the time to actually read any. Faced with nine of the ugliest covers he had ever seen, he was unsure which to pick—he knew he had to pick. All of them were dark and scribbled on, and most written in languages he couldn't read. And yet he saw the words clearly and understood what they said. The Great Library's *In Tray* slipped his mind entirely. Fate had offered him a new role.

Before he knew it, that first small book, blue and damaged, sat snug in his palm. He read the title allowed.

'Stupid.'

STUPID

R *aining? In space?*
'Stupid,' said Samson, an overly pimpled teenager with long and tangled hair, probably light coloured but too greasy to tell. Of course, everything appeared stupid behind the veil of adolescent-tinted glasses.

He was staring into the vast expanse of the universe through a barred window, rain pattering against the glass. There was little that boys his age didn't find stupid, especially ones forced from their homes and sent to trudge across a foreign galaxy. The other half-a-million people crammed into that feeble excuse for a *luxury* shuttle didn't help either.

'Shut up, Samson,' came a firm response from his mother, her exterior as grey as the tiny room they shared. 'Stupid this. Stupid that. It's a wonder you don't think breathing is stupid and just give up altogether!'

Samson didn't turn away from the window. 'It is stupid though.'

'Nonsense, we get to see the stars!'

His mother's attempts at brightening the mood fell on deaf ears, the blackness outside their window more than enough to dampen her light. She had been hanging the washing all morning; Samson hated it when she hung out the washing. As if it wasn't wet and cold enough in the squalid, ten-by-ten metal box they called home. Adding the stench of rags washed in stagnant water

15

was hardly helping his mood. 'I've seen the stars. And it's not the stars that are stupid either, stupid.'

Samson's mother bit her tongue as she had grown so accustomed to doing. Somebody had to be positive. Not another soul on the giant shuttle, all packed tightly into their colourless, mouldy boxes, had smiled since they set foot upon it. The Gov was just asking for trouble.

Thankfully, so far, the mother-son duo had avoided bunking with other unlucky refugees as so many had already been forced. Pulling rusty chips off the bars however, Samson saw little difference between the Hope-14 and the slum beneath a slum from which they were fleeing.

Even outside the cruiser's walls, the beauty of the universe became an inescapable irritant. The bright purples and blues of a far off galaxy, which were reflected in rainbows upon the glass that morning, just served to send Samson into an inward frenzy of glumness. Having to shift about on a soggy, bug ridden bed below his window was just the out-of-date icing on an already stale cake. Outside's serenity taunted him.

His face jiggled against one of the vibrating bars that covered the window. Too damn depressed to heave his head off of it, he let the hum of the ship's engine madden him further. There was little else to do. That morning, the melting pot that was Samson's head boiled all of these thoughts together without reprieve. His mother had told him that such stewings were not good for him, but Samson was certain that the resulting meal would be the most nutritious he had eaten in weeks.

Samson wanted off the Hope-14 the second they next docked, no matter what part of the war was taking place there, or what atrocities the Gov was committing. If he had to go down to that dining hall just once more, to break bread with those hideous aliens, or smile pleasantly at the Wolves...

The Wolves.

'Dickheads,' Samson growled as they slipped into his thoughts.

Everyone turned a blind eye to their sordid exploits. The thousands of refugees held up in the Hope-14 might have been drifting through space, but sound travelled easily through the metallic labyrinth. The many vents protruding into Samson's room, which caked the corners of his dwelling in a thick unknown muck, hid little of what happened behind closed, or even open, doors. It was no wonder why so many souls broke against the shrill cries of night. Even those untouched by the Wolves developed nervous ticks, and Samson could feel himself tapping the sides of his legs with his fingers that very moment. It happened whenever he imagined his mother or himself in danger, which was far too often. He justified those ticks as a necessary evil, deciding that those random shakes were just his body's way of keeping him on edge, keeping his eyes keen, keeping him safe.

'Who the fuck did that!?' Samson launched at his mother. It was difficult not to notice the bruise below her right eye and the others below her ripped and tattered shirt. The shirt had always been tattered, but the shoe prints were new.

'Oh, it's nothing,' she replied, although her voice broke through the last syllable.

'Nothing!?'

'I'm alright, just a little run-in on the way back from the wash chambers. They were fine though.'

'There's no such thing as a little run-in with those fuckers, Mum! Fine? What did they do?' Samson was up off his manky bed, flakes of skin bustling into the air—not his, they probably belonged to the previous occupant.

'I said nothing, Samson.'

She was still putting out the clothes as routinely as ever. Samson couldn't bear the mundanity of it. 'No, fuck that!'

'Must you swear like that?'

'Well, yes, my Mum's been beaten up! Or worse!'

'I'm surprised you care...'

'Surprised I... Oh, I'll show you how much I care!'

Samson grabbed a rusted pipe that had been hanging loosely from the wall. He had been planning on how to use it for weeks. Tearing it free, he knocked a stack of his mother's books onto the ground, knowing full well where he wanted to thrust it.

'Now look what you've done!' she huffed, like it actually mattered. Samson shoved past her towards the door. 'Samson, no!'

He planted his foot against the door frame and then heaved the rusted wheel handle towards himself. He poked his head into the biting cold hallway. Empty, save for his breath. One of the first things to break on the Hope-14 were its lights, most of which now hung limply from chewed wires. It meant seeing any further than halfway down the walkway was impossible. From there on out half a minute's worth of travel was shrouded in a stomach sinking blackness.

Samson didn't know whether it was the Wolves, the bugs, or the mutated rats that had cut those lights, but it was without a doubt those rabid gangsters who benefited most. The thought of catching one of their sickening grins in the darkness steadied his enthusiasm for a moment. But it was just a moment.

'Fuck it,' he said, taking a step out onto the grated floor.

Not that he had much chance of surviving, but to be honest, a quick, bloody, and quite violent death was more enticing in that moment than the slower option of being cooped up and gnawed out of existence over a period of months by the insects living in his bed sheets.

'Please, Samson,' his mother said, finally taking the situation seriously.

Samson leant against the door opposite, across the narrow corridor. He stared back into their pit and his mother's terrified face. He was ready to tear each one of those Wolves a new one, but deep down, as all of us do, he didn't really feel like dying today. He didn't fancy being beaten to a pulp, nor the rape that would follow. But he sure as hell didn't want to go back into that room either. He blew the hair out of his face, his heart beating so hard through his back it was knocking on the door behind him. To his mother's relief, he dropped the pipe. It clanged and rolled away into the pitch black end of the corridor. His mother's eyes were overflowing, but she kept her cries damned with an impossibly strong, matriarchal smile.

'Thank you,' she said. 'I'm sorry.'

Samson didn't say anything as he made his ghost-like return, readying himself for another torturous day of staring out of the window. The rain brewing outside had grown stronger. A nauseating cliché if ever there was one.

'Uh oh, what do we have here?' A voice from the sightless part of the hallway caught Samson and held him in the corridor. He knew that condescending, hateful tone all too well. It belonged to a Wolf.

That smile Samson had envisioned running into belonged to one in particular who went by the name of Jarr. A stupid name, for a stupid person, but you would be the stupidest of all if you said that out loud. Samson stood firm and unwavering outside the open door to his home, but inside he was as structurally sound as shattered glass.

Jarr leaned out of the darkness, goofy teeth first, holding the pipe Samson had dropped a moment ago. He rattled it against the other misshapen pipes and vents that lined the corridor walls, playing a broken tune upon them as he strutted whimsically forwards.

He was a thin, long limbed cross-dresser, draped in a cluttered mismatch of dresses and cardigans, their previous owners no doubt victims of the sick society of carnivores he had grown to become the leader of. Thin chains dangled between piercings in his face and other parts of the body Samson shuddered to think about. Jarr twirled as he approached, his spotty dress billowing gleefully from under a striped, tight fitting miniskirt.

Samson wanted to punch him square in the jaw mid-twist but his mother had a hold of his hand, beckoning him inside. The Wolf stopped an inch from the teenager's face, having to bend his neck ninety degrees as he towered over him. His breath stank awfully, his mouth somehow filled with as much grime as his exterior. Samson grimaced. Jarr smiled. 'What's the matter? Don't like the way your mum smells?'

Samson took a deep breath and closed his eyes. He was shaking with anger. His mother screamed at him through trembling palms not to try anything.

'Oops! Sorry, missus. Didn't see you there.' Jarr bent over and put his head into their room, wrapping his knuckles on the door three times. He was probably scanning it for any valuables. 'You should come away with me,' he said, 'don't you think? Not a very nice place for a lady, ay? I know you'd have fun, even more than earlier.'

Samson looked past him and saw the crooked grins of other Wolves lurking in the shadows. Dogs were pack hunters, and their presence meant any chance of getting a cheap shot in on Jarr without having to answer to his cronies was doomed to fail.

'Fuck off,' Samson said, unable to control himself. Any hope of survival flitted through the bars of his window on the back of those two words.

'Fuck off? That's a bit rude isn't it, missus?' Jarr laughed, looking back at Samson's mother. 'Very fucking rude!' His nasally, coarse voice echoed through the Hope-14 as every orifice of Samson's body snapped tight. 'Very rude indeed. Why would you say such a hurtful thing?'

Samson fell silent again. He prayed for the heroic arrival of an on the level Hope-14 guard. *Yeah, right,* he thought.

'Seems to have lost his speech,' Jarr said, bending over so they saw eye-to-eye. Samson refused to catch his gaze and turned to his mother instead. 'After what me and your Mum went through we're practically family. This is no way to treat family, is it? We're not that bad. Here come, come. Let's meet your cousins.'

He grabbed Samson by his greasy hair and pulled him away from his bawling mother who dropped to her knees after a brief, limp tug of war.

'Help!' she screamed.

'Heeelp!' Jarr mocked her as he dragged her son away. 'A bit louder, love. I don't think the Gods can hear you.'

Samson tried grabbing at the Wolf's hands, fearing for his scalp should he be wrangled any more violently. That should have been the least of his worries as he approached those hands lurching out of the darkness, their owners squawking like hungry baby birds promised a scrawny worm by their mother.

'Help!' Samson's mother screamed again.

But help wouldn't come. In fact, help was just meters away in the form of a Hope-14 guard, who slobbered just as eagerly as the other Wolves at the front of Jarr's pack. Samson's eyes bulged, begging the man in the uniform to help. Nothing. *Fine then!* Samson spat at the guard who barked back furiously. Jarr continued to laugh and gripped Samson's hair even tighter. Samson felt his neck cramping. The whiplash was unbearable, he had to do something. If this was going to be his end, be damned if he wasn't going to be beaten and humiliated without a fight. He swung his arm out blindly... Bulls-eye!

Jarr dropped against the wall, gasping for breath, his hands flinging groin-ward. Samson ripped himself away and ran back to the safety of his mother and their room. His neck was numb, and his shoulder wasn't in particularly good shape either, but Jarr's high pitched squeal had put an extra hop into his step. He didn't even care if he got caught because, judging by how he felt Jarr's genitals turn to mush against his fist, he knew for certain that monster's favourite pastime was history.

'Get him!' Jarr squeaked.

The other Wolves revealed themselves in the same sickening garb as their twisted leader. All of them were notably shorter, and their dresses more scruffy and torn, if that were even possible. Not that Samson took the time to look back. He was heading straight for his mother and the promise of a few minutes sanctuary before the Wolves broke down their door.

He held out a hand, expecting his mother to do the same. She did not. She wasn't even looking in his direction. Instead, her puffed eyes were fixated on something in their room.

'Mum?' he called.

No answer.

Suddenly, a monumental sound rocked the entirety of the Hope-14, sending Samson and his pursuers cascading into the ice cold walls of the corridor. The ring that followed was ear piercing, a soul shuddering pitch of bending metal.

Whipping about, doll-like, Samson's head crashed against the wet steel. A layer of condensation drenched him and his vision blurred as his body flopped onto the floor. The bright lights above buzzed on and off. He shook his face, desperately searching out his senses. The Wolves were gawping blankly in every direction.

'What was tha'?' said one.

'It came from outside space!' droned another.

22

Sound? In space? 'Stupid,' Samson said.

'I'll show you stupid!'

Jarr was clambering over his confused underlings towards Samson, ignorant of the cataclysmic event that had just taken place. Thankfully, the teenager had already picked himself up and spun around the doorway into his room. His mother was there, shaken but unharmed, stood statue-still beside her tipped clothes horse. Finally, Samson saw what she had seen.

The rain had stopped outside their window. The stars were still shining, but from the blackness, pointy nightmares of metal and wiggling organs slithered from hyperspace. They were thin vessels, long, their wings spindly. Samson had never seen anything like it. They were a thousand times smaller than the Hope-14 but made up for it in number.

We're under attack, Samson thought. Another loud, unnatural shriek boomed again. The force sent Samson and his mother sailing from their room into the neighbour's door across the hallway. The twang of the impact was so deafening that Samson whited out, if only for a moment. After a firm shaking from his mother, he awoke to a red pulsating tunnel of despair. Two of the Wolves head's had caved in, and yet the torrents of blood pouring from their skulls were nothing compared to the deep hellish flashes produced by the emergency evacuation lights. Shaking away his dizziness, Samson heard the screams of other families and travellers, the opening of doors, and frantic running. The corridors were alive with the scruffiest and most desperate people in the universe fleeing in any direction that wasn't their current position.

The intergalactic collection of men and women who occupied the Hope-14 trampled over the Wolves, and each other, hollering in one succinct language: fear. The villainous hierarchy that had been established meant nothing in the wake of whatever was happening outside. Samson had to know. He hadn't seen where that high pitched noise had come from, and those pod-like ships attacking the Hope-14 didn't look to be carrying weaponry. Although, in this war lusting universe, who knew what kind of deadly tricks some races carried up their sleeves. If a combination of those two events was going to kill him, he wanted to know exactly why.

He limped his way back into his room. One of the brown ships whizzed past the window, its engine whirring and kicking out smog. He ducked. Once he was sure it wasn't coming back, Samson hopped onto his bed and grabbed the bars. It was manic out there.

'Samson, we should go!' his mother called from the corridor. She was watching Jarr, who was beginning to stir. The Wolf didn't care about the madness, his bloodshot eyes were fixed on her.

'And go where? Stupid.'

Samson whispered that last insult under his breath. His mother had probably been through enough that day. He squinted, trying to make sense of the carnage. Both the alien crafts and the shiny, Gov issued Hope-14 defence drones spun about each other, unsure of what to do with themselves. There was little rhyme or reason to any of it. The drones were attacking the puss-drenched ships, but the invaders themselves weren't fighting back, they just darted about insanely. Samson's mother grabbed his shirt, 'Please, we should go!'

'A moment!' Samson squinted harder. Then he saw it. The very wall of the universe moved.

Samson stopped breathing, his brain deeming it pointless. It had laid witness to a leviathan of the stars, a body blacker than dead space, and larger than the very planet he hailed from. He couldn't tell what kind of beast it was, its impossible scale invisible against the infinity it inhabited. It was only as the star-like photophores lining its limbs moved could Samson make any sense of what he was seeing.

Behind the creature's slow-opening jaws it revealed a luminescent green tongue, alone and gigantic. Then erupted the sound that had rocked the Hope-14 two times prior, a scream imbued with slobber. The horrid, metallic noise charged as a wave towards the ship.

Samson grabbed his mother and the two held onto the barred window. When the wave hit, their shoulders almost ripped free from their sockets. Alarms rang out, loud and constant. Freezing water burst and sprayed from the vents in their room as a licking fire sprouted out of nowhere. The wailing from the bowels of the Hope-14 grew ever more perilous. But Samson and his mother were still fixated on the monster. Suddenly the flight paths of the foreign ships became clear; they were fleeing this creature, poorly, without thought to their movements.

'They're just pissing it off!' Samson shouted, his eyes widening as he saw the outline of a gigantic tail swing towards their part of the ship. 'Okay, now we go.' He grabbed his mother by the hand and they ran into the corridor, now bent and twisted in the wake of the sky monster's cry.

He could hear the tail moving, but how? *There's no sound in space!* Samson discarded the thought; the mysteries of the universe would have to wait.

Jarr was still crawling along the ground, digging his fingers into the floor grates. Despite the number of people who had stampeded over him, he made to grab Samson's leg. What he found instead was a firm, nose-breaking boot to the face. Samson felt like cheering as he hurdled the Wolf but there was no time; the swinging tail he had seen from his window had just hit its mark.

The hallway folded into itself. The walls ripped and splurged unconstrained towards him and his mother. For a moment the alarm bells stopped and Samson's mind shut down. His mother's cries felt a million miles away. It was over. Exploding steel ricocheted behind and in front, above and below, and the dead-eyed response to his demise was met with a tight embrace from the woman who had brought him into this world. The tears of that woman stained his cheek as they prepared to leave it together.

Death was painful, more so than Samson expected. He and his mother were consumed by catastrophe and their tight grips of each other did nothing to stop their separation. Now alone, the heat, the pressure, the pain, their extents were indescribable. Samson's next few seconds were a vicious blur, a blind pummelling that came in the form of large rods and sheets of melted steel. He couldn't see, his eyes forced shut by hot, buffeting gusts, and the picture painted by every strike and burn was a frenzy of whirls in his mind. Disorientation didn't cover it. One moment he was being scorched by flame, battered by severed limbs, and drenched in blood, the next, as he finally gained the courage to pry his eyes open, he found the universe spinning as he spiralled through a tube of destruction. He didn't know where his mother was but he reached out for her regardless, hoping against hope his fingers might take a hold of those grey rags.

He couldn't think. Oxygen wouldn't pass his lips, let alone reach his brain. There was no air, which meant he was in the merciless embrace of space. His chest expanded until a large thump from behind his rib cage forced out a final breath. His lungs were empty, his sternum lob sided. As he writhed like a crushed insect he saw the broken extremities of the Hope-14 floating, sparking, exploding. He instinctively focussed on those shapes, anything to keep his mind busy.

His current trajectory had him coursing straight through the centre of a huge fissure struck through the ship's middle, the result of that galaxy-sized monster's tail whip. He was burning, the hottest he had ever felt, so much so he began clawing at his own skin to remove his flesh. It was like being stuck in some reverse microwave. How long before his skin fizzled away to reveal his freezing innards? How soon would it be before a rogue Gov drone ran him through, or he was caught and torn in two by a haggard piece of debris? This was worse than death. His time on the Hope-14 had been the most deplorable month of his life, but popping intestines first from the inside out seemed a suffering more brutal than any fate its confines would have offered.

Soon enough, he was caught in a trail of his own vomit and the Hope-14, running wild with sparks, began to fade from Samson's reality. His head was light. Dizziness crept over him. Alone, eyes streaming, he was gliding harrowingly close to a wrecked girder that poked menacingly from the edge of the Hope-14's gaping wound, the final bastion before he would be lost to the infinity of space. Samson prayed for unconsciousness, but the pain was still so real. He had a few seconds left before he slipped into his final sleep, and judging by the claw-like mutation of the girder, those last few seconds promised to be quite uncomfortable. He flailed about and hated himself for acting so undignified in his last moments.

Those useless, reaching instincts didn't save him. Instead, his saviour came in the form of an escape pod that had launched from the innards of the Hope-14. As the stout tube rumbled past him, Samson was buffeted by its shell. The sour, terrified faces within recoiled as Samson's ghostly limbs pummelled the windows.

Although broken-ribbed, at least he was no longer headed at that girder. Caught in the pod's jet stream, half of his face sizzling off in the process, Samson was sent tumbling back towards the Hope-14. By some absurd luck, the trail of flame propelled him straight into the escape hatch the pod had just jettisoned from.

Samson was, of course, too busy dealing with the traumatic event of his face bubbling down to the bone to be appreciative. Narrowly avoiding other protruding parts of the wreckage, he slipped back into the cruiser. Those nauseating lights, which once highlighted its dingy halls, had become beacons of safety. The hatch snapped shut, air pressure returned, and the ship's gravity kicked in. Samson gasped hard after slapping the cold white floor. His liquidised skin glued his face to the surface. The hangar was circular and too short in diameter to stand straight in, it was barely big enough for that one escape pod. At either end was a door; one a fully windowed hatch that peered back into space, the other solid steel that led into the ship. It was probably the cleanest part of the entire vessel, sparkling in fact.

But this was no time to rejoice. In this panicked state, his mind regressed to that of a young child. He wailed out, clutching at his deformed cheeks and puke stained clothes, sipping maniacally for the breaths that, for what felt like an age, had been absent to him. Half a minute was all it took; the fear, the pain, the sorrow, the hell spawned barrage of emotions had thrown him into a mental breakdown. Clasped in the foetal position, all he could do was bawl. He shook uncontrollably, his insides cold, his outsides seething. Samson screamed in agony but his body retracted into a shell of still sorrow.

His breaths were hurried, every inhale pressed his splintered ribs against the organs they used to keep safe. With eyes wide he played the events of the past minute affront them, he and his mother's separation taking precedence over most of the memory. That final slip, as her hand left his, still tingled his palm. She was dead, had to be dead. Samson was struck by more than one severed limb before he fell into the nightmare of space, one must have been hers.

'Stupid,' he whined into the quiet of the hangar.

He didn't even know what he thought was *stupid*, only that if he ever felt hard done by that word came bobbing to the surface of his lips. Had he not previously in life claimed suicide as a stupid thing to do, he would have been searching for a button to expel himself from the pod hangar and back into space for good.

Even as he calmed, the bold contemplations of death apparently enough to pry him from his shrieking, he couldn't move. He would never move again. How could he? Why would he? What was the point? There was nowhere to go now. He doubted the strength he had left would be enough to open the door leading back into the Hope-14. He was stuck in the hangar's blissful whiteness until the air ran dry.

Even if he could get out, the thought of running into another species other than human made him shudder. They all stunk something awful and looked horrid, every single one of them. Plus, they were stupid. Samson fancied his chances finding more relatable companionship with the bugs he used to share his bed with. No doubt that bed had been blown to oblivion by now. At least the one thing this new tubed room appeared good for was keeping the destruction firmly locked out. The fires licking at the frames of the hatch window were hypnotic. Samson could feel vibrations through the floor, loud and strong, deep and booming, and he was rocked dreamily by them in his safe cocoon. He could have gotten used to that.

Peeling his face from the floor with grim determination, he leant against the door leading into the Hope-14. There he sat for a moment clearing his head, and although he was finally able to quieten himself the tears never truly stopped. He hadn't heard those titanic screams of the monster outside his window since it battered the side of the ship, nor could he see it through the window opposite. Although, if it was close, it would have blanketed the view of space entirely anyway.

Staring out at the expanse, the boy felt a cold serenity within his apparent tomb. His sorrow was maxed to the point where it had levelled out entirely. His mother was dead, and it wouldn't be long until he joined her, the rumblings around him a clear sign. It was impossible to truly process.

Once all of those morbid thoughts had made it through his mind, for some reason it was the rain that irked him the most. No matter how terrible a situation, rain always made it worse. Beyond all explanation, its cruelty had followed Samson all the way into dead space. The injustice of it drenched his soul in grey defeat.

The universe was so huge, it stretched so far, that any combination of any event was plausible. As a boy, Samson had heard stories of parallel worlds, but staring out at the rain that morning he knew that no such places existed, for the universe was so large it had more than enough room for them all anyway. If there were planets made entirely out of diamond, creatures born of all shapes, and rogue celestial bodies coursing through the skies ready to pluck entire races out of existence, then it probably made sense that somewhere within the great limitless expanse it was raining. He never had a chance of making it out of that randomness unscathed.

The sight of that rain was preceded by the view of a mighty beast, probably one of a kind. A war, unparalleled throughout history, had stretched and torn its way through every galaxy, and Samson knew for a fact that not one single side of virtue or selfish desire could stand against such a creature, no matter what immense firepower they carried. In a way, Samson felt a little proud to have survived this long. He had faced impossible odds and was still breathing; an obliterated spaceship, the torturous extremes of space, even a collision with an escape pod. Samson could have done without the melted facial features and broken ribs, but that didn't stop him feeling lucky all the same. If there was such a place as heaven, he would have one hell of a story to tell when he got there, or, 'Maybe this'll all just blow over,' he joked with himself out loud, certain that if he didn't find the time to laugh he would just be crying.

The white lights of the next life were mirrored by those within the tiny hangar, but as Samson lay still—in what he thought would be his final moments—a dark red hue fell over his confine.

Samson felt a twinge behind his ribs. Was this it? Was he dying? The world had certainly fallen dark enough. Tiny bulbs around the window's edge flitted dimly, the low power barely able to sustain them. The Hope-14's faint hum became a low throbbing. Somewhere far off, alarms were sounding again.

Samson got to his feet, crouching low to avoid hitting his head, and found his heart pounding so heavily it was no wonder his ribs ached so badly. The ship was going to blow.

Knock, knock, knock... Knuckles rapped against the outside of the door leading into the ship; there went another rib. Clutching his chest, Samson whipped around. Apparently some people must still be alive. Not that they would be able to get into the hangar. Another explosion sent Samson crashing into its curved wall. Then came another three knocks.

'Go away!' Samson yelled at the door from his stoop. No way in hell was he going to share his tomb with some hideous alien. 'The shuttle's gone! You're going to die. Just... get over it!'

Knock, knock, knock, they came again, the same pace, the same strength. Something about it felt wrong. Very wrong. *Knock, knock, knock.*

'I said go away!' Samson shouted again. Why did they sound so familiar? 'Please...'

The knocking stopped. What replied instead was far worse: another hellish scream from that star dwarfing beast. Grabbing his damaged ears, Samson rushed to the circular window only to witness that far off monster, with its green slobbering tongue, burrow face first into the bulk of what remained of the Hope-14 and barrel through the other side. The impact took a moment to reach Samson's side of the ship, but when it did, there was nothing he could do to stop his inevitable casting into the air. His body kipped up and rattled about the hangar as it broke away from the Hope-14 in its entirety, spiralling into the depths of space in an unbridled blaze.

The red lights were still pulsing but that didn't matter. Samson's eyes were closed, swollen from the battering they had received. He tried to shield his face from more punishment only to find the rest of his body clattering against the rods, wires, and pistons that once held the escape pod in place. But this was no escape pod, merely its shell, and as Samson tumbled about it he knew there would be no lucky escape this time. It wouldn't be long before either the oxygen or his body gave out. The red lights and warning alarms did nothing to help. They were but a haunting reminder that this was the end.

Knock, knock, knock.

Samson awoke suspended in the air. He was still in the escape pod hangar. He stirred, pawing out at flakes of his own skin and clotted blood that had matted about in various globule shapes. Sorry to say, that wasn't the only liquid he saw stewing in his gravity-absent chamber. His heart hummed against his chest at the sight of it. He could do nothing but cower into himself.

Aside from the missing music of mighty booms, sirens, and screams, it was a familiar environment. Those red lights around

32

the circular window pulsed as gloomily as ever, but instead against a backdrop of silence. A few of the bulbs had shattered during the Hope-14's destruction, shattered against Samson, judging by the shards of glass that needed picking free from his limbs.

Dreamy minutes passed in his wounded, floating state. Every time he came into contact with the blood formed stalagmites protruding pointedly from the walls he wondered how things could possibly get worse, careful not to linger on those thoughts too long, lest he tempt fate with the challenge. If he was to fade dreamily out of this life, as it appeared he was doing, it would have been the first moment of actual luck to befall him in years.

Samson's body counter rotated against the twist of the hangar. His head arched back and he looked through the window, now painted with an eternal starry landscape. He felt like a drowning baby, suspended in a tube of water. At least he would be unconscious by the time his eventual suffocation began, or so he hoped, his education on such matters was thin at best. It probably wouldn't be long until he crashed into that object anyway.

Object? Samson asked himself. It couldn't have been, and yet there it was, in the universe's usual emptiness, as clear as day. Against all laws of physics, the hangar was drifting straight for it, somehow pulled from its line of travel as if beckoned by a siren call.

At first it resembled a small piece of debris, blown apart from the Hope-14 just as Samson's chamber had been. Or it could have been much larger; Samson's depth perception had taken quite a knock, a testament to his broken eye socket. As he drew nearer, it reminded him of an engine, a dead black heart ripped from some giant craft. It must have come from the Hope-14, the shoddy craftsmanship was unmistakeable. The metal work was no doubt any less worse off before the ship blew apart.

It was hexagonal in shape, prismal, with a flat top and bottom, and it dwarfed Samson's hangar. Various tubes and electrics sparked and emitted gases from its steely skin. In fact, they did in such a violent way they rocked the escape pod shell as it began to dock. Samson's fingers squeaked against the bloodied walls, bracing himself for impact. *Stupid*, he thought, d*ownright ridiculous*.

Samson thumped the bottom of his fist against the wall. He wanted nothing more than to escape life and yet fate kept throwing him back onto the uncomfortable blade's edge between this world and the next. Now he was about to calmly land in, for all he knew, the next nightmare of that morning's chaotic offering. That's if it was still morning.

A section of the Hexagon's plated roof slid open, moments before Samson's hangar made contact. The hangar drifted into a dark expanse of potential horrors, the roof shutting swiftly once clear of it. The red lights around the window revealed little of this new environment. The rust covered, grated flooring right outside was all Samson could make out, anything further was shrouded in a dead black. Dead, but not quiet. Gravity had returned, so it made sense that sound would follow suit. Unfortunately, it brought with it a hidden scurrying. Samson wanted to hide, but the mockery of that sightless being transmogrified him into a caged animal under red spotlight, and the instinct to cling onto life regrew within him. With no other option, he glared out at the scuttler, letting whatever it was know that he had survived too, and he had come too damn far to give up now. If death was on his plate he was going to tear into it with vicious enmity and grind it to mush. He was determined to clang his fist against the testicles of hell, as he had Jarr's.

Regardless of his enthusiasm, that rare, optimistic mindset wasn't helping him. Samson squatted right next to the window, fingers tapping the glass, racking his mind for an escape plan. From where he sat he had two options: He could ram his way through the glass, at the expense of what was left of his already mangled body, or he could call for help and wait until whatever lurked out in the dark came to his aid, or the opposite.

'Probably more likely,' he said to himself. Whoever it was, they must have been as frightened of Samson as he was of them, though it was also doubtful they were as miserable and determined to put up as big a fight. Samson smiled to himself as he came to his conclusion; he was going to break out of there and claim this vessel as his own. It was probably the teenage angst and its nauseatingly misplaced sense of superiority welling up within that sent him on this course of action, but he figured he hardly had much blood left to lose anyway.

Drawing back to the door of the hangar shell, he propped up the toes on his front foot and lifted his fists. He drew breath and waited for the starter's gun to fire in his mind. His body tightened, ready to expel all of his pent up energy. He let out a breath and tilted his head forward like a stag ready for collision. The pistol sounded. He was off!

Knock, knock, knock.

Samson felt the cold hand behind that knock ruffle the bloodied rags draping his back and he tripped away from the door. As if his lungs weren't screaming out enough, his ribs were now all but ready to release them onto the hangar's floor. He swallowed hard, hoping to combat his fleeing organs with phlegm, and then shuffled back towards the window, gasping for both air and understanding. He was drowning in panic. Every piece of courage he had built up had been abandoned in front of the white metal door he was gawping back at.

'No way! No way!' he screamed at it. How could he have forgotten about those knocks? They were the last sounds he heard before being knocked out, and filled him with so much dread he was surprised he could have fallen unconscious at all. It was as though they let him forget, allowing themselves the chance to sneak up on him again.

'Stupid, stupid, stupid!' Samson clutched at his hair, tangling it over his face as he tried to forget once more.

Nothing aboard the Hope-14 could have survived in space. 'Nothing!' Samson screamed. There wasn't a chance in hell that the one responsible for those knocks could have survived the journey all the way to the Hexagon.

No chance in hell, indeed.

Knock, knock, knock. Was it that hidden scuttler? Had it crept around to the other side of his hangar?

The window behind Samson's head shattered and rained over him in a storm of razors, carried by a flying swivel-legged chair. As the seat clattered into the hangar Samson rolled backwards into the darkness of the Hexagon. He hit the back of his head against something, not that a bruise upon a bruise was anything to worry about now. He was far more concerned with the invisible barrage of attacks coming from both in front and behind.

He felt about the floor around him, searching for a weapon, for something heavy. When his hands found nothing but dust and the edges of the desk he had clunked his skull against, he scarpered beneath it. Statuesque in fear, Samson peered back at the red rim of the hangar window, waiting for the still scene to unfreeze.

'Fuck,' he whispered.

'"FUCK."' came an impossibly loud response. It was so loud Samson jumped and cracked his head against the table again. The lights of the room he and his hangar had descended into croaked into life and illuminated a green, rusting confine. The room was booting up with whizzes and bangs as the instruments scattered throughout attempted to power on, most failing. '"FUCK" COMMAND NOT RECOGNISED. PLEASE TRY AGAIN.'

The robotic woman's voice grabbed him by the heart and strangled his arteries. The corners of his mouth tugged his face south as he looked this way and that, as erratically as you would expect, hoping this new light might fall on whoever was hurling chairs at him.

From what he could see and hear, there was nothing. The only oddity of note was planted in the room's centre: the hangar shell. Wires and panels obtruded from it, its broken spikes reaching out to stab the floor and ceiling. It was in similar shape to the Hexagon's exterior. Samson breathed long and hard and rocked on the spot, holding his hair in his hands again. How he made it this far seemed ever more ridiculous. Maybe he imagined the scuttling? Maybe his post-juggled skull had sent his brain rumbling against the inside of his head, and that was the cause of the sound? Judging by the chair, set on its side with wheels still spinning, it probably wasn't.

Surrounding the hangar were four work consoles set at right angles, one being the table Samson had taken refuge under. A wheeled chair was stationed at each, save for one of course. Further out from those were the walls of the rectangular room. Tiny lights covered in mould, most yellow, presumably once white, flickered in various patterns in some vague response to the Hexagon's new life. Clusters of these were flanked by panels of varying buttons and do-dads of which a teenager from an off-galaxy slum would never understand.

Samson crept out from his hiding spot as the room shuddered into life. There was zero confidence in his step, the necessity of having to check the grimy hovel weighed heavy on his feet. Circling the hangar, he came to the other side of the door where he had heard the knocks. There was no sign of life, just a monumental dent in the metal. Not the kind of mark a hand would leave. Maybe whoever it was had escaped further into the Hexagon? The only way out was through another door, parallel to the hangar's, with a glowing red "*LOCKED*" sign slapped above it.

'PLEASE TRY AGAIN.' The mechanical voice echoed impatiently.

'When did computers get such an attitude?' Samson said, choosing to ignore the voice that had scared him witless for the third time. He continued searching for answers.

The scuttling had stopped, which was a good sign. Maybe it was just something to do with the realigned air pressure that sent that chair coursing at him earlier? *Yeah, that had to have been it*, Samson thought, with no authority to base his theory.

By the looks of things, the run down control room had been dormant far longer than the Hope-14 had been travelling, meaning that this Hexagon couldn't have been part of the Hope-14 and no one besides him had been there in years.

'I AM PROGRAMMED TO SPEAK WITH—'

'Shh!' Samson hissed at the ceiling. His head lashed about in search of the source, but the crack in his neck quickly put a stop to that.

'VOLUME DECREASING. I am programmed to react organically, for the sake of user familiarity.'

'Stupid.'

'"Stupid" command not recognised.'

'That's because it wasn't a command. *You're* stupid,' Samson whispered, not wanting to evoke another ranting explanation. 'You're taking the mick now,' he added, a little too loudly.

'User Michael: Not recognised. Passenger Michael: Not recognised. Life forms on board the Hope-14: 3; Passenger number 210291J: Samson; Passenger number 150192R: Deldrah; And Subject 01. User Michael not found.'

Samson grimaced at being interrupted, but it was safe to say this particular tangent had peaked his interest. 'So this *is* the Hope-14?' he asked, leaning into a microphone poking from the console he had crawled out from.

'Correct. Would you like to search for another passenger on board the—'

'No. Just answer my questions.'

'Confirmed.'

Samson couldn't believe this Hexagon was part of the Hope-14. Not that where he lived in the shuttle was much better, but at least there weren't any weeds growing out of the walls back in his room. Not yet anyway. 'How long has the Hope-14 been travelling?'

'The Hope-14 will reach its destination in seventeen years at the end of its one-hundred-year journey.'

'For those of us who've hit their head one too many times this morning?'

'Eighty-three years.'

'Eighty-three years...'

'Confirmed. Eighty-three ye—'

'Alright, alright... And these three life forms, is that just within this Hexagon place? Or do you have tabs on every bit of scrap left of the Hope-14?'

'I am aware of every functioning unit of the Hope-14 with access to life support operations. Functioning units: 7. Life forms: 3. Passenger No. 2102...'

'Ok, ok. Is there a setting to make you less long winded?'

'No.' The voice was sharp. It sounded offended.

'Easy! I'll just cut you off when you start to ramble, ok?'

'Confirmed.'

'Am I the only passenger on board this... functioning unit?' Samson asked, scrambling his tired mind for the right words.

'Negative. Life forms on board the Hope-14's Primary Function Unit: 3.'

A chill ran up Samson's spine. He felt it popping through the cartilage. He hunched over the console, trying to make himself appear smaller. The scuttling had been real, then.

'Primary Function Unit? What is... *was*... the Hope-14's primary function?'

Samson thought this should have been obvious; they were being shipped away from the war-zone. But if that was so, then why would its '*Primary Functioning Unit*' have gathered so much dust? Why would it exist in the first place?

'Classified. Experiment information restricted to the highest ranking Gov or Hope-14 personnel only.'

'Classified? Experiment? Are you fucking kidding me?'

'Negative.'

'Wait, there are only three people left, and so...'

'Confirmed.'

'Would you stop interrupting!' Samson roared, unable to catch his irritation. He slapped his palm over his mouth and chewed the calluses as a replacement for a gag restraint.

'Confirmed.'

'Brilliant,' Samson whispered with a snap, bringing his voice back to a hush. 'Well, by that logic, as one of the only survivors, I have to be one of the highest ranking personnel?' He was met with silence 'Ha! You have to tell me, don't you?'

'Negative.'

'Gah!' Samson thumped his hands on the console then took a moment to cough up blood.

'Please refrain from spreading germs on the work station,' the voice insisted. 'For information regarding hygiene protocol, please list th—'

'Spreading germs on the workstation? Are your sensors faulty? You've got mouldy flowers growing out of it.' As he said this he twirled one such example through his fingers. 'When was the last time anyone was even here?'

'Experiment completed three hours into voyage,'

'And since then nobody's been here? In eighty-seven years?'

'Negative.'

'What?'

'Eighty-three years. Experiment completed three hours into voyage. Automatic lockdown of Primary Function Unit—'

'Can we just call it the Hexagon?'

'Confirmed. Automatic lockdown of the Hexagon was issued upon the experiment's completion. All Hexagon personnel were expended before lockdown. Lockdown will be lifted upon completion of the Hope-14's journey.'

'Argh,' Samson moaned, 'still so many holes.'

'I apologise.'

'You don't care. All you can do is respond.'

'Fine.'

'A machine with an attitude, I'll give you that. Okay, show me where these other two survivors are.'

'Booting monitor.'

Sparks flashed and banged from a mossy growth on the work station. A bowl of broken glass kicked up smoke. After returning from beneath the desk, Samson hollered, 'Do you have any idea what's happening here!?'

'I know ev—'

'No, you don't! You're fucking inanimate! How can you tell I'm spreading germs on your desk but not know about the broken monitor, or the fact you've got trees growing out of the walls? How can that even happen?'

'I—'

'And then I'm supposed to believe that after everyone died in this Hexagon, somehow three of us managed to get in despite it being thoroughly locked down for nearly a century? Is this the fucking experiment? Trying to drive me crazy!?'

'You are clearly unaware of the experiment.'

'Well, duh. Enlighten me would you!'

'Negative.'

'I order you to tell me.'

'Negative'

'Fuck's sake!' Samson wheeled away from the console.

'What are you doing? I sense hostility in your voice.'

'You're going to sense hostility in your face!'

Samson returned from the hangar shell with the chair that had been thrown at him earlier. After hoofing it onto his shoulder amidst winces of pain, he crashed it onto the desk, tripping and flapping his arms about in silent anger as it struck his knee in recoil. He stared at the last wheel left on its leg, spinning about frantically. At last something he could relate to.

'Are you okay, Samson?'

'Fucking jolly,' Samson said as he sat on the floor and bounced his head repeatedly against the table leg.

'I apologise for not being fully aware of the situation. The result of the experiment has been the one adapting the Hexagon's physical makeup. It does what it pleases. I am unable to—'

'The result of the experiment? Subject 1?'

Samson got up.

'Confirmed.'

'And it let me in here? And is responsible for all this weird plant life?'

'Confirmed.'

'What in the hell is it?'

'Classified.'

'So. Fucking. Close. Alright fine, where is it?'

'Booting new monitor.'

A light popped up on a different console. Samson hopped over. There, he was met with a bird's-eye schematic of the Hexagon, through a fully functioning screen this time. In its centre was the control room where Samson was standing, a faint blip representing his position. Circling that were six evenly sized rooms that backed onto it. A corridor led from the control room to another hallway stretching around those six, making up the hexagon shape. From there on out more corridors, blocked and chopped up like a maze, onioned outwards with more layers until they reached the Primary Functioning Unit's edge. Tucked away in one of those tiny segments were two other blips, virtually on top of one another.

'Hey, is this Subject 1 thing dangerous?' Samson asked. He couldn't look away from the blips. One was dim, the other danced with a frightening vibrancy.

The robotic voice wouldn't reply.

'What's your name?' Samson asked.

'I was referred to as "Shez" by my initial users.'

'Does that stand for anything?'

'Confirmed.'

'Aren't you going to elaborate?'

'You usually command silence when I begin to elaborate.'

Samson smiled up at the ceiling. 'I actually like you, Shez, but I seriously need you to answer; is Subject 1 dangerous?'

'Confirmed.'

'Can you say "Yes", instead of "Confirmed"?'

'Yes.'

Samson was overcome with a brief smugness, and then returned to his situation.

'Now, is there any way I can escape, or send out a message? I don't like the idea of being trapped in here with that thing.'

He could have sworn he heard a scuttling outside of the door with the *"LOCKED"* sign above it.

'Negative. You will die.'

What did he expect to hear? This was the worst day in history, it was never going to end nicely. Fortunately, an acceptance of this fate had already flooded him a multitude of times.

'What about this other passenger, what's Subject 1 doing to him?'

Samson stared intently at the monitor. He could almost feel the pulse of the more active light bubbling through his fingertips. It was but a blip, and yet the longer he gazed upon it the more he was sure he could see a hideous face looking back. The other light was almost dead, and Samson grew more uncomfortable the longer he lingered over the image.

'Passenger number 150192R: Deldrah. Has been present within the Hexagon for 46 years. *She* is a Blendorin. She was in too close a proximity to the Hexagon and Subject 1 absorbed her into the unit.'

Samson wasn't sure if he could ever get used to hearing how this creature could bend the world to its will like that. He gulped. 'What's it been doing to her for 46 years?'

'Classified.'

That answer was all the boy really wanted; specifics would have been too difficult. Samson's top down view of the pulsing dots was enough information already.

Samson hated aliens. Truly hated them. As if teenagers weren't smug enough, he looked down upon those of different colours and shapes with vile disdain.

On his home world only he, his mother, and a hand full of others were human. The rest within his cramped upbringings were a mismatched torrent of ugly, stupid creatures that he couldn't understand and didn't want to. Each of them were the representative arse-feeding dregs of their respective races. Samson didn't have much else to go by. When he first boarded the Hope-14, he looked to the heavens with gratefulness for his escape, only to find that every class, of every race, were as stupid and putrid as the others. Even humans. *Especially* humans. It certainly put his prejudices into perspective, but that xenophobic subconscious mind of his still tugged at the string that turned his nose up at other species. And yet, as he watched Subject 1's blip jumping about its prey, his heart palpitated with sorrow and he let out a pained whimper. Life would be so much simpler if its characters were just blips. How much more sympathetic we would be to those we deem lesser. It wouldn't be long before this creature, to which the laws of physics bowed and gave free reign, came for him before he even had a chance to rectify his bigotry.

'Stupid, kid,' he whispered.

'It won't be long now,' Shez said. 'You must leave.'

'Why? You said it best: I will die.'

'It knows you're here.'

The scuttle returned, forcing Samson to break from the Hexagon's blueprint. He turned to find an empty control room. The escape pod shell he had arrived in was gone, a murky skin of fleshy matter lay moist and thinly on the floor in its place. Samson's mouth was tight, his neck stretched as if his head were trying to escape his body.

'Better to die than let it catch you.'

'I can't kill myself,' Samson said.

If he had the courage to put himself out of his own misery, he would have done it long ago.

'Then you must reach the edge of the Hexagon, there is a hatch, let space do it for you.'

'Thanks, Shez. I think.'

The control room faded dim and those scurrying footsteps grew louder.

Samson's broken frame hunched over in the light of the control room's doorway. His breath crept into the blackened corridor as tentatively as he had approached it. The void he was faced with felt endless. He wasn't sure how Shez had done it, and the AI had become eerily quiet since the door light switched to green, but it appeared Samson had received free reign to wander the Hexagon until he met his fate at the other end. Of course, that was if he didn't stumble across Subject 1 first.

'Subject 1,' he mumbled to himself. 'Pfft... The scuttler more like!'

Those jeers were the only thing propelling his fragile silhouette forwards.

'I've survived galaxy sized monsters for fuck sake.'

A hiss and shooting noise caught him off guard and he yelped as the control room door snapped shut behind him; he immediately blamed Shez. Rolling his eyes and catching his breath, he proceeded on slowly, so slow if he went with less pace he would be retreating backwards.

A dim green glow buzzed at the end of the stout corridor, which branched off in two directions. As he made towards it, Samson's path met with spores of dirt that danced slow and sporadic, and glinted in what he sensed was a false light. They looked like dust particles, and scratched his throat. Holding back splutters, Samson reached the crossroads. The sound of scuttling came from the low arching hallway to the left, and a creeping in the ventilation system came from the right. *I'm being toyed with,* Samson thought. Samson knew. All that power, he could feel it gawping at him through the shadows.

In the end, it was the creeping direction that won out. Down this corridor, the remnants of Subject 1's expendable creators stained the vegetation growing out of the walls, and Samson felt a sticky squelching beneath his feet.

A victim of youthful curiosity, he outstretched his arm and grazed those bloody marks. Freshly clotted red stained his fingers, and Samson adopted a sour face, pondering whether or not it belonged to the Blendorin, or if the scuttler had decided to keep fresh his handy work of eighty-seven years prior. Samson shuddered as he failed to shake the blood from his hand. It wasn't long before he refused to trust his senses altogether. Was the blood even really there?

Twisting past the frost blotted windows that peaked into the Hexagon's different rooms, he could hear many a disconcerting thing that couldn't possibly exist. Far off groans of multi-voiced animals sang distorted in the air. It had become clear Samson had moved from a metaphorical nightmare into a real one.

Only someone as stupid as me could have stumbled across this, he thought. *A smarter person would have let himself be impaled by that girder.*

Further and further he crept away from the bowels of the Hexagon, hoping that as he did its illusions would dissipate with the distance.

Stupid.

Samson lost himself further in its maze. He smelled rotting flesh, and saw the metal walls become skin. He limped on regardless, his light-headedness proving an asset. With his vision so matted he could blot out most of the gruesome details and focus on chasing the end of corridors. He couldn't imagine what

Subject 1 looked like, or how it would reveal itself. Whether it was male or female, alien or human, or like nothing he had ever seen. It would probably disguise itself to match the decrepit state of the Hexagon.

Samson had no idea where he was at this point, or where he was going. It was no use trying to remember the map he had seen in the control room; as far as Samson could tell, its walkways were spiralling around each other like a child's rampant scribblings. The floor felt tilted, the air that kicked through the vents sounded twisted and misshapen, and for all Samson knew, he was now scrambling through the intestines of Subject 1 itself. Soon enough he had forgotten his mission to drown in space. He just wanted to move forwards, refusing to be swallowed up by his own madness.

All this time I spent being negative, expecting nothing better of the world. Well congratulations, now it can't get any worse!

As he admonished himself in silence, afraid to utter any words, the world strained back into reality. This real world felt far more perilous than any twisted hallucination. He stood in power-stance in an empty room, weedless and clean save for dust, with no idea how he had gotten there. He didn't know how far the room stretched, but it was long and thin, and at the end of the light's touch, Samson finally saw Subject 1, vague and distant, but unmistakable.

It didn't need an introduction or an explanation. Only one of the two creatures Samson shared the room with was Subject 1, and the tortured alien beneath it didn't look in form strong enough to distort reality. In truth, neither did Subject 1.

It was humanoid, gaunt, and brittle looking, but as its chalky-skinned body lurched over the Blendorin beneath it, Samson saw a harrowing strength deceptive of its frame. The fear of that juxtaposition pinned him still and he watched helplessly as

Subject 1 drank the Blendorin's life force. Green and glowing, the Blendorin's soul drifted into a deep, black chasm that was the entirety of Subject 1's face. To see it wasted on nothing but skin and bone struck a deep chord within Samson.

The Blendorin shook uncontrollably, tears dried upon her blue face; hardly blue anymore. Her pigmentation was now a washed grey compared to what Samson remembered Blendorins to look like. He could see it, she wanted to call out but found herself unable, her vocal cords torn over the course of her torture. Her eyes hung like a hammock in the top of her head and fell upon Samson who gulped as Subject 1's dome followed their line. Its neck cranked back onto itself to reveal nothing but that life sucking hole that refused to close, drooling over Samson's rigidity. Two blank, golf ball sized eyes glinted and sat lopsided in the top corners of its face, pushed aside to make way for that gaping hideousness. There could have been other notable features but Samson had absorbed all the macabre sights his mind would allow.

Subject 1 rose like a cheap, stop-motion animation, elements of its movement somehow missing. Its limbs clicked and twisted to the point where it keeled over on itself, its spine too weak and fragmented to bear much of anything. Samson was uncomfortable just watching it try to drag its feet. Every ligament fought to hold the monster back, only to fail and allow the painful clockwork kinetics strain against their own misgivings. Every slide of its feet bore a nasally groan that echoed throughout the Hexagon. The sound came breathless and filled with stink.

'Heangh... Heangh... Heaangh... Heaaangh.'

Samson ran, finding it hard to believe he still could. He hadn't even realised it until his knee began to ache early on into his sprint. The sight of Subject 1's rise and chase played before his eyes despite refusing to look back. He wanted to, but couldn't.

The rotting panels, poles, and frantic blipping lights of the Hexagon flitted past him as he charged without any thought to his direction; away was his only concern. The word *"Please"* sat constant at his lips' edge, but too afraid to speak it, it regurgitated over and over in his head instead. He didn't know who he was pleading with; there was no saviour on board this vessel. He was a mouse fleeing through a demon built maze. All he could do was move.

But time stretched, and in that space, Samson's ears overflowed with Subject 1's whines. 'Heangh... Heaangh... Heaaangh!' It didn't matter how many rooms or corridors he ran through, it was inescapable and growing. Samson's injuries weren't helping either. Aside from an all-consuming, sharp ache, the burns were the worst. They held his flesh taut, and when he forced full motion out of his clobbered limbs the searing strains of his hide would wrench tears from his eyes. They ran over the lumpy disfigurations of his face and stung the wounds.

Throbbing all over, he wondered how much more damage Subject 1 could possibly do. Maybe he would be afforded a quick death, like those who had brought it into the world. Not likely. Chances were, it could have killed Samson the moment he docked.

If it can change the atmosphere, why not blast me into oblivion? Why am I even running?

'Fuck it.'

Samson halted at another crossroads. Panting, he spread his arms wide.

'Come on then!' he shouted, his voice echoing back at him through the green haze. Subject 1's groans ceased, but somehow the monster felt closer than ever. Samson twitched as the tingle of claws grazed his tattered hair. 'Get it over with!'

Silence.

'This is stupid.'

'Stu-piiid,' a pained voice gurgled ahead of him. Subject 1 had learnt a new word. Samson's favourite.

At the end of one corridor, the light fizzled out. The little that was left cast unfinished shadows over the teenager's pursuer, crooked and sickly as ever. With his mouth dried out, Samson found his fighting talk stuck in the back of his throat. A twitch, a snap of the neck, a broken knee winched backwards on itself and Subject 1 began crookedly dragging itself at Samson again. The world bent around it, as distorted as the creature itself. Samson didn't care how bravely his last stand had played through in his head, nothing was going to keep him routed on the spot.

A door! It appeared out of nowhere, right on his shoulder. *A trick?*

'Heaaangh!'

Trick or not, Samson ploughed through, slamming the heavy pallet closed, harder than his body should have allowed. It was deathly cold behind it, but quiet. There was no gurgling, no dragging feet, just quiet. Samson experienced a brief moment of relief and deflated. He slipped to the ground against the door, as if his body would be any sort of barricade. Alone again, it was like being back in the escape pod hangar, and a calm acceptance clothed him. He was happy to face the stars once more, their sparkles glistening against his damp cheeks. Sat adjacent to him was another door, a tall window in its middle, an isosceles trapezoid, a gateway to the heavens. It let forth a light with sharp edges, rendering anything outside their touch unseen. It would have made sense to get up and attempt suicide, but that rare moment of serenity, that visage of space aloof of foreign space crafts, destruction, and planet-sized beasts, had caught Samson off-guard. His eyes were strapped to its beauty, and he allowed himself a moment's comfort. After a life of suffering, topped with his current ordeal, who could blame him? In the quiet, he took solace in his mother's early demise. She may have gone out in a blaze, but Samson was glad to know her suffering was over, if not slightly ashamed that she had to spend her life caring for such a miserable sod.

Faced with his doom, a little familiarity wouldn't have gone amiss in front of the cosmic masterpiece. His mother, the only friend he had ever had. He was never quick to show it, and this beautiful fix would have been just the eye-candy she deserved for being so wonderful against every odd.

'Well, here we go.'

Now it was time to join her. Whatever death held, Samson didn't care. So long as he wasn't in the Hexagon, he would be happy. The walk along his self-paved green mile was slow, the tall door growing more imposing the closer he got. Once he reached it, one last brain storm thundered desperately for another option. Samson's finger tips tapped wave-like over the handle of a big red switch, stalling for a few more precious seconds, one swift pull and it would all be over. He frowned at his own hand as if to convince it to take the plunge. He was ready...

Knock, knock, knock.

The world slowed. If he was looking for a reason not to pull that door open, he had found it. Now, he didn't want to look at the window at all, let alone allow himself to be sucked through its door. Just inches away, he saw someone in the corner of his eye fogging up the glass from outside. Fighting his better judgement, Samson's dark side pulled his face to meet them. Any face in the universe would have been welcome so long as it didn't belong to Subject 1, save for one. That one carried the pointed features of Jarr, leering still and spitefully back at him from the outside with the same broken nose Samson had afforded him earlier. The boy tried to shake the image free but it wouldn't go. That merciless gangster really was there, as plain as could be, the chains piercing his pimpled face glistening with frost.

Knock, knock, knock.

'No,' Samson whispered.

A flash memory of Jarr knocking against he and his mother's door hours earlier spiked through his head. He retreated, refusing to break eye contact with Jarr, his hands reaching behind as a guide. The way back into the Hexagon's corridors was no more. Instead, Samson was met with hard, featureless steel. His legs gave way, broken at the sight of that once precious landscape stained with Jarr's hideousness.

Knock, knock, knock.

Face unmoving, Jarr robotically slammed his shoulder against the window. After all the blood soaked impossibilities he had witnessed, Samson knew better than to trust the *fact* that Jarr wouldn't be able to enter the Hexagon. Those fears were quelled by a more terrifying sound than the three knocks; the scuttling was back. Subject 1 came wriggling out of the darkness and halted in front of Jarr. It looked up curiously for a moment, almost in awe. Its three twisted digits, barely passing for fingers, pressed against the glass longingly. *What's happening? Is it in love with Jarr or something?* Samson wondered, holding back vomit, curling his knees up to his face.

It wouldn't have surprised him. The leader of the Wolves was probably the closest thing that walking freak show could relate to. It must have been like looking into a mirror.

Clunk. With a free hand, the scuttler pulled down the red handle. Samson's eyes expanded, unsure whether to be terrified or relieved. This was it, he was going to leave the Hexagon and die in the great black vacuum, Jarr and Subject 1 in tow. But there was no rushing of wind, no suffocating expulsion of air as Samson had come to expect from his all too recent experiences. Instead, the door swung calmly into the Hexagon. Its base scarred the floor and Jarr's still body was guided delicately into a kneeling position beside Subject 1.

The moment the door slipped shut behind them, Jarr looked alive. He was startled, even more so than Samson if that were possible, but alive. He pushed at his own face and piercings, gripped at his grotty dresses, unable to believe it. Finally, he dropped a fearful eye on his saviour who sat between him and Samson, just beyond the light's full touch, as if eagerly waiting for some morbid show to begin.

Jarr was understandably confused. Subject 1 rose, frustrated with the stalling, and Jarr recoiled. Barely giving the Wolf time to adapt to his new found life, the monster wheeled around its new toy and placed dry, white hands on Jarr's shoulders, leaving a powdery residue on his cardigan. It whispered into his ear, face so close that its crusty lips pushed the gangster's greasy hair about. Samson felt that puke rising again and he sank further into his shaking ball.

Deep down, he hoped Jarr would snap and attack Subject 1, just as he would anyone else who got that close. Either that or Subject 1 would put an end to Jarr. Samson wasn't sure which alternative he'd prefer but, if he was being honest with himself, so long as one of them survived he was in for a rough time. What he was one hundred percent sure about, was that he didn't want Jarr to grin like he was doing. Subject 1 continued to whisper dread into the lone Wolf's head and Samson shifted. He couldn't hear what was being said but it had to be evil because Jarr was loving it, so much so he salivated over the very sight of Samson.

You're in this together now, aren't you? Samson said with his eyes. He was surprised he could hate Jarr and Subject 1 more than he did but, at that point, his disdain felt limitless. Jarr stood and cracked his neck.

'Well, well, this is going to get rather uncomfortable for you. Shame your mum couldn't be here.'

Subject 1 was hopping about, if you could call it that. Samson just scowled back with all his might, too weak to run or fight. His hand scratched at the ground, trying to escape without him. It connected with dry paint that flaked beneath his finger nails. The paint belonged to an old Hope-14 logo, usually seen dotted about unused utility stations within the ship. The image was an equal cross with thickly drawn edges and a circle covering its centre. Upon that the arms of a compass pointed to nowhere. There were a thousand questions running through the boy's head but only one thing painfully clear; when the Gov piled him and his mother, and a million other unlucky souls into the Hope-14, it was just to feed their suffering to this pale monster. That compass pointed nowhere for a reason. Grief was the only destination. There may have been hope in the Gov's plan, but it was sure as all hexagonal hell never intended for the passengers of the Hope-14.

Samson looked past Jarr at Subject 1, his mind a warped collage of what he had witnessed it do. This beast could never be controlled.

I bet they didn't expect their little science project to have such a bold imagination. When I'm gone I'm going to look down with glee as this fucker rips them all apart. I'll be laughing on my warm fluffy cloud.

He refused to shudder as Jarr placed a false hand of comfort on his shoulder.

'Ready, son?' Jarr asked with putrid warmth. Samson could have spat right inside that ridiculous grin of his.

You're going to get it too. 'Stupid.'

THE BULLET BOY

'Mummy, can you see the Bullet Boy?'

Dandy only ever asked that question once. But what kind of reply did the six-year-old expect? In a world where everyone knew everything about anything, the idea of knowing nothing about something was torture.

'He gets it from you, you know,' he heard his mother tell his father once. Dandy didn't like his mother or his father. They didn't seem to like each other either. Regardless, never afraid to step over others to get what they wanted, the family of three had landed one of the nation's most luxurious Victorian properties, a classic design imbued with all the technological trimmings expected in a world four centuries its junior. Today was moving day.

The new house, although decorated warmly, was as cold to Dandy as were his parents. No wonder he found better company with the Bullet Boy. When the other child Dandy's parents couldn't see appeared, he was glad that at least made two of them.

At first, it was scary when the shadowy figure stumbled out from a low cupboard and into the kitchen. He didn't look like a normal boy. He was slightly shorter than Dandy, his legs and feet dumpy like a baby's. So were his hands, although his forearms were so long his knuckles dragged on the ground. His head was like a balloon, smooth and without feature. With skin as black as oil, it was no wonder Dandy leapt out of his and trundled behind his mother's legs for safety the first time he met him. The Bullet Boy was a depressing sight compared to Dandy's light curly hair, yellow jumper, and bright blue dungarees. When Dandy looked closer, he thought the Bullet Boy might be hurt. The shell casings of war protruded from all over his body, thin reflections glinting over their edges. Most were small, pimple-sized, others a few sharp inches longer. One must have been under his foot because a *clink* echoed every left step.

After being shooed away by his mother, Dandy followed the Bullet Boy upstairs, keeping a safe distance. He watched as the Boy shuffled unpacked boxes aside, and began scribbling on the creaky floorboards with a stick of chalk. Occasionally, he looked up at Dandy, who would quickly gasp and duck out of sight. When he was brave enough to spy again, Dandy noticed the Bullet Boy was far more interested in his drawings than him. With his head fixated low to the floor and his back arched uncomfortably, the dome-headed child was overly meticulous. These were no childish scribbles. A collection of white circles resembling star systems, connected by lines and patterns, were drawn so precisely they appeared mathematical.

When he was finished, the Bullet Boy picked himself up and moved onto the next room, head bowed as if weighted by some great depression. When the coast was clear, Dandy scurried over and gawped at the mural. He had seen similar pictures before, hung in his father's office, though he had only ever caught peaks of those cosmic diagrams through cracks in the door. He considered running to his father's new study, to unpack one and show it to the Bullet Boy, but then he remembered what his mother said; 'Your father is a soldier, Dandy, his work is too important. Don't you dare go in that room, Dandy, ever.' Dandy didn't like soldiers. Whenever they came to the house they smelled funny and sounded mean. His father was never happy when they were around either.

The sound of chalk on board began again and Dandy hurried to see the next room's instalment. They were different to the first drawing but the theme remained the same, as did the process. After hours of following him through his new home, Dandy's fear of the Bullet Boy passed. Rather than hiding, he grew comfortable enough to sit right there on the floor with him. The Boy didn't mind. Sometimes he had to gesture Dandy aside so he could lay more chalk, but otherwise he was content. He would even stop and rest, sitting with Dandy silently, occasionally looking over as if to speak. Although, the lack of a mouth made it difficult. In that one day, Dandy felt closer to the Bullet Boy than he ever had his parents, so a sorrow befell him as the Boy crawled back into the kitchen cupboard at sun down.

All that was left for Dandy was fear; fear that the Boy would never return, and fear of his mother's reaction to their handy work. That fear was realised in the form of a rather painful spanking, so much so Dandy was left walking funny. It seemed pointless to try and explain the truth. Instead, he took the punishment, knowing he would go back to his normal, lonely, pain-free life soon enough. Unfortunately for his backside, it didn't stay lonely for long.

A few days later the Bullet Boy returned, same routine, same drawings. This time, he gave Dandy a friendly nod after clattering past the pans that filled the kitchen cupboard. Dandy followed the dark figure upstairs to the first room, Dandy's room, a place stuffed with simple toys for a simple child. He desperately wanted to see how the Bullet Boy's picture panned out, but at the same time his bottom was still raw.

'Could you stop please, Boy?' he asked.

The Bullet Boy continued.

'I think they're very nice, but Mummy will tell me off.'

Still the boy drew. Dandy slumped in a sulk.

'Why are you drawing?'

The Bullet Boy tapped an empty bullet casing on the side of his head. Dandy frowned.

'I don't get it.'

This time, the boy reached for one of Dandy's colouring books. In it were images of worldly characters; a nurse, a doctor, a farmer. The Bullet Boy landed on a page displaying a soldier. He held the picture to Dandy's face, tapping the shell in his skull more frantically. He then nudged Dandy and pointed.

'You don't like soldiers either?' Dandy asked, worried about the soldiers that frequented his house. 'You think they will hurt me?' The Bullet Boy nodded then continued to draw. 'But these drawings will stop the Bad Soldiers?'

The Boy nodded again but paused as a creaking sounded above. Dandy held his breath. He was used to being left alone by his parents, he wasn't used to noises when he was so.

'What was that?' Dandy whispered.

The Bullet Boy picked up the pace of his work. Dandy was scared. For most of the day an over-sanitised smell followed them. Dandy stuck close to the Bullet Boy, who in turn refused to move on to the next room without him.

When the drawings were finished, the stink subsided. Exhausted after a manic art session, the two sat back to back in the living room, chalk laid over the rug, tension still rife.

'Would you like to play?' Dandy asked, knowing few other ways to relax.

He could feel the Bullet Boy shuffling uncomfortably before leaving the room. Dandy wasn't surprised; the Boy must be tired.

To Dandy's surprise, a bright red ball bopped in from the grand hall and rested beside his leg. Dandy beamed. From that day on, whenever the Bullet Boy visited, they always played with the red rubber ball in the breaks between star drawings. His mother was always angry when she came home to the mess, but when Dandy tried to explain about the 'Bad Soldier' she would never listen. He spoke much more openly with the Bullet Boy.

'I miss Nanny,' he told the sketching shadow one morning. 'She smelled of biscuits. I used to go every day. Now I'm inside all of the time. I like being inside with you, though. We have fun. But it's sad you have to draw all the time.'

The Bullet Boy tapped his skull again.

'I know, I know. Do you kn—' Dandy was cut off by that same creaking sound they hadn't heard since the Bullet Boy's second visit.

Their hearts battered against their rib cages, fully expectant of the following smell, but somehow this presence didn't feel as malevolent. It came from downstairs. Dandy's mother was home early. The Bullet Boy was normally long gone by the time she returned.

They rushed through the home but she had already set to work, wiping away the chalk on the kitchen floor. The Bullet Boy was noticeably distraught. He bounced around her, pleading desperately with waving arms, but she couldn't see him. His panic was justified. At some point during the display that sterile stink from before had returned. Dandy's arms flared with goose-bumps and without a moment's thought, he leapt at his mother.

'Dandy, what's gotten into you? Enough!' she shouted.

'No Mummy, no! Or the Bad Soldier will come!' he screamed back. His words swung along with him from her arm. She eventually shoved him aside, his elbows burning as they squeaked against the wooden floor. Retaining her composure with a harsh straightening of her jacket, she resumed her scrubbing. The Bullet Boy stopped jumping and ran to Dandy's aid.

'This ends now, Dandy,' she said sternly.

His mother was unaware of how true her words were until it was too late. She stormed away, huffing deeply, pausing when her nose twitched with the smell her son was already suffering. Reaching the door to the hall, she winged her arms outward in quake survival mode, holding onto the frames as an ear splitting crack waved over them. When the rumble subsided she shot Dandy a glare as if he were to blame. Of course, she couldn't see the things that he could see. Dandy looked past her and saw, beside the staircase, a second short, balloon-headed boy. Its skin was perfectly white, reflective like ink yet to dry, but there were no bullets in this body. There was nothing at all. No feature, no personality, just an emptiness that willed to erase any iota of happiness.

'The Bad Soldier,' Dandy mouthed.

The new arrival lumbered away, set to wander the house as the Bullet Boy had done. Dandy didn't want to follow this time.

Unlike the Bullet Boy, the Bad Soldier never left at the end of the day. Dandy knew it didn't actually look like a soldier, but he could sense a violent nature within the creature that only the worst ones held. He only ever saw the Soldier shuffling about the home as if lost, shoulders frowned, replacing absent brows.

At night, Dandy's mother would check his room, hearing those same sorrowful footsteps but unable to see the cause.

Dandy unfortunately could. In the darkness, he would often wake to find the Soldier stood over his bed, still as a rock. He yearned for those mornings when the Bullet Boy visited. He would hug his depressed friend the moment he appeared, the cold ammunition comparatively warm to the Bad Soldier's company. But the Bullet Boy would no longer draw his starry displays across his home sized canvas. It appeared his reason for doing so had passed. Dandy tried to play with him but little effort was returned, with good reason. Whenever his mood appeared to rise so too would the Soldier's eerie presence. Dandy could tell the two had a past.

And so, the friends had to tread carefully through their days, the quiet time spent with each other all they could pull joy from. But even that wouldn't last.

One day, as they were sitting silently, watching the television, scared to even breathe loudly, Dandy made the mistake of subconsciously rolling his red ball on the arm of the sofa. He and the Bullet Boy were absorbed in a news program. Dandy didn't understand the long words, but the action was kind of exciting, albeit upsetting in places. Really, Dandy had wanted to watch cartoons, but that would be too much fun and the Bad Soldier had already taken issue with his ball.

The spectre made a beeline straight for him and snatched away the red ball from his hands. When those chubby fingers made contact with his, Dandy almost wept. In that brief moment, he wanted to die. The kind of feeling a child should never know. The Bullet Boy was furious. He sprung from the sofa, chest puffed, and let it carry him past Dandy. If he could speak, the air would have trembled. The Soldier was unphased, and sure enough the longer it remained hunched and still, the more frightening it became. The Bullet Boy was shaking but wouldn't back down.

'Come back, Boy,' Dandy whimpered, and reluctantly his defender returned. That was the last time for a long time that Dandy saw the Bullet Boy.

For weeks, Dandy found himself waiting by the cupboard in the kitchen, worried that the Bad Soldier, always present and never welcome, had done something to the Bullet Boy.

'Poor Bullet Boy,' he would say to himself every morning.

Dandy hated the Soldier, who was now always playing with Dandy's ball. It was gloating, and Dandy wasn't going to put up with it anymore. In some directionless act of defiance, Dandy decided to follow the Bad Soldier for the day, determined to find its weakness, determined to put an end to that monster. After hours of senseless meanderings, he followed the creature right up to his father's office door. Dandy hadn't seen his father in months and was still nervous to go in there. He waited outside for a long time, hidden behind a house plant, dreading the idea of being stuck in that room with the Soldier. Eventually, the Bad Soldier emerged and Dandy slipped inside before the door shut.

After entering, he immediately wished he hadn't. Paper was shredded everywhere, his father's star maps torn from the walls. Books, stationery, guns, and glass, all strew broken about the office. With its old uniformity now littering the ground, the blank walls were plastered in all manner of terrible imagery. Dandy couldn't fully grasp the violence, the sexuality, the profanity of such drawings, his innocence acting as a shield against its true terrors, but he recognised the stars and planets, and felt every sharp, tearing shape that intertwined them. They shook his insides to a point where he felt guilty just looking. He daren't imagine how his mother would react to these new chalk drawings.

That is if he ever saw his mother again. A choking bleach stench rose within the room and a cold hand snatched the scruff of his dungarees. All of a sudden, Dandy found himself being dragged from the office and down the stairs. *Thump, thump, thump,* his back bounced off each step. Red faced, Dandy bawled, struggling against an impossible strength that threw him into the grand hall.

Why are you doing this!? his mind screamed, mouth stuffed with cries. His parents weren't home, the Bullet Boy was gone, what rotten luck that the Bad Soldier should reveal the extent of its malice now.

A flick of the Soldier's wrist sent Dandy rolling towards the kitchen. Every angle of his body bounced against the hard floor beneath the rug. His elbows and knees throbbed, which made crawling away impossible. He looked back helplessly and watched the blurred outline of the Bad Soldier lift its long, gorilla-like arm. Dandy felt the floor disappear beneath him. He was floating in the air, being squeezed so hard he thought he might pop.

Then suddenly, *thump!* Dandy was free, strewn in paralysing pain, but free. His eyes were busy chasing stars when he heard the familiar clink of metal on stone. That bullet ridden left foot had returned, and its owner stood in the kitchen doorway. Dandy welled with joy to see his old friend, the Bullet Boy, ready to do battle with that evil, Bad Soldier. Dandy could have lived in that numb, happy moment for all the rest of his life. But the hallway was long, and the race towards the youngster had already begun.

Charging forth, their knuckles plunging into the rug to aid their speed, the beings of black and white moved like primal beasts destined to lock horns forever. The Bullet Boy had moved fastest, hurdling the crying Dandy, clapping his heavy arms against the Bad Soldier's. The world strained, bending beneath their collision. Locked together, the Bullet Boy gestured Dandy to make safe, then rammed his skull into the Soldier's. The two ghouls rattled away into the walled decorations. Room was made for Dandy to flee for the front door.

A moment away from reaching the handle, Dandy had to duck after hearing the Bullet Boy's hurtling body whistle ahead of him. It crushed the door frame. Splinters rained and Dandy was forced to stumble in a new direction. He fell into the living room right before the Bullet Boy regained his feet and threw out his arms. The bullets in his body unleashed like a fiery nail bomb, laying mercilessly into the approaching Bad Soldier. Dandy's ears rang with the explosive sound and he clasped them tight as he dived for cover.

The Bullet Boy won, Dandy thought. *He had to have won.* Smoke shrouded his vision. A black figure fell behind him into the living room. Using the furniture as cover, he snuck closer, not wanting to risk the wrath of an injured Bad Soldier. But Dandy's legs gave way when rather than bloodied, white skin, he saw smoking craters where the Bullet Boy's bullets had once been. Dandy fell to his friend's side. 'No...' he said. Back in the hall way, through the smog, Dandy saw his red ball bouncing.

Orange embers danced about it as it lit brightest red. Then, the unharmed, unphased Bad Soldier hurled it at the Bullet Boy. The smoke made a whirling path, and the few windows left unshattered sang as it struck the Bullet Boy's chest and the force snapped his ribs flat. Dandy squirmed along with the Bullet Boy.

As the last act of a battle he had no chance of winning, the gloomy spectre revealed a stick of chalk between his fingers. He wrote on the charred floor "S... O... R... R..."

The apology was cut one squiggly letter short as the Bad Soldier wrenched the Bullet Boy's neck sideways.

'It's okay,' Dandy whimpered.

He stared hatefully at the Bullet Boy's murderer and grew more enraged as the Bad Soldier just shrugged. Dandy wanted to hurt it, and would have tried had it not faded away into nothing. Its wicked job was done.

'You should be the one to say sorry!' Dandy roared into the empty space left by the Soldier.

He went to lay a hand on the Bullet Boy but found his palms falling on nothing but the floor beneath. Dandy shuddered in his old loneliness.

A struggling light drifted through the home's broken walls and dust coated air. No matter how thick that mist, it wasn't enough to drown out the sound of marching boots. Dandy tilted his round face upwards as soldier silhouettes stormed his home. Suppressed claps from concealed weapons filled his ears. Blackness.

An age passed, or a few seconds, time lacked relativity wherever Dandy was. He woke in a foreign place, a shack of some kind. A creature was barking at him. It wasn't a dog; Dandy didn't know what it was but he didn't fear it. He held a stick of chalk in his blackened hand, responsibility heavy within it.

SHUTTLE SPOTTERS

'I'm bored, Darren,' Rollo moaned, 'Bored bored bored!' You wouldn't question him. The security guard's jolly rotundity did little to liven such a dull existence. His past month had consisted of dreary night-time hours sat lopsided on a tiny stool at the centre of a derelict building site, not an iota of drama to give his girth purpose. Darren wasn't much company either. The toothless pensioner sported a height and weight deficiency and wasn't much to look at, nor had he spoken a single real sentence in their time working together. The geriatric's features squeezed northward until his bottom lip tickled the brim of his hat, eyes forever below its shield. Rollo couldn't even be sure Darren was awake at times. Talking to Darren was much like talking to oneself, aside from the occasional murmur.

The pair were hardly the dynamic duo, and it was rather shocking either of them had been hired in the first place. But with nothing to do, and communication hardly a necessity when one's job entailed nothing, the two weren't ready to complain; although small joy could be taken in how well the job paid compared to its dullness. Even the scenery, the role's most attractive feature, had grown stale. Once upon a time, Rollo would gawp up at the unfinished innards of the city's latest abandoned spire. The site's naked girders stretched skyward around his dirt pit station, decorated with sparking chords and flitting tech that Rollo could never understand. Seeing the skeletal foundations spike the stars from their spiralling tunnel until they merged with the city's densely stacked skyscrapers was a buffet of texture for the eyes. The dazzling gleam from the all too sleepless world struck the girder's peaks and cast gothic shadows, reminiscent of ancient expressionist films. But the lights could never funnel to the depths the guards were destined to patrol. Nothing but a tiny generator lit their charge and its reach was feeble. It wouldn't be long before the light packed in all together. And so, no matter how distorted and magically technological the scenery above them was, the view below, mixed with the sand in Rollo's shoes, was quick to coarsen the mood. By then, in his mind, *if you've seen it once, then you've seen it, and that's that*. It was nothing compared to...

'A Hope-15 X-Nine New Era Class!'

Rollo's blubber hoola-hooped about his person as he leapt from his stool. A giant shuttle coursed overhead, blotting out the only patch of stars the unfinished tower showed them. It couldn't have been more than two miles above the highest girder's reach, and the posts rumbled dustless as it pummelled the air with its passing. The engines were an unfathomable size, each propellant larger than the city itself. Rollo found his face burning against their blaze, his cheeks aglow akin to his childlike enthusiasm. Darren, on the other hand, couldn't care less. He blew the dust from his aged chops and laughed as he watched his gelatinous friend scribble the ship's ID number into a flimsy notepad.

'Yur feckin' weir' you are,' Darren slurred.

'*You're* the weird one, actually,' Rollo scoffed. 'Compared to you, I'm the damned... erm... Prime Chancellor!'

They had to shout as the Hope-15 engines were deafeningly riotous.

'Nor you feckin' ent.'

'Shut up. Let me enjoy this!' Rollo continued scribbling as the Hope-15 ruffled his hair and clothes while its endless lights skimmed the sky. 'Can't believe it. Do you know how rare these are?'

Darren shook his head. 'Fehin' shuttle potters.'

'Shuttle Spotting isn't something to turn your nose up at, you know.'

Darren chuckled.

'Yeah, laugh. If you knew the stories behind those New Era Hope ships you'd be a bit more interested, I reckon. I mean just look at it. What I wouldn't give to be up there, behind all that power!'

'Arr give a lot n'all!'

The Hope-15 flew out of sight, the wind still rife with life in its absence, its sound still minutes from muting.

'At least I can take joy in something. What do you do? Besides wake up in puddles of your own dribble?'

'Ay!'

'Sorry... But come on!' Rollo was wiggling with delight as Darren retreated beneath his hat in bewilderment. 'We'll probably never get to see something like that ever again! I'm so chuffed I managed to get down the serial number on its hull. Must have been really close. Might even be illegal to be that low... Lucky us ay!?'

'Or yer...'

'You can still hear it now!'

You really could; the floor was shaking and the engines continued to blaze in a far off storm of their own making. A whistle could even be heard, low like thunder at first, but gradually increasing in pitch.

'I could have reached out and touched it.'

Rollo began a jig at the thought, happy at last to take something positive away from his meaningless existence. But, as his belly bounced jovially, he noticed its shadow growing. He knew it was a large stomach, but not to that extreme. He plunged his porky digits into the girth, confused, only for his enthusiasm to quell beneath the shrill pitch of that high whistle accompanied by a bulging light behind him. Rollo turned to see a smooth metallic rock, larger even than he, tumbling from the heavens, clattering against the steel frames of the unbuilt skyscraper.

He scurried away as it pelted towards them, the excitement of the passing Hope-15 replaced with terror. He snatched the lightweight Darren from his seat and ran with him as if he were a paper streamer, leaping with uncharacteristic agility for cover. A deafening thud kicked dirt over the quivering pair and the generator beside their shattered stools whirred into silence as the scene sunk into pitch black. Before they had time to poke their heads from behind a pile of cement blocks, the projectile had rolled out of sight and an unusual breeze swam about the area.

'The 'ell war tha'?' Darren asked, his mouth shakier than usual.

'I don't know. What should we do?'

Darren replied with a *"How the hell should I know?"* kind of shrug.

'Erm, okay. Well, let's check it out then.'

'Wha'!?'

'Come on, it probably came from the shuttle! Oo, what a souvenir!'

'Feckin' 'ell.'

'Come on!' Rollo tugged him from hiding and they both fumbled for their torches.

The light was weak in the face of this new darkness, the bulbs flickering as if afraid to give too much away. Whatever it was they pursued had steamrolled into a labyrinth of high metal and stone. Rollo would never complain at the job's lack of action again. They moved slowly, following the broken earth and torn wires, the shattered foundations reaching claw-like about them. Their torches faded, something unnatural was playing havoc on the batteries. The wind creeping behind them felt misplaced, its whip usually failing to reach them at these depths.

'I thin' we shu rayio.'

'And radio who?'

A banshee scream launched from Rollo's chest, setting his heart into overdrive. He ripped the walkie-talkie pinned to his pocket free and hurled it away after it refused to silence.

'Must be interference of some kind...'

'We shu gur bah.'

'Nah, this is our job, we've got to investigate. Also, we could become famous for discovering something!'

Rollo kept pushing into the derelict cold. A strange air stung his tongue and the two didn't feel as alone as they should. The breeze was an alien breath that lifted the hairs on their necks, but to be so close to part of a Hope Cruiser was too good an opportunity for Rollo to pass up. Feeling their way forward, their torches now useless, Rollo sensed Darren shivering behind him. He was slowing them down in order to rub feeling back into his wrinkled arms, and Rollo felt a pang of anger at the stalling.

'Would you stop it!' he snapped.

Usually building up that kind of anger required too much effort for someone so obese, and he felt a twang of guilt at Darren's immediate silence. He didn't apologise.

With their torches discarded, they relied instead on a cool blue hue that beckoned them forwards, twisting the usual gothic shadows into something even sharper. Then, there it was, tucked within a web of broken steel and crumbling concrete, a boulder glowing with a cobalt hue. It was still, and yet the earth trembled, along with Darren. Rollo, on the other hand, was beside himself, his fears eradicated. Despite the object's natural, rocky form, it had to have been a part of the ship. Man-made rods and wires protruded from it in spiky ferociousness. Rollo wanted to touch it. He had to touch it.

'How beautiful...' He held out a hand, trembling with joy.

'Wha' ur dur!?' Darren was shaking too, for different reasons.

'Sh!' Rollo hissed. There was no pang of guilt this time.

'Ror-yo...'

'Shut it.' Rollo's eyes bulged red and then quickly paled as if nothing had happened. 'Remember, I said if you knew the stories behind the Hope ships you would be much more interested in them?'

'Ye...'

'They were horror stories, Darren,' Rollo said, gawping at the rock, his fingertips tingling in their closeness. 'They used to transport people during the War. Poor souls. They used those people in experiments, to test and create weapons.' He laughed. 'Terrible weapons.'

'Let's go...' Darren's voice was the clearest it had ever been.

'What I wouldn't give to be in their place.'

Rollo's palm flattened against the stone. Once it connected with the living frost, his hidden perversions and fantasies over those stories finally manifested on the surface, and his body took a contorted turn.

To Darren's horror, the fat drained from Rollo's skin. It was replaced with gaunt shadows stretching across a skeletal form. Rollo's mouth opened to the rock and that high pitched siren call, the same one that erupted from the radio and crippled their ears, sounded again. His eyes, nose, ears, and mouth, were replaced with flashing white lights and a dead, manic laughter erupted from every shining orifice.

If only Darren had known of Rollo's true passion, a passion of the most bafflingly vile and hateful things. Darren tried to run but found that his once minor arthritis had taken a hold of his joints and they became frozen, cracking locks. He looked to his escape routes, knowing he would never reach them, knowing he shouldn't have followed Rollo. By the time he turned back, Rollo had become a dreaded, hollowed out cosmonaut, the tales of such space ghosts told over frightening campfires in his youth. Rollo's tight, white, flaking skin had merged with the stone. His featureless skull, bloody and void of mind, cackled from its rocky podium surrounded by a halo of thin rusted metal.

'I am no shuttle spotter.' Rollo's voice was cutting and high pitched and of multiple tongues. 'I just like the stories, and now I am one.'

FAMILY

The rusty blades of a space cruising chopper had spun for a month straight, or so it felt, causing a whirlpool of rotten air to fill the cabin. In the thick of the musk, wrapped in chains, Terrora huddled against the wall separating her and her fellow prisoners from the cockpit. The red skin of her species couldn't hide the darker shades splayed over her wrists, creeping from her tight shackles that wrapped around her and beneath her rusted, rotting seat. Weary from the long journey, she embraced those chains, latching onto them for comfort. All other colour had been drawn from her face. Its paleness, however, was inconsequential for the porcelain texture of her people's stone white facial patterns, in particular, a crescent shaped moon that reached from her eye to the top of her head. Despite her predicament, Terrora's pigments hadn't drained out of fear of the cruel men she was forced to travel with, nor of the mystery of their destination. She was definitely afraid, though. So afraid she couldn't breathe, her anxiety and confusion heavy hands that crawled over her body.

The other prisoners had leered over her with lustful intent since their departure, their various hulking shapes slobbering over a woman so beautiful they could barely believe their luck. Terrora could have laughed off their intentions, their grizzly demise a certainty were they to act on their impulses, but instead she shivered beneath the dark haze that was the memory of her own crime. She didn't know for sure why she was being shipped to the Gred'lough, an edge of the galaxy prison planet reserved for the most hellacious evildoers, but she knew there must have been a good reason why her chains were far more fortified than the others'.

The cabin shuddered, forcing hideous visions of that night to flicker through her mind like a zoetrope riddled with missing frames. Whispers rippled behind torn silhouettes, plastered against the screen of her closed eyelids. She had heard those voices many times, and in the cold shell of her capture, her inner family stirred just below the surface once more. She hated them, feared them, feared herself. Her father had too.

'Five minutes until drop,' the pilot's voice called over the cabin's speakers. The voices in Terrora's head suddenly woke and began to chatter. She slammed her skull against the wall but they wouldn't stop.

'Aw, come on now, dearie,' snarled a bulging Dicerous, a leathery, thick humanoid who took up two seats. He had a chubbed, pimple doused nose that hung past his chin. Most of the sounds he made erupted from it. 'It's not so bad. Free reign down there I hear, hardly a prison. Every man for themselves.'

He chuckled deeply, and his flab rattled uncomfortably close to Terrora. She sunk further into her little corner as the other inmates laughed along with him. The whispers in her head sent a twitch shooting through her fingers. She gripped them tightly with the other hand, welling up as she failed to soothe them. She had only embraced that twitching once before and, judging by her current position, it had not ended well.

'Two minutes until drop,' the pilot came again, distracting her. He had left the cockpit and was making his way to the back of the cabin, careful to avoid the jeers, tentacles, and lashing limbs of the prisoners. He remained stern in the face of it all, his sharp features a match for his military uniform. After taking an electrified baton from a sheath tied to his back, and jamming it into the face of a particularly aggressive snub-shouldered Groober, he addressed the cabin.

'You, the stains of the Rothrum Galaxy, will be dropped from this carrier in approximately one and a half minutes. The estimated drop time will be two minutes, at which point half of you will plunge to your deaths upon the Frenz Mountains below. For those of you lucky enough to catch the pack of parachutes and essential items following in the chopper behind, once you land you must immediately report to the first Gred'lough Guard you find and he will transport you to your detail.'

'What if we feel like killing the Guard when we find him?' the Dicerous asked.

The other prisoners were genuinely eager to hear the answer, drooling over the prospect.

'Then your souls will be ripped from your bodies,' the pilot replied, quite matter-of-factly. 'Gentlemen, and madam, do not think the Gred'lough Guards the same as you or I. If you test them, they will neither hesitate nor fail to destroy you. Death will be reserved for the lucky.

'Survival on the most effective prison planet in the universe's history is not something to be taken lightly. No ship has landed there since its inception, its very atmosphere is a punishment and technology an impossibility. There is no escape, there are no means to take power, and you will serve the rest of your lives on its surface alone and in pain, just as you deserve. Now, any questions?'

'I have one—' the Dicerous began.

'No? Good.'

The pilot whacked a worn out button on the ceiling. The cabin filled with a red pulse and Terrora's heart paced rhythmically with the manic flashes. She wasn't ready. This chopper had been her home for a solid, uncomfortable month, but in the face of her fate, she would have gladly traded the paper thin, threading cushion of her chair if it meant not being thrown out of it. Then, before she could utter one last plea with her eyes, her stomach leapt into her mouth as she and her seat fell through the floor and into the foul stink of the Gred'lough cloud system.

Panic set in immediately as grey fluff rumbled past Terrora's hairless head, swimming over her like icy water that squeezed her lungs. Her fingers froze, she could barely bend them around the shackles anchoring her to the chair she was desperately trying to wrench free from. In the ever-quickening descent, all she could do was latch onto the passing seconds and beg time to slow, to give her an extra moment's clear thought before she met the peaks of the Frenz Mountains. She may have feared the approaching prison world, but she didn't want to die either. Given the unusual guests in her head, how could she know what horrors the life after promised?

In her increasing delirium, the bulbous physique of the Dicerous sped past laughing, causing what little concentration on survival she had to scatter. He lashed out as he passed and clobbered Terrora's arm before disappearing into the rainy void. It took all her might to quieten the voices in her head; she was not going to die in their possession, even if she agreed with their vengeful sentiments. The brief collision caused the princess to spin away uncontrollably, and her arms and legs clattered against the metal of her chair. She couldn't tell which way was up. But as the world stretched into streaks of varying grey shades, her eyes glimpsed a dark green object falling with her: a parachute pack.

She flung her arms wide, stifling her rapid spin for a brief moment, just enough time to take a hold of its straps. She tore open the top and rummaged through. The family in her head took immediate offence and screamed out together. Terrora's ears panged and she pulled her hand free. They didn't want her to survive. 'No!' she screamed at them, and then plunged her arms back inside. She closed her eyes, trying to blot out the pain, and wailed along with those voices as blood poured over her ear lobes and down her arms.

A few more precious seconds sailed by before Terrora's numb fingers felt out hollowly against a key, just as her body broke the base of the clouds and she entered the last stormy mile between sky and mountain. The twirling trails of the Frenz below made a bullseye of its harsh tips and curled around its ridges before they met a roaring ocean. Terrora jammed the key into her cuffs and her family's screams became quiet, fearful pleas. She threw the cuffs aside, and then kicked the chair away, fumbling the clips of the pack across her chest. They clicked into place, just as vertigo set in and shook her senses into uselessness. But now she was set and ready, she was going to make it over this first hurdle, and all she had to do was pull the parachute promising cord dangling beside her hip.

She heard the waves of the southern sea, clashing against themselves in god-like, nautical combat, dwarfing the sound of the wind that layered her pointed red ears with frostbite. She prayed that the ice might plug them, damning the sounds of her family, which still begged her not to release the cord. The storm's raging blackness was nothing compared to their coarse language, rattling the inside of her skull before she defiantly shook her head and pulled...

Too late.

Her body met with whipping wind, sharp and unforgiving stone, and the heart stopping chill of shallow water, all within an unrelenting instant, and she fell to the shadow of the Gred'lough landscape. A small, forgiving whisper petered into the blackness along with her dead mind.

Hiking through the winding Frenz Mountain trails, two Gred'lough Guards patiently awaited the arrival of the new inmates. Both were of equal stature and build, and were human in form, but rather than skin their bodies appeared to be wrought from clear glass. Instead of organs, their sleek transparency yielded only dark blue smoke intertwined with starlight. They both wore identical, stone black suits that refused to catch even a speck of dust kicked up by the storm. The faces poking from their sharp collars were unmoving, eyes closed, but they could see. Oh, how they could see. Where a human's brain would normally be, a galactic wisp of bright colour twirled behind their stoicism.

The one whose wisp was a saturated red led the way, issuing his partner a breakdown of the incoming prisoners and their crimes. The other Gred'lough Guard, whose wisp was light yellow and releasing subtle streaks of lightning, replied with a simple, 'It is understood.' Although his mouth didn't move. His voice was fair yet deep, as was his partner's. As they walked together, they seemed to float over the landscape, traversing the perilous ledges and slopes without a single thought given to the steps they had to take. This had gone on for several hours without issue until the Red Guard spoke of the final prisoner.

'Princess Terrora Faus Sen: Female,' he said as if reading, although there was no list in his hand.

'A princess?' The Yellow Guard questioned, breaking their systematic routine for the first time.

'Is that a problem?'

'No.'

'Then it is understood?'

'It is understood, but—'

The Yellow Guard didn't know why he was suddenly so interested. Considering the war and its ongoing power struggle, royalty was far from a rarity when it concerned inmates destined for the Gred'lough. He lamented the seconds he had wasted, knowing he had few to spare. The Gred'lough Guards were powerful, so powerful that outliving the decade was not an option. It took too much energy to fuel such beings. But they were efficient, or at least should have been. The cosmos behind his face should have quashed any query he had instantly, and yet there was something about the name Princess Terrora that the Yellow Guard's vastness couldn't quite grasp.

'But?' the Red Guard said, equally perturbed.

'I don't know,' the Yellow replied. 'I suspect the answers to my concerns will be revealed in the reading of her details. Please, continue. It is understood.'

The Red Guard paused, the wisp in his head swirling off axis, then continued.

'Her crime is that of High Murder against Prince Trus Far Sen, her father and Under Lord of the planet Sen, and his guests on the twenty-seventh evening of The Half Age of their native calendar. Total body count: Fifty-two.'

'It is understood.'

'She pleaded not guilty but, after a lengthy trial, was convicted due to irrefutable evidence. She achieved High Murder through a series of methods; cutting, impact, and shock.'

'Shock? The guests were scared to death?'

'Correct.'

'It is understood.'

'Her most prominent threats are unknown. Due to the logical impossibility of a young Senthri girl, not twenty-one Senthri years of age, overpowering an entire High Council and their families, as well as five armed Senthri Officials, we are unable to determine the full method behind those murders and the true dangers she possesses. Due to the amount of deceased, it is determined that we be on Highest Alert.'

'Fascinating.'

'Pardon?'

'It is understood.'

'Distinct features are that of most Senthri females; red skin C63434; humanoid; bald; white plumage on the face. Terrora's plumage is unique due to a distinct crescent shape reaching from the corner of her left eye to the top of her skull. Her eye colour is full blue 3487C6. She is considered an aesthetically pleasing member of her species and, in keeping with Senthri culture, she was fully segregated. Because of this lifestyle, she is found to be nervous around males. She is five feet and seven inches tall, and weighs approximately one-hundred and twenty-seven pounds.'

'It is understood.'

'Is it?'

'Pardon?'

The Red Guard turned to the Yellow as they reached a pebbled slope leading to the rough shores of the Gred'Lough's Southern Ocean. 'You are going about your duties rather haphazardly this morning and have been insufficient in your reading of this inmate. I worry that you have not absorbed the information correctly and therefore will not be fully capable of handling a difficult situation should it arise.'

The Yellow Guard didn't respond at first, although the reflection of his partner's fears were swirling aggressively within his own glass head.

'That will not happen, it is understood.'

'Pray that it is.'

Flashes of lightning lit the ocean's black horizon with a harsh gradient and, as the Guards approached the beach, they saw seven of the fourteen bodies they had expected falling from the clouds. The remnants of the prisoners' limp scrambling fell on forgotten sympathies from the Gred'lough locals, who had seen so many before them plunge into the planet's face and splatter into the next life. When their bodies hit the Frenz, thuds echoed across the mountain range. The Guards waited patiently for the next wave.

Those six bodies petered through the cloud line in much more delicate fashion, parachutes unleashed. The Guards of Red and Yellow watched them slowly descend into the mountains, judging how long it would take to reach each one, and which routes would be best to take. One inmate was unlucky enough to land in the Southern Ocean, a mile's break from the shore; he wouldn't survive those waves or the hungry, violent beings that dwelled there.

That final landing should have been the Guards' signal to begin their search, but instead they redoubled their focus on the clouds. Neither could wrap their heads around the absence of the final prisoner. It wasn't like a Gred'lough Guard to miss something so vitally important, and even more unlikely that two should miss it. They looked at each other, then back to the sky as that prisoner finally fell, desperately struggling to attach her parachute.

How she had reached the planet last without being the first to unleash her chute was a mystery, and the wisps behind the Guards' faces swirled wildly as they searched every morsel of information they retained on both physics and the supernatural, demanding an explanation to the anomaly. Before they could find one, the body of the girl hit the shallow water where the sea met the shore, barely half an hour's hike from the Guards' position. This was going to require further investigation.

The Dicerous hit the ground hard after his parachute caught and ripped on a jagged ridge. After a brief battle with unconsciousness, the beast shook his head like a dog and steadied himself. Blood trickled freely from a gash where his ear used to be, all the way to his hoofed hand, an injury that would have claimed any weaker species. In all his murderous years spent traipsing across the galaxy, he had quickly learned that he was far tougher than anything death could throw at him. Rather than bow to the pain, he stood straight, bawled both his hands into fists, and plunged them into the thick of his spine.

'Ah!' he moaned. 'Now, I wonder where that little princess has got to.'

He grinned at the cavernous trail ahead. The grey walls of the Frenz Mountains reached over like the inside of a sharp mouth fit to close and he slobbered at their challenge. Like stampeding animals, the Dicerous people had a one track mind, and this particular specimen knew exactly who he intended to meet at the end of it; he had known the moment her red skin graced the light of his eyes. He had no intention of seeking out the Gred'lough Guards as instructed. As far as he was concerned, he was a free Dicerous, and he would not be refused his first meal as one.

He left his pack behind, deciding that nothing it held would aid his already enormous frame in surviving, and made his way to higher ground. The howling winds, which tore chunks out of the mountain itself, were no stronger than the wings of a moth to him. He used his bulk as forward momentum and paced for ceaseless hours through the Frenz's different pathways, hoping to reach an unimpeded viewpoint.

He hadn't seen a single Guard or prisoner and took pride in assuming he was the only one to survive the drop, as well as the sulphur thick air. Still, he trudged in search of the princess, his mind somehow skipping the thought that she may well have died too. After scouring the mountain for half the day, he reached a maze of head height stones. He took a moment to turn his face against the skin-peeling rain and drank the sour water. The Dicerous choked when he heard a voice call to him from the other end of the maze.

'Burta!'

With the aid of six moist tentacles, a thin, slithering alien crawled out from the confines of a cave system across the maze from him. The Dicerous recognised the creature's long, aqua colouring from the chopper, and took immediate cover behind a nearby rock. He struggled to squeeze his bulky arms behind it, but his rough skin merged seamlessly with the stone.

'How does he know my name?' the Dicerous growled quietly to himself.

'Taejon? Dreaden? Hem?' the slitherer called again.

'Or does he?'

Burta poked a yellow, vertically-slitted eye over the lip of the stone and saw his fellow prisoner reading from a paper list clasped in its front tentacle, no doubt found in the pack bouncing against the reptilian creature's back. Slunk low to the floor, it reluctantly made its way into the stone maze in search of an ally.

'Hello? Hem? I saw one of you out here. We need a plan; we can rule this place together.'

Burta's bloodlust became insatiable as the creature's words bounced off its nerves. Not to take advantage of one weaker than himself would be an insult to the Dicerous' very modus operandi. He could surely spare a minute from his busy schedule of stalking the princess to tuck into an appetiser.

Crawling around the maze, both of its hearts beating against the dusty floor, the tentacled inmate grew more and more fearful the longer it went without hearing a response. Its tail lagged behind and its wobbling limbs shook whenever a crack of lightning sounded overhead.

'Burta?' it whispered. 'Come on, if we stick together nothing can stop us.'

'Oh?' boomed the Dicerous.

The slitherer jumped and crawled on top of the closest pillared rock for a better view. It couldn't see anything over the field of stone. The lines of its face contorted.

'Enough! Where are you!?' But it could not discern the stone from Burta, who remained surprisingly light footed in his approach. 'You can join me or die, Dicerous! Whatever your name is!'

'Doubtful.'

Burta's voice echoed all around and the reptilian grew more aggressive.

'You weren't the only great power aboard that chopper you fat fool, and you'll see!'

The lizard bounced agitatedly atop the pointy rock, ready to leap at the first sign of movement.

'Really?' Burta asked.

'Really!'

'Please.'

Then, as if a vice had clamped around its tail, the reptile hollered and turned to see the meaty hoof of Burta clasping it tight. The Dicerous snatched the creature from its perch and pelted its tiny frame against the flat of another. Rather than stars, although they too pulsed on the back of its eyelids, it was blood and rogue teeth that spun about the reptile's head before it crumpled into a heap on the ground. But what the lizard had claimed earlier was true; the Dicerous wasn't the only dangerous passenger to be dropped on the Gred'lough that day. As Burta laughed carelessly, the body of this particular captive seized up through some obscure defence mechanism and sprung onto the Dicerous' arm, tentacles wrapping around and latching into his flesh. Burta tugged at the creature but the slimy skin only lubricated his hand. Suckers on the underside of the tentacles were drinking the very colour from Burta's arm and he dropped to a knee. His growl broke into something higher pitched as the reptile snapped its wide mouth over his shoulder. Tiny, scalpel-like teeth cut through the Dicerous' tough hide like butter. Burta was growing woozy, and in every spot where his arm had been punctured, a creeping green pigment began taking over. The reptile laughed with a mouthful of blood, the overflow of which splattered Burta's cheek, but Burta wasn't done yet.

He stood and staggered over to the face of a tall flat stone and lined up his fist. With all the might he had left, he plunged his arm into the wall, all the way up to the elbow. The sharp rock broke off in both his arm and the parasite draining him of life. The reptile's grip only grew tighter. In his panic, Burta pounded the standalone rock to rubble and then tripped over the debris. His head was swirling but he rose again. He threw himself into other stones, whipping his arm about violently, levelling the entire maze; no matter what he did he could not shake the lizard. His vision doubled, then tripled. The Frenz spun so rapidly about him that all he could do was feel out his surroundings and hurtle himself arm-first into whatever was closest.

That was until the Dicerous' toes went numb, and he slipped onto his knees for the final time. His heart slowed, all he could hear was the gurgling of the reptile as it fed upon his flesh. It was a sound he imagined far worse than any intimidating laugh he could have mustered should the tables have been turned. It became quickly apparent that Burta was not stronger than death.

A passing Gred'lough Guard, the wisp behind his glass face blue and icy, had stopped to watch the fight unfold. When he was sure it was over, he entered the arena of broken stone. At its centre, the mangled body of Burta lay beneath the reptile who continued sucking whatever life was left.

'Greysin Cules?' the Guard asked, without a hint of trepidation.

The lizard was startled and scuttled behind Burta's corpse, limping.

'Greysin Cules? The Télagardian?' the Guard asked again.

'Yes,' Greysin hissed.

'Come, you must report to your detail. Take my hand.'

A wry smile stretched across the Télagardian's face. He slowly made his way to the Guard, eyeing up the arm and body that had been presented to him, looking hard into the Guard's face for any inkling that he knew what Greysin was planning. *Two meals in one sitting?* Greysin couldn't believe his luck. Of course, nothing could be read in the Guard's face, which lulled the Télagardian further. Greysin was excited to learn how this being's insides tasted. Before judging the situation further, Greysin took the outstretched palm and attacked. A barrage of flailing tentacles and dust kicked up as he coiled about the Guard. Being much smaller than Burta, Greysin easily wrapped his tentacles around both of the Guard's arms and latched onto him like some heavy, scaled stole. There was nothing the Guard could do now that Greysin had locked his mouth around the Guard's throat. Or so Greysin thought. The glass skin would not break, and Greysin's teeth cracked and chipped against it. Even the sharpened suckers on his arms failed to tear through the Guard's suit. All that was left to do was squeeze.

After a few more moments of struggling, dread eclipsed Greysin's confidence. The Guard stood straight, flexed his back, and puffed his chest. Greysin felt an invisible force take a hold of him. It was a burning sensation that travelled through his arms and towards his hearts. He spluttered and saw the Guard's blue wisp thrashing about its owner's skull. In the eye of that storm, Greysin became light-headed and drained of energy. Somehow his grip broke and he felt the exact pain and fear of those he had murdered skulking across the universe. The pain and terror washed over him in a spiteful flood all at once. He slid groggily from the Guard's shoulders, but before hitting the floor the Guard snatched him back into the air with a telekinetic wave of his wrist. The Gred'lough Guard raised a steady finger and held Greysin still, unable to writhe, unable to breathe, and walked away from him. Alone and unmoving, the reptile felt every individual cell that comprised him turn on each other. He was eating himself from the inside out, but his body would not deplete. After all the battles he had survived, after all the situations he had managed to worm himself out of, after he had so easily vanquished the massive Burta, this was his end, and it would not be quick.

The Télagardian's mind was easily read, and as he left the flattened maze, the Gred'lough Guard looked back and said, 'We haven't the time to suffer fools, Greysin. Your sentence has been amended, you will suffer yourself forever.'

Six bobbing glass heads, filled with a different coloured wisp each, sat atop the shoulders of six Gred'lough Guards travelling aboard a rusty, eight-legged clockwork carriage. The handle of a giant key poked from its front, rotating slowly. It would be hours before it stopped and the carriage would need winding again, and it had been hours since that the Guards had left the Frenz Mountains with the three inmates they had found alive. A slender red hand, dangling from beneath a dark green parachute, lay across the floor of the carriage, taking up much of the room.

'Why can't we just kick this lump overboard?' a human prisoner asked, his body laden with scars, some old, others not so much.

'No, she must be brought to Menoheth City with us,' said the Guard with the yellow wisp. 'She is an anomaly; she must be investigated.'

'She's not an anomaly. She's dead. She's nothing now, you bizarre lightbulb.'

Another prisoner, taller than the Guards by a foot or so, whose body resembled a dark purple, skinless muscle diagram, said, 'Do not insult them, Hem. You, yourself, saw what they did to the worm.'

'Oh no! I didn't mean no offence, but they can understand my frustrations, can't they?' Hem said, shuffling uncomfortably as the Blue Guard sat opposite him had yet to turn away. 'Shame though, she was quite pretty. I could see me settling down with a girl like that.'

'Is that before or after you murder and eat her family in order to... What was it you did in that cult? Drain her life force?'

'Collect, not drain. And it would be my King who received it.'

'Then why are you here and not him?'

'Probably 'cause I was a little overzealous with my sacrificing. Sacrificed faster than he could receive. But you know, like my mummy said: you've got a talent, you've got to let it bloom. Over three thousand souls I presented to the Great Ori King!' Hem's chest puffed proudly. 'Bet you wish you could achieve such numbers.'

'Why would a man wish to drown in all that blood? I'm not a murderer, I do not enjoy killing. I was High General of the Atlan Clan and defended my realm from all twelve of the Black Planets for countless seasons before a cowardly betrayal led to my arrest. I have seen too much of death already. You can keep your numbers.'

'Please, you're no less murderer than I am. Proud I bet too. Bet you've thought about fighting your way off this carriage more than once.'

The general did not reply.

'What about you?' Hem continued. 'What are you doing here?'

He addressed the third prisoner, a robed man sat at the front of the carriage. The figure had kept his face hidden beneath the deep red robe ever since the chopper first set off for the Gred'lough. He trembled at being spoken to.

'Oi! I'm talking to you!' Hem raised his voice, now far too comfortable in the presence of the Guards who had, for the most part, ignored him.

He reached over the red wisped Guard to tug on the shaking man's cloak but the Guard grabbed his wrist. The bone beneath Hem's skin buckled. The storm ceased, the legs of the carriage paused mid climb, and the ocean their path overlooked held back its crashing waves. The only sign of life came from the other Guards, who turned to Hem in unison.

The purple general was free to move too, and his face dropped. The general's stature and battle prowess were nothing compared to this mysticism, and he felt foolish for even considering escape, as Hem had rightly predicted of him. The Guards could stop his heart just by commanding it. 'Apologise, you fool!'

'I'm sorry, I was just playing,' Hem quivered, frozen in fear, afraid that if he tugged himself away his world would end.

His soul shuddered beneath the grip of the Guard, and the faces of all those he killed fluttered before his eyes and he felt a nibbling on the back of his neck. He remembered the lizard, who the Guards had left squirming, alone and broken, back in the mountains.

'No more talking,' the Red Guard demanded. 'Is it understood?'

'I understand! Please, I'm sorry!'

The Guard let go. Once he did, the Gred'lough returned to its usual self. Hem looked down and rocked in his seat, trying to forget the faces he had seen, the teeth he had felt on his spine. He nervously chewed the back of his palm and noted the similarity of the bite. Shame kept him silent and still for the rest of the journey. Rather than talk, he fixated on the body covered by the parachute at his feet. If he didn't know better, he could have sworn he saw the red hand twitch and heard a whisper sing softly beneath the rushing winds. He presumed it a delayed trick of the Guards and kept quiet.

The day remained constant as they travelled. The Gred'lough didn't get any warmer or colder, lighter or darker, it was consistently dreary. By the time the party reached Menoheth, it could not be told whether it was day or night.

Menoheth City was a slum fishing port built of innumerable shacks, stacked high and deep over a long valley that bled into an estuary that joined the Southern Sea to the mainland rivers. The clockwork carriage crawled into a dank, semi-circular harbour, painted with grime. The odour of fish guts swelled with the planet's pre-existing sulphur stink. The city's villainous inhabitants skulked about the seafront's shanty shops, carrying lamps that shone with sickly yellow flames. Hem, the purple general, and the cloaked prisoner, were ordered into a line beside the carriage. Despite the clear danger that each of the Menohethans possessed, all of them alpha villains in their own right, they paid little mind to the new arrivals. They bustled around them, arms filled with baskets containing hideous fish, or minerals taken from the cliffs that bookended the harbour. Thin streets crisscrossed towards those cliffs, a giant slope of tightly packed homes reeking of disease and overpopulation.

'Do you see that? Skulls in the walls,' Hem said, leaning into the purple general.

He was right. Boulders, jutting from the cliffs, decorated with sunken alien bones, sat away in the distance at the end of his shaking finger. They appeared to have absorbed a being each and had pulled their victims flesh so tight across the stone that they had become skeletal. Occasionally, but never in unison, the skulls would glow faintly white, their lights casting no shadow.

'The Rothshao Stones,' the general said. 'They are not from this world.'

Hem felt the scars on his face being pried open by dry and unseen hands, and tiny streams of blood began streaking down his cheeks; the Rothshao were responsible. He knew because every single prisoner waddling past them spluttered relentlessly upon themselves and one another. They were all broken, either in mind or limb, and beyond the help of medicine. Those cackling heads that cocked and whined in the cliffs above them loomed like poisonous overseers of struggle. The Gred'lough did not hold its captives with chains, but by exaggerating individual weaknesses.

'What planet are they from then?' Hem asked, coughing onto the back of his hand.

'No, this *world*. They do not breath the same air, nor abide by the same rules, they are ghosts sat between this life and the next, present only by absorbing the living. You and they have a lot in common.'

Hem scowled. 'You seem to know a lot about them.'

'It was my job to know everything I could about the Black Planets.'

'I see. Any ideas on how to escape this one?'

'I wish.'

'Only three?' a new Gred'lough Guard called out. He marched towards them from the heart of the crowded docks, a pink galaxy behind his face.

Every Menohethan bowed before him and hurried aside as he approached. This Guard wasn't like the others. He strode with a proud gate and exuded an essence that almost pulled Hem, the general, and the robed prisoner onto one knee before him as well.

'Most did not survive the drop,' the Red Guard said. 'Two died through in-fighting and one—'

The Pink Guard raised a hand. He looked past his underling to the body below the parachute, now dumped unceremoniously beside the water, protected by the other Guards who made a path for their pink leader's gaze.

'And one what?' he asked.

'We aren't sure. We thought—'

'You thought foolishly. Thinking takes time. Time allows chances. We cannot give inmates chances. Name?'

'Princess Ter...'

'She was high priority. Stand aside. Her soul must be eliminated.'

The Pink Guard moved hastily, but as he drew close the Rothshao Stones broke into a chorus of coarse squeals that cut the air. The Guard stopped. Hem saw the anger in the Guard's pink wisp, and the ground rumbled. The air was alive with hate, and the Pink Guard cocked his head as he addressed the cliffs.

'Quiet!' he roared.

Most Menohethans dropped what they held and took cover behind anything close. Hem wanted to do the same, but the general held him firm. 'Don't do anything stupid!'

Hem had only ever heard the Guards speak in tones of mild disinterest; this one packed a temper. The Rothsao refused to obey, and their lights coursed the sky and flashed over him. Pink lightning ebbed between the Guard's fingertips as the sirens grew more out of control.

'I said quiet!'

Any Menohethans not hiding scattered into a manic frenzy for cover. Something terrible was about to happen.

'This is new,' the Yellow Guard said, standing beside the general and Hem.

'They've never done this before!?' the general bellowed, covering his ears, darting his head about to try and escape the screams and lights of the Rothshao.

'Never.'

'Should we run?'

'That would not be wise.'

Just as the cliffs looked ready to collapse, the third inmate, who was trembling so violently at this point that he looked ready to disrobe, randomly took off into the thinning crowd.

'Enough!' the Pink Guard shrieked.

A bolt of furious magenta exploded from his fingertips, all of his pent up anger behind it. It ruptured the attempted escapee's spine, and the impact filled the docks with a squelching sound. The bolt lurched low and then high, lifting the inmate into the air before driving him back onto the wet, cobbled floor. Forgotten already. A new stink of burnt flesh swelled into the Gred'lough's filthy cocktail.

'Her soul will never be yours!' the Pink Guard howled at the cliffs. 'She must be cast to the winds!'

Silence. It was not calm. A vicious anticipation hung in the air, and gravity tugged hard on the faces of those still present.

'Good.' The Guard stood straight and regained his composure. But he had not seen what Hem, the general, and the other six Guards had seen. The parachute from the carriage hung tall beside the water, floating with a ghostly sway. A red hand loomed from a tear in its side.

'Wake up, daughter,' an unseen woman sang. Terrora's eyes stayed shut and the darkness pressed her to the floor.

'Wake up,' said another. 'We're sorry we had to be so cruel.'

You're not sorry, Terrora tried shouting back, but her lips were numb. *You wanted this.*

'We want you, daughter, to embrace us. For we are you,' a man's voice added.

I'm nothing like you.

'Then why fight so hard to be rid of us?'

Because I don't want to hurt.

'It's okay, sister,' a young child said. 'Hurting is natural. It makes you strong.' Terrora couldn't tell if it was a boy or girl. To hear it speak of pain so fondly sent her nerves into spasm, the first thing she had felt in hours.

You made me kill all those people... There were children...

'All with their own selfish agenda,' the child said. 'There was talk of marriage you know, at the party.'

The other voices hissed at the word and began to bicker incoherently, even Terrora's eyebrow furled. *Father would only want the best for me. Maybe... Maybe I would have liked to get married.*

'And become nothing but meat! Would you be a man's meal, sister? To pick at when he wanted, sister? Did you

95

enjoy being locked away? Will you enjoy being locked away still?'

No…

'No indeed! They must know you for you, they must know us, know what you are; more than your curved scar. Unleash us…'

But how? No… I will not see your side again!

'Our side is your side,' the man said. 'But this isn't about sides, daughter.' Terrora liked his voice, even more than her real father's. 'This is about change. We must let the mortals know we are here and that we will not be shackled.'

Terrora felt a hand on her back and she cradled into it. She felt so comfortable beneath the soothing palm. It would protect her. It always had. It knew what was best. She had always thought of herself as good in heart, would never hurt a fly lest the family in her head instructed it, but now, in the presence of their voices, she dreamt in blood, in carnage. The vibrations of her family's soothing tones rippled across an ocean of it, gently rocking her heart into something she finally recognised.

'You have a choice now,' the woman said. 'Alone you are dead, your flesh broken upon the rocks, but together we will rise again, you and your family, as one. Just as it should be.'

Where did you even come from? Terrora wanted to come across defiant, but there was nothing to her words.

'You will know when you rise.'

But mother…

'Hush, daughter. Follow those twitching fingers.'

Terrora rose, cruel hands lifting her broken soul, and she felt a veil upon her, heavy and rough in texture but it did not block her view. She saw straight through it, at a man whose anger was pink and tangible. It paled in the light of hers, and the more irate he became the more her sight vignetted and her soul grew wild. The grey, pulsing border around her gaze made a target of the pink man and she began to pant like a hungry beast, her tongue slobbering in kind between teeth fit to scar the air with their sharpness. She had become what she had always feared of herself: a monster, unstoppable and propelled by a family of equally wretched things, and she was glad. She no longer feared, for herself or her people or her future, for in this form there was nothing more that could claim her, and she was hungry. So very hungry.

Her hand was cold. She felt the fears of everything close by swirling between her fingers, tasting it through her skin. Her hand clasped shut so tightly that she cut into her palms, her nails transformed into picks of ice. The pink man took a step forwards and she lost the last iota of her old self. Not knowing how, she whipped her veil at him and chased after it, crawling on all fours. Like a spider, she clambered onto her prey and sunk her teeth into his skull. It cracked and shattered and she swallowed the bright liquid and smoke that oozed into her mouth along with her own torn flesh. She knew that others were watching, could feel exactly where they stood and where they were moving to. They were but panicky zig-zagging heart beats and she was drawn to their terror like a bloodhound.

There was screaming all around, muted by her own as she leapt from one victim to the next. Bolts of bright energy tore into her, but web-like, stringed flesh pulled her limbs back together as she charged at the other coloured men. The favour of their attacks was returned tenfold as Terrora absorbed all that they were, splaying herself at them with more limbs than were countable. She grew to an unfathomable size and tore up the earth with her advance before changing direction. She followed a crowd of rushing heart beats fleeing into a boxed city, the walls of which hid nothing from her fiery eyes. She tore into their bodies, ripping souls from their cages, entering the homes where they hid through vents or key holes, or by tearing down the walls and banshee wailing her shuddering victims into the next life.

A trail of destruction lay behind her, of blood and wreckage and organs that fell from the sky like rain, until she reached the cliffs. The mountainous stone wall was filled with faces she hated more than the pink man's, beings of similar power and origin, and their calls battled against hers. But they were weak, she could smell it. A wave of her now winged arm stripped those skeletal boulders from the walls with one apocalyptic flap and the rubble coursed comet-like at the ant sized beings left scurrying in the ruined city below. The destruction of those monsters filled her with a twisted joy and her carnage lust bubbled over further. She foamed at the mouth, bursting at the seams with it.

She took to the air in a flaming arch of light that cut the sky and plummeted back into the harbour, her intentions a blur and unknown even to herself. She had become a frantic animal, more dangerous than any beast the physical world could produce. When she hit the ground a cloud of energy mushroomed into a burning mountain of hellfire. Weightless bodies flung helplessly into the air and turned to ash as the ocean turned to flee her. Just two faint heart beats remained, locked in her sniper's vision. She drooled over the weeping shapes, her jaws contorting in anticipation of the coming meal, when a pair of arms wrapped around her shoulders and began to squeeze.

For a moment she saw herself; face redder than it had ever been; arms long and multiplied; tails, wings, horns, all growing into various shapes before dissipating into stews of smoke and piles of crushed insects. Her hate tripled, but it was aimed inwards. Her hazy, blackened vision cleared, and she saw what she had become. In a desperate longing to escape the truth, she coiled her neck around her assailant, who was fighting with all he had to feed her with the imagery of her own hideousness. A moment later, the yellow man shattered and the glass stuck in her throat, only to melt away into nothing.

The young Senthri princess, who Terrora used to know, had returned, but she was trapped in her new ugly guise and teetered on the spot. She could not vanquish the image of what she had become. Her mind swirled with confusion. She could hear her family, guiding her murderous claws as they saw fit, leading them towards the two souls she had drooled over previously. But she was a girl again, she didn't want to choke on their blood, she didn't want to hear their bones snapping. She cried out but it crushed the cosmos and sounded villainous. She had been tainted forever. She had succumbed to her own fear and would be forced to poison the universe in a demon form she shared with her abusive family. This would not stand.

Yes, she was but a fraction of that demon, but an equal fraction. She would leave these two bodies before her, whoever they were, even if it meant tearing herself apart.

She wheeled away towards the cliffs and ocean, and clattered into its rocks and shallow water, her own body pulling itself apart. Whirling chaotically into the Gred'lough coastal regions, she left the wrecked city behind her, as well as the knocking knees of the two men she had spared.

Hem and the General were holding each other. The Yellow Guard had told them not to move and those words of wisdom held true. Menoheth was awash with blood, its walls decorated with mosaics of entrails, its architecture torn like paper. What they had seen could not be repeated, and they were left so afraid that it was difficult to trust the image of those black and red leviathan tendrils disappearing around the cliff's ridge and out of sight. They felt for sure they had met their end.

Hem dropped to his knees, watching the tears drop from his nose onto the stone floor. Holding his nerve and acting rationally did not come easily to the aptly nicknamed Ori Slasher, and he keeled over, dry heaving on an air rich with death.

'Did you see how she moved?' he said at last.

'She was all things, yet nothing,' the struck general replied. 'One moment smoke, the next shadow, or liquid, then a marauding plague.'

'And beasts! I didn't recognise one of them.'

'A shapeshifter, with a million crooked eyes. I can't—'

'Do you think she'll come back?' Hem asked, getting to his feet and into a panicky state more natural to him.

'No.'

'How'd you know?'

They both stared away at the coastline, a shrill call of the demon still echoing over the Southern Sea.

'Look around you, she sent this place to hell. If she wanted us dead, we would be.'

DOCTOR DOCTOR

On the eve of a most important decision, the faces of seven Medi board members strew as straight and serious as the no-nonsense conference room that housed them. Four men, three women, each dressed a match for the sharp black walls, nervously shifted amongst themselves as a flat-screen monitor at the end of the room's central glass table flickered into life. The screen's image was faint at first and cast its content in a hue of overbearing blue. Once the signal grew clear, the pointed features of a scruffy, white coated man crowded the lens.

He stood in a room cluttered with papers and film tapes, with no further space for anything but. Nose tilted up at the camera, he addressed the board as nervously as they looked.

'Sirs and Madams, good morning. I have Mr Toffman's testimony on file when you're ready. I know you also have some questions, so, if you please...'

None were brave enough to speak.

After a prolonged silence, the most stone faced woman of the group, her lips drooping from heavy lipstick, took a deep breath and said, 'Very well, if no one else has the fortitude; Doctor Parker, can this man's story be corroborated? Is he going to cause headaches in the future?'

The doctor looked unsure of himself, unsure of the question. 'Well, no. He was the only survivor, and given his current mental state he wouldn't be fit to testify against the company in a court setting, but that shouldn't be the issue here—' He tried to continue but was cut off by the flood of relief spilling over the board members. They were all too busy wiping the metaphoric sweat from their brows and bursting with silent elation to listen further. Many a handshake was had before the woman finally responded.

'Well then? What's the issue here? We're safe, the company who pay you are safe.'

'The issue here is that it shows how clearly defective the Medi program could become, could already be.'

'This is a rare circumstance.'

'Potentially, but can Medi afford another episode like this happening in one of our public sectors? Although this was a military Doc, his manufacture was fundamentally identical to every other Doc within Medi's jurisdiction.'

The woman issued a shrill laugh. 'Don't you think, given the scale of this operation, that something would have happened by now? We have Docs stationed in every Medi facility, in every city, on every habitable planet, in three galaxies.'

'And that doesn't worry you? Given that scale it may have already begun without us realising!' Doctor Parker's previous nervousness was now buried deep below a moral high ground and tone of disbelief. 'All public Docs are reaching an age similar to that of the Mandar Doc. It would be foolish not to at least hear Toffman out and take the according measures, which so far Medi has been unprepared to do.'

'Okay, okay, Reginald.'

'Doctor Parker.'

'*Doctor Parker*, we'll hear him out, but don't expect a majority vote for your proposal given the cost.'

Doctor Parker had to stifle his agitations beneath a huff and turned to a stack of tapes on his desk. After rummaging through the pile he slotted one into a nearby player.

'Patching through now, I hope you make the right choice.'

The screen cut to a scrawny man sat alone in an empty room of overbearing white. He leant over a tiny square table, head in his hands, hair matted between his fingers. The board members watched him intently, listening to the hum of the speakers until an off-screen voice called out to the man.

'I know this is hard Mr Toffman, but we just have to hear it once more, from the top. Then we can get you somewhere safe.'

Mr Toffman looked up at the camera, his eyes deep and black, heavier than they should ever be, and said...

You know this is hard? You know this is hard!?

Just one more time, Mr Toffman! Just one more time!? Fuck you and your one more time! It should have been one more time three times ago. I doubt you could handle a more detailed report even if I could muster the strength to give one.

Do you know what it's like to see something so beautiful picked apart until that beauty becomes nothing more than an unfinished puzzle of mangled flesh? A slippery heap of blood that you can only assume can't be desecrated further but is? Do you know what it's like to relay that shit over and over again in your head and then be expected to speak it aloud in concise detail?

The violation that Medi has perpetrated with its Doc Program isn't just against the flesh, but the very souls and memories of those caught up in the aftermath of their vulgar profit experiment. I just... No, I won't. I can't. I... I know nothing could have happened between us. I could have gone on living with a broken heart, I don't know if I can go on living knowing what happened to hers. You won't tell her story right so it stays with me!

The film cut to black as Mr Toffman kicked away his chair and began lashing out at the walls. Some of the board members were on the cusp of laughter, shaking their heads, overjoyed at Mr Toffman's clear lunacy. In this form, he was no threat to their salaries. Some rose out of their seats before the film resumed with Toffman sat back in that same hunched position.

Fine. As my retelling is the only true account that will ever be told. You'll hush it all up in the end anyway.

We were a communications team, small, military, but none of us had any practical combat experience. We were sent to Mandar to re-establish communications with the human forces in conflict with the people of the Dygon Galaxy. Which is stupid you will say, because as we all know after four years into that conflict, communications suddenly went dead: The Mandar Blackout. Within a few months, most of our forces had returned home unscathed, as had the Dygons returned to theirs. Mandar was deemed uninhabitable by both sides and the campaign was dropped. Mandar became a listed Dead Planet, unwanted, unused, uninhabited. Well, apparently not so uninhabited after all.

Fast forward eight years and some tech savvy nobody hacks into an ancient cy-mail address from one of the Gov's abandoned basements and finds eight years' worth of unchecked one-way medical reports; everything from procedures performed, medicine administered, fatalities. Lots of fatalities. They were as frequent as one might expect from a full blown battle and had been updated consistently all the way up to the present day. Because of the blackout, the Gov figured that a coms bubble had been produced and a small combat force was still active in a more rural location and had no clue that the conflict had ended eight years prior. It wouldn't be the first time that the Gov left someone behind. The only logs getting through were that of one Doc, painstakingly reporting back to Medi the entire time. That's why we were sent in.

I don't know why they couldn't have just sent a team with more combat experience, to tell the soldiers that the war was over and then brought them home. It probably had something to do with money. Although, if anything, I got the feeling the Gov seemed interested in Mandar again. I guess that's just wild conjecture on my part.

Whatever their reasons, me and the rest of the team headed to Mandar, with a decade's worth of improved tech, to get the Gov linked up with the ground team still fighting.

Oh, you wanted to know my colleagues, didn't you? Well, there was me, obviously. Ryan Smithy, he was our pilot. Then there was Digby; I didn't know his last name, he didn't even speak the common tongue. He'd grown up on some backwater planet just outside Dredba. I doubt Digby was even his real name, but he was good with wires. Crazy good with wires. And then, of course, Ara. She was the *beauty* I mentioned earlier. You know, the one your sick fucking experiment... Whatever.

The four of us left Tothri station, what, two months ago? We went into cryo and popped a month later after hitting Mandar's orbit, directly above the source of those medical reports. It was weird looking down at the planet. We knew it had been deemed a *Dead Planet*, but I couldn't believe it would actually look dead. We've all seen Mandar in the pictures; it's a bright warm red disc in the sky. But, just outside the atmosphere, it looked like a black claw had reached in and torn up the landscape. Lacerations and pits cut their way across both hemispheres, scarring hundreds of thousands of miles worth of terrain. Typical, that this whole fucked up situation should begin after dropping smack bang in the middle of it. We tried sending out a signal to the medic source but didn't get a reply; took us four hours just to pick up static, by then we'd already landed.

Now, when I said the medical logs looked fit for a full-scale war, they couldn't have prepared us for the world that we entered. The ground itself was as lifeless as it looked from space, a faded red rock covered in patches of black ash. We opened our door to a post-apocalyptic, city-sized base of Gov military operations and housing. Vehicles were upturned, barricades broken, bodiless clothing strew the streets. There wasn't a single plant, which wasn't surprising; even if there hadn't been a war, the winds would have easily uprooted the place.

There was this constant howl that gets in your head and shakes your brain, and the black ash kicks up and cuts you like glass. The entire city had been levelled and surrounding the rubble were rocks that had melted into piles of mucus shaped mounds. You couldn't pay me to go back. Hideous place. I was shocked the air was even breathable because aside from that there wasn't one viable extractable from the planet.

It was strange though. Despite the carnage, the cause was non-existent. It was a ghost town. The only sign of the Dygon's came in the form of their bent and rusted rifles stuck in the ground like tombstones. Dygon's aren't hard to miss either; what are they, ten feet tall or so? And if any of our guys were around they covered their tracks tremendously well. We spent three days wandering through that waste land and didn't come across a single ration packet, foot print, nothing. Any sign of life was eight years expired.

I stuck close to Ara for most of the mission, we were essentially the admin team, so most of our time was spent filling out forms. I loved hanging out with Ara. She was Homo-Nox, you know, *"The next stage of human evolution."* I love all those guys. I think she was older than me but she looked about twenty. Not a single hair on her body but for the blonde on her head, skin as pale as cloud. They've got those eyes too; just the pupil, no iris, gets right inside you. I'll never forget those few days together. The work we did was boring as all hell but I'd do it all over just to share another glance with her.

The *fun* didn't last long though. After two days, we realised we were being tracked by some Mandar locals; not that the Gov had told us there were any. I presumed *Dead Planet* meant there was no life, but upon further reading, it means no *"Threateningly Intelligent Life."* Although, these little fuckers were far from stupid. Kept their distance for the most part, testing us, waiting for signs of fatigue, rats the size of dogs that hunted in packs. I can still hear the pitter-patter of bald, lumpy claws. The sound was constantly at the edge of any perimeter we set up: primarily a buzz scrambler defence that animals with a heightened sense of hearing can't bear.

I remember one afternoon Digby coughed, just one time, and that night a chorus of fluorescent green eyes floated around our camp, three times as many as before. It's like they could sense weakness. None of us could sleep, and that morning, I saw one gnawing on the hatch of an abandoned tank. A tank! Chewing and slobbering over a plate of metal like a chew toy. They were getting hungry. We were probably the first meat they'd smelt in years. We had to find this Doc quickly or we were going to be supper. All we had to defend ourselves, aside from the buzz scramblers, were standard issue pistols; one each, but only a couple of full magazines between us.

The whole of the next day those mutant vermin kept a close eye on Digby. Then you'll never guess what that idiot did; went ahead and split himself off from the group. He needed the toilet, but apparently pissing in private was more important than keeping his leg. Just as me and Ara were filling out a request to return home, his scream erupted from behind a pile of rubble, about fifty meters away. I still can't believe how far he wandered off. Smithy was first on the scene, and by the time Ara and I arrived our pilot was busy kicking in the skull of a rat that had Digby's thigh in its mouth; hardly in the job description, ay? Another three of the vermin had begun a wild, excitable dash towards us over the pile of broken concrete. Ara and Smithy started shooting and covered me as I made a grab for Digby.

The idiot kept fighting me off. I couldn't tell what he was saying but it must have been something idiotic. I dragged him back within range of the scrambler, the lower half of his right leg hanging on by a haggard fragment of knee cap. I suppose I should let him off being a little delirious. I was pissed though. My clothes were ruined, covered in blood, and he was pinching me so hard it left these scars... I couldn't tell which blood stains were mine or his when we eventually made it back into the scrambler's safe zone. Then I heard a great smash and buzz and turned to find that some of the rats had made it past the scrambler barrier and had broken our equipment.

As they were busy tearing into our food hampers, I felt damn near ready to leave Digby, to call out to the others and make a break for it. I was both frightened and bloody furious. My heart was pounding. I could feel Digby slipping out of consciousness in my arms. I didn't really have a choice, I was going to have to leave him. Then, just as I loosened my grip, a siren sounded.

It was high pitched, something I imagine only a dog might catch, some far off blip every three seconds. My ears pricked and tugged my searching eyes left and right. Smithy and Ara were back, the former championing a shattered eye socket, the latter as stunning as ever. Do Homo-Nox sweat? She wasn't even out of breath.

We desperately sought out the origin of the blip and caught a tiny white light, about two hundred metres off a derelict trading street, flashing in rhythm to the beeps. It was a beacon on top of a cubed building. Well, half-building, half-mountain of avalanched concrete. It didn't look particularly inviting, but it was the most secure stronghold Mandar could have offered right then. I still half wanted to drop Digby for being such a moron, but the hero in me cried, 'Fuck it!' And the three of us picked up what was left of him and made a rapid dash off the street. Once clear we hit a strip of parted rubble, sectioned off with wire fencing, kind of like a run way.

The rats were right behind us and moving a lot faster now they had something to chase. They would have run us down had Ara not emptied what was left in her pistol. She caught one of them in the ankle and the rest scarpered, for a moment. Once they realised she was just clicking the trigger the hunt resumed. Again, the idea of dropping the now snoring Digby became hard to resist, especially with the tongue of a slobbering wolf-rat on my calf. Then a window in our cubed safe haven unleashed a hail of gunfire.

It must have been a turret because the carnage was unholy. It cut down the rat just behind me and tore like a laser through the rest. As the ground shook with the impact, a stray bullet bounced off the concrete and lodged itself in my thigh. It wasn't too devastating, and adrenaline kept me hobbling on, but holding onto Digby with one arm whilst dragging my numb leg with the other wasn't easy.

Vermin guts rained around us as we hit the two tall, steel doors belonging to our sanctuary. Smithy broke the rusted chain and shoulder barged his way through first. Once Ara and Digby were safely through I hopped in after them.

Unbeknownst to me one of the rat's pointy snouts had followed. Ara kicked the door shut as I wheeled away. The rat's nose got caught and snapped, sprinkling blood and mucus into the dank hallway we'd entered. Not that I was complaining, at least the door was definitely shut! Smithy shoved a thick rod between the handles, followed by the rushed placement of a heavy cabinet, and we all fell to the floor exhausted, blind, and shaking for the sound of bullets and rat-wolf squeals still raging outside.

At first, given the hallway's abandoned appearance, we weren't sure if the beacon we'd followed was manned. That turret could have been sensory, the flashing light on a timer. We slumped in the corridor for a good quarter of an hour in silent contemplation as our heart rates returned to normal. It wasn't until a profusely sweating and deep sleeping Digby began gibbering that we decided to move deeper into the cube. Smithy was in bad shape too, and I had no idea how long the makeshift bandage around my leg was going to hold. That's when we met the Doc.

Have you ever met one of the Medi Docs in person? I'd seen pictures before but even I was taken aback. Not the most comforting of diagnosticians, but if you were bred in a lab, with cost efficiency in mind rather than patient care, you probably wouldn't look too wonderful either. This Doc was particularly worse for wear. He loomed out of the darkness at us, approaching slowly, quizzically, holding a torch fainter than the galaxy's furthest star. He was no taller than my elbow, and stood with an overbearing hump, from the top of which his long head dangled. It was loose on his neck, stretched, permanently fixed with a gawp and one eye so large it bore through us. The other was covered by a red glass dome, strapped tight over the top quarter of his face.

Notes I couldn't read typed themselves across the glass, and the eye we could see twitched like it was reading. His arms were long and gaunt, finishing just below his knee caps, and, rather than form one forearm, his greyish-brown skin wrapped about his ulna and radius separately, leaving a thin hole between his brittle elbows and wrists. I don't know what race the Doc's were modelled after but it wasn't human.

He was draped in the blue scrubs of a hospital orderly. Bloody hand marks and chunks of flesh decorated the uniform, and dirty tubes poked in and out of his arms after what I can only assume had been a rushed self-surgery. At the time we thought nothing of these things, that anybody immersed in war this long would look as equally dishevelled. To be honest, we were just too desperate, and the lighting was too low, to look further into his appearance.

After an awkward standoff he introduced himself, pleasantly enough, but with a robotic, nasally rasp.

'My name is Doc Forty-five, how can I be of service today?' he said, and then proceeded to look over Digby before receiving our answer. The poor guy winced in his sleep as Doc Forty-five enthusiastically pushed about his leg and then clicked at me and Smithy. 'Bring him. We must be quick.'

He may have sounded rude but we could tell he had Digby's best interest at heart. We could see him glowing at the thought of helping someone so we did as we were told. Ara helped too, she could tell me and Smithy were both too hurt to be much use.

We descended deep into the ruin, spending many a minute awkwardly traversing a cluttered stairwell filled with dirty mattresses, medical equipment, and makeshift weapons, all weathered and unusable. Any wall light we passed was either broken or too faint to be useful, so we followed the ghostly sway of Forty-five's torch. We must have been half a mile underground by the time we stopped. The Doc kept us entertained, though. We asked him about the war and he regaled us with a few crooked tales and assured us it was very much still going on.

'The players are few but the game's still afoot, lurking in the ash, waiting for me.'

He kept saying how survivors were waiting for him. It was all a little ominous. He broke that talk up with randomly placed *Doctor Doctor* jokes, as if they'd been programmed within him in some vague attempt to make him more relatable. The wheezy laugh after each retelling of, 'Doctor Doctor, I feel like a pair of curtains... Well, pull yourself together then!' made that difficult. He must have told the joke ten times. As I say, it kept time from dragging; he was more quirky than threatening. Soon enough, we broke away from the stairwell and entered the surgical ward. It was the only one with working lights.

The three of us hoisted Digby onto a three wheeled stretcher and trollied him further into Doc Forty-five's labyrinth. It was no surprise the Doc lasted so long down there; it was the last place on Mandar I would have wanted to search him out.

'Where are the other soldiers?' Ara kept asking him, but the Doc's responses were always misty.

'Above ground, fighting in the shadows, the war rages on...'

'You know the war has ended?'

'War doesn't end; pain and suffering, only I can stop it.'

'Who's in charge here then? Who's your superior?'

'General Packroni.'

'And where is he?'

'Isolation Ward, although he is in a world of hurt. It is okay, he is being monitored, as are the others.'

'Others?' I asked.

'Monitored.'

'No, where are they?'

'The Isolation Ward, or above in the lightless sun.'

'Can we see them?'

'It is hard to see that which can't see itself...'

At the time we didn't fully understand that last statement, but we would. We hit the double doors to Forty-five's surgery.

The tiling of the once shimmering white walls bore a green mould, made worse by the reflections batted about by various rusting metal rods, cutting tools, and magnifying spheres. An uncomfortable air filled the place, it's toxins rising into a black hole above our heads where the ceiling used to be. Mounted, transportable lights hid none of the surgery's disheartening stains and, even if I was still harbouring an ill feeling towards Digby, I found it difficult to let go of his stretcher.

We transferred him onto a rotting bed, low enough to the ground so the Doc could get a good view, and then took our seats, deciding together without words that it would be best if we didn't leave the two alone.

'I'll see you two next,' the Doc said to me and Smithy.

We tried to force a thankful smile. There was no way this cluttered surgery could have been fully operational; I mean, how could their stores have even lasted eight years? I feel foolish for ever following Forty-five down there. Even in the thick of war, nowhere should look like this. But the Doc carried himself so well, it genuinely looked like he knew what he was doing.

After hurrying around the prostrated Digby, reading from his eye-mount, Forty-five withdrew a crooked needle from a hingeless cabinet. Without hesitation, or even taking aim, he jammed it into our teammate's neck. Ara grabbed my hand, and I clenched hers tighter, as Digby seethed. It didn't look like there was any fluid in the syringe at all and that the Doc was just going through the motions. Smithy was ready to object until Digby shook and went still. 'There we are,' said the Doc. 'Let me relieve you from the darkness.' Digby was still breathing, I checked thoroughly before allowing the surgery to continue.

The Doc pulled a power saw from his instrument table. Its buzz sounded broken, off-axis, too old and bent to spin properly, but I suppose the luxuries of laser technology had long been exhausted by this point in the Doc's war. After a rather unsettling glance my way, Forty-five thrust it into the meat of Digby's thigh.

Digby sat right up!

I'd never heard a scream so curdling, and Smithy, Ara, and I, jumped up too. We ran to his side to hold him down before he hurt himself.

'The anaesthetic hasn't worked!' Smithy shouted at the Doc.

'It wasn't anaesthetic!' Forty-five shouted back.

Ara and I were too busy holding onto Digby's flailing limbs to cuss the Doc out. Ara stared deep into Digby's eyes, telling him everything was going to be okay; the blood spurting from his leg into the ceiling hole told a different story.

'It was lyso fluid, to aid with correct healing,' Forty-Five said. 'Here, his forehead, do it hard!' The Doc pulled what looked like a tiny computer chip from his scrubs and handed it to Smithy. *Wham!* Smithy slapped it onto Digby's forehead.

Digby convulsed for a few seconds, and his legs and arms became even more difficult to hold onto, before he suddenly fell still. Smithy stepped back, horrified at himself. We were about to call the whole thing off before a more fatal mistake was made, but the Doc continued his amputation. The saw erupted back into its asthmatic whir.

The cut was smooth, but accompanied by Forty-five's own angry mutterings and a rather rushed amputation, so much so we had to take cover behind a curtain for the sake of Digby's flying flesh.

It was hard to leave him, even by a few feet, but the Doc seemed genuinely under pressure with us there. It was all such a catastrophe that any attempts to help on our parts were going to cause serious delays or injury. None of us were medical professionals after all, maybe this is what surgery in the heat of war looked like. For what it's worth, the surgery was a success...

Back in the conference room, the screen distorted into a pause. It froze on a sickly looking Toffman who was clearly becoming more agitated. His hair was knotted, some of it pulled out.

'I don't think we need to hear anymore,' the thick lipped woman said, dropping the flat screen's remote control impatiently on the table. 'This is becoming increasingly uncomfortable to watch. Can we all just agree that it would benefit everyone if we just *lost* this video? All I've heard so far is the tall tale of an inexperienced, gullible, and, quite frankly, foolish Gov employee who put his faith in a clearly traumatised Doc. There is no case.' A chorus of "*Here Heres*" boomed from the other board members, only to be cut short by the return of Doctor Parker's voice through the screen's speakers.

'Why have you stopped watching?'

'We've heard enough, Reginald,' the woman replied.

'You've barely heard anything.'

'We shouldn't have to waste any more time here.'

'You've already wasted too much time. This man's full story must be heard, be felt, and in full.'

'Isn't it all summed up in the documentation you've prepared for us? We're all far too busy to deal with these trivialities.'

'No, it can't just be summed up! Good grief... You're all in charge, you're all responsible, you have to be prepared.'

'Nonsense, and you had better watch your tone, Doctor Parker. You forget yourself.'

'I know myself well. Perhaps you've forgotten what it takes to be a person but I won't and—'

'And this meeting is adjourned.' The board members got to their feet and slunk towards the door.

'It is not. You must listen!' Doctor Parker thundered, and the video of Mr Toffman resumed.

A success. Funny how he made us believe that. It's frightening to know how easily we were manipulated. That bloodshot beady eye, full of the Sandman's dust, somehow didn't appear so without care as it would should I see it again. I can assure you, I'm not an idiot, and I know how this may look. None of us would have run so blindly into that situation without reason. The Gov doesn't hire just anyone, you know. How... How did we let this happen?

I... I'm sorry...

After the dust settled from Digby's surgery, Ara and I followed a map that led to the Isolation Ward where Forty-five said we could find General Packroni. Smithy stayed behind with Digby and the Doc. Forty-five could only work on us one at a time and, much to my everlasting thanks, Smithy offered to receive treatment first.

'Don't worry, he won't make any mistakes with me.'

That was the last thing he said to me, with a wink for good measure.

A lot of the rooms had been crossed off or cut out of the map, but it was a relatively straightforward journey, if not a little eerie, the makeshift bed and chair barricades we passed helped add to that. I could feel the still lingering shadows of shuddering men sheltered behind them and feared the worst pressing forward.

We smelled the ward before we saw it. After ramming the stuck doors, we entered. It was twenty feet long from front to back, ten beds in total lining both left and right, with an extra bed at the far end. They looked old, rusted, and still bodies lay beneath the sheets. Glowing grime crept over several of the patients and their groans hung low in the air. Monitors beside the beds beeped infrequently, not a single heart rate as it should have been.

'What have we walked into,' Ara said. It wasn't a question.

That ward was a pit of festering disease, and any further horrors were hidden beneath the bold black lines cast by a single spotlight at the end of the room. I suppose it was better that way.

We didn't get a close look at the patients, stopping short at the charts hanging at their feet:

Initial Condition: Cough
added Complications

The mangled body wheezing in the bed certainly didn't reflect a cough. I picked up another:

Initial condition: Finger laceration
added Complications

Another:

Sneezing fit leading to complications.

Again and again, they were the same. The most barbaric and life threatening procedures I could imagine were being performed to treat injuries and ailments that wouldn't normally have warranted a plaster. It hit us that we shouldn't have left Smithy alone with Doc Forty-five.

'He lies!' called a voice from the lone bed at the ward's end.

The chart accompanying it read:

Lower General Malcolm Packroni.
Initial condition: Wheezy voice.
added Complications

Wheezy voice? Can you imagine reading that and then seeing a man whose throat had been flattened and left to fizz beneath mounds of blue goop? Both of his hands had been amputated, and his legs had been bent in all different directions, their true definition hidden below dirty sheets. How he was talking at all seemed miraculous, although that wheeze he once owned had evolved into more of a dry gurgle that made me clutch at my own neck.

I wanted to leave. Whatever the Doc was doing down here was way over our heads and the last thing I wanted was him to preside over my injuries. If he was cutting off hands for a sore throat, I couldn't imagine what he'd do to my leg that still had a bullet in it.

Ara and I tried to sneak away quietly; we didn't want to hear what Packroni had to say, we didn't want to put him through the pain of speaking. Alas, speak he would. 'He lies!'

'Who lies?' I asked, deciding to humour the poor soul, knowing full well the answer to my question.

'He lies. He acts like he cares, plays it off like a mistake. He lies. He tricks. He steals. He jokes.'

'You mean the Doc?'

'Doctor Doctor, I can't tell how long I sleep... Take a ruler to bed with you then!' Packroni laughed, or what might pass as a laugh.

'How did he do this?' I asked. 'Why?'

'We can't call home. We can't. He finds us, hiding on the surface. We can't call home. We can't leave. Not many of us left now.'

'How long have you been here?'

I felt bad asking him so many questions. I think I'd convinced myself I was going to put him out of his misery anyway, might as well try and find out we could through the gibberish.

'I don't know,' he wept. 'I don't know! Before the Blackout.'

'Eight years?'

'Before the Blackout. Others come and go; Dygon, man, rat. He keeps me here. He keeps others here. He lies.'

'General Packroni, Malcolm, we need to find a communications grid,' Ara said.

'Gone. All gone.'

'They can't all be gone, the Doc is still sending medical reports.'

'Gone. All gone!'

'I think we need to go,' Ara urged, turning away from Packroni.

But I needed to know. *We* needed to know. If we couldn't get word to the outside we would either die there or on the surface with the wolf-rats.

'Where does he send the reports from?' I asked one last time.

'Basement level,' came a robotic reply, but it wasn't Packroni.

For an agonising moment I pleaded with the heavens that the General had spoken without moving his lips, but Packroni's eyes shuddered in his skull like one who recognised hell. The Doc had joined us.

How much else had Forty-five heard? Did he know that we knew what he'd been up to? He looked out of breath, sweat mounting in his various wrinkles. I tried to play it cool as we faced off, the dwarven monster stood crooked in the ward's doorway.

'Th-thanks,' I stuttered. 'If you don't mind I think we'll head down there.'

'I wouldn't advise it,' Forty-five said, 'you're standing very poorly on that leg. Too many stairs for you. But first I should see to the lady.'

This, this is where things get uncomfortable for me. It was like he signed a death sentence with his voice. Obviously, we were confused; aside from being a little grubby from the journey, health-wise, Ara was in her prime.

'No, no,' she said. 'I'm fine, thank you. How's Smithy?'

'Fine too, fine enough, a few complications but he's holding out.'

Complications... that word held worse connotations than it should have.

'Come,' Forty-five continued, 'we must hurry.'

Ara and I were rooted to the spot. A small hand saw hung from the Doc's droopy arm, fresh blood falling along the blade's edge. He cocked his head as we refused to move.

'Come. The doctor will see you now.'

His mouth was clicking angrily... his tongue or teeth, something. Ara and I scoured the room for a weapon to defend ourselves with, but the only thing that wasn't tied down was a nearby bed pan. To be honest, I wasn't thorough. I was too busy watching the twitch in Forty-five's eye.

'Come,' he said for the last time. I felt like dying.

He hadn't said it loud but the word lingered. It was followed by another strange clicking, like someone lighting a gas stove. I couldn't see the source, or smell anything over the ordinary rot, but my head felt light, the world went white, and I fell. I fell onto Ara who was already on the floor. That was the closest we had ever been. The closest we would ever be.

'He's setting traps! He's, as Mr Toffman describes, lying,' Doctor Parker said over the speakers. 'What number of other Docs are doing the same thing? The forty-four that came before Forty-five, and all the other military Doc's after, all died in combat before reaching an age that their engineered structure was not fit to stand. They are clones after all, unaware of the world and what dictates proper care other than what's been programmed into them. They understand and enjoy one thing: cutting people up! We have to investigate this thoroughly.'

Most of the board members had retaken their seats, standing hardly an option after hearing Mr Toffman's story. On the screen the clearly traumatized subject had broken down entirely; orderlies were restraining him again, thankfully the action had been muted.

'Is there more?' one of the quieter board members asked. He was short, an alien hybrid of some kind from generations passed.

'Yes. As dictated by your orders, the full story, in detail. We're lucky he got through it all.'

The scene on the monitor calmed. Toffman was back to his usual head bowing self. His eyes were puffy, and his voice often muffled by slurps as he held back the tears he earned to let out.

I woke in an even brighter light. We were back in Forty-five's surgery, the glint and haggard sharpness of his tools more apparent than ever, as was the ripe stink that stained everything within.

Digby and Smithy were there too, propped up in the corner of the room covered by a grubby sheet. I knew it was them, contorted and more still than I thought possible. My arms were tied to a chair in the opposite corner. Its padding was torn and the jagged metal beneath dug into my back, and yet that pain was nothing compared to the sight before me. In the room's centre, Ara had been strapped to the surgical bed Digby had been maliciously pulled about on earlier. I wish he chose me first.

'Far too pale, a sickness I haven't seen before,' Forty-five said. His head was so close to Ara's cheek, and his mouth was clicking again.

I wanted to kick it off his shoulders, and tried, as the Doc wrestled a gas mask over my face and knocked the switch to its adjoining canister. There was a hiss but no anaesthetic. I quietened, but only through confusion. He was just playing doctor! Going through the motions. I was speechless as he did the same to Ara, who looked back at me for a supporting eye, anything to give her courage. I couldn't, there was no look I could afford her that spoke of anything but terror.

Those bizarre arms hovered over her with sharp utensils, the fluid about the Doc's joints popping in tense anticipation. He was loving it. He had seen what he didn't understand and drooled over its ruination. In that moment he looked like a spindly insect, doing the duty of something that lacks empathy in its remotest sense. What a hateful creature. A sad sight to behold and sadder still to watch at work. My eyes locked onto the bone saw that had plunged into Digby earlier, still plugged into the wall, and I dreamt of all the horrid things I could have done to the Doc in that moment.

My breath caught in my throat as he began to work, this time with the tiniest of knives. I... kept looking at Ara... I kept... I can't... No.

I kept looking at her, into those endless eyes, and she did not turn away from mine. I wasn't sure what my winces could have done. Maybe I believed in some spiritual sense, that if I kept her gaze, she might be able to offload some of her suffering onto me. She leaked tears, which free-flowed into the sheets beneath her, as the Doc slotted a triangular knife beneath her flesh. It cut her so easily. She refused the Doc her cries as he flayed the skin from her body, toes first. He was being intentionally slow, careful to tug and prod at the muscle beneath.

My stomach was too empty to puke. My innards rocked and I was unsure how I would ever eat, or sleep, or breathe again without seeing the pain in her face. I didn't even care that I was next. It turns out there's a level where you can't feel anymore, and unsurprisingly my breaking point was watching someone I loved skinned alive right in front of me.

After what felt like an age, guilt gripped me by the throat. I knew it wasn't my fault, there was nothing I could have done, that no matter how many different circumstances I dreamt up in my head they would have all failed in that moment. And yet I was being smothered by the wish that it was me on that table instead of her. The cutting stopped at her neck, and I was glad, in a relative sense, if only to see that the rest her beauty would remain untouched.

Idiot. Of course that wasn't the end.

I don't know why I believed it could be. The Doc switched to a thin, jagged knife, something so large you might hunt a Dygon with, and moved it over her face. I'll never forget Forty-five's last joke before he made the stab; 'Doctor doctor, I feel like I'm at death's door... Don't worry, we'll pull you through.'

Then Ara screamed as he plunged the knife into her eye. It was the first sound she had made the entire operation. He finally broke her, and in that moment I broke too. I may have cried even louder than she did. I was swearing, kicking out, cursing the Doc so badly that the next life just has to be hell for him. It has to be! He looked so happy, that little fucking animal.

'Complications,' he said, then tutted and choked her.

Those rough hands throttled relentlessly. He wasn't even trying anymore, and he called over to me, 'Don't worry, I'll be finished here soon.'

He kept reassuring me, even told me how routine my appointment would be, that I may only need to take antibiotics. He was still playing the character. It was unfathomable that he could still act this way as he stole the life writhing away in his palms. Ara twitched into death, her heart fit to burst through her ribs before falling still. I lit up.

Maybe it was adrenaline, maybe some psychotic recess of my brain had snapped and given all strength over to my right arm, maybe the Doc had been sloppy, but I ripped one hand free from my shackles. Moving faster than I believed possible, I reached for the gas canister and flung it over the top of Ara's prostrated body. Its base thumped the Doc square in the chest.

He flew back into the bodies of Digby and Smithy, their severed limbs and disembowelled organs spilling over him. With my free arm, I pulled at the other bind and it came loose. The reds of rage tinted my sight and mixed with the blood mounting within the surgery. I must have looked mad; I was. I grabbed the tool I'd fantasised putting through Forty-five's skull the moment this ordeal began, that wonky bone-saw. It was mine now and he was too stunned to react. I hurdled the surgical table and was inches away from the shaking monster of Mandar when the saw's chord reached its tether. I slipped on part of Digby and crashed onto my back, winded. The Doc got lucky.

I didn't need the air, I was running on rage. I had barely hit the floor before launching at the Doc again with fists and clawing fingers, anything I could to grab a hold and do my worst. He was slippery and deceptively strong and squeezed past my flailing attack. He hopped onto a cabinet. I tried to pursue him but, like a spider who knew his web far greater than his prey, he fled into the black hole where the ceiling should have been. The ghoul had become part of the architecture now, one with his environment. I could hear him breathing heavily in the darkness, somewhere hidden, loving every moment. By this point, I was thinking clearly again; I ran.

I stole one last look at the heap of flesh that was Ara, hoping the view may have been different than I remembered. It wasn't.

Wiping the pools of water from my eyes, I hurtled into the corridor, trying not to look back, knowing that the image would be with me forever anyway.

As I ran, the ward twisted in ways that I couldn't recognise and the failing electrics cast shadows of confusing villainy that would have halted me had my legs not refused to stop. The fear of just waiting for the Doc to fall through the ceiling and smother me with some monstrous surgical tool kept me moving.

I'd forgotten how cluttered and murky the cubed hospital was, how filthy and slippery the floor had been. My leg was throbbing, still bullet riddled, and I stooped lower to the floor with every step. I was slowing drastically and it was then that Forty-five re-emerged. I looked over my shoulder as the demonic form of the Doc charged me down with arms outstretched like thin tenebrous wings. His syringe wielding hands clattered the same overturned clutter as I had done, wagging psychotically, accompanied by that insectoid clicking in the back of his throat. He was getting closer and closer, I could hear the lathering of saliva gathering behind that long mouth. The little light there was in the hallways bounced off the glass dome attached to his face, causing a red beam to hang over me just as I was giving up.

Without realising, I crashed the double doors leading into the stairwell. It was lucky, I admit; I had no idea where I was beforehand. Now I had two choices: up or down. If I returned to the surface, I risked being massacred by the Doc's machine gun fire or becoming a wolf-rat's dinner, and below was the only communication system still working on the planet. If it was even possible, the stairs leading to the basement were hung in an even greater darkness. I didn't have a choice at all. I headed south.

My journey was all guess work, feeling around, shoving unseen lumps out of my way, some far too squishy to bear remembering.

After a couple of minutes I hit a wall and discovered that I had reached the bottom.

The Doc wasn't far behind, I could hear his wailing penetrating the air of the stair well. The faintest ray of light seeped through the crack of an open door to my left. Looking up I saw Forty-five, spider-like again, crawling down the bannisters faster than I could have run the stairs at full health. He made a demonic leap and I threw myself to the side. Rolling, spinning onto my backside, I awkwardly shuffled into the room, quick to slam the door shut behind me with my working leg.

I was there, the communications room. *Wham!* The Doc hit from the other side. *Wham!* He struck again. The door was locked, I was safe. *Wham!*

This went on for hours. He must have turned his shoulder to mush, and certainly complained enough. I couldn't just sit there and wait for him to break through. The comms room welcomed me with an array of fading red and yellow bulbs. It was an ancient system but I got it working. I flipped the right switch, issued my own medical report with accompanying distress audio and... And I...

And I guess that's it. That's it.

Five days later, even if I still despise them for sending me in the first place, the Gov pulled through and got me out. The wait was agonising. Forty-five was relentless. He used saws, hammers, kind words, anything to try and coax me out of that room. It's when he was quiet though, that was the worst. Being left alone with my own thoughts was hell, being left alone with the image of Ara. During those five days, I would hear the surgery's retelling through the walls; the Doc knew how much it hurt to hear. He would whisper horrid things during the night.

He could get everywhere but in that room and made sure that his poisonous words counted for something. That last day I heard shuffling in the vents right before the Gov rescue team showed. I thought that would be it. I had no energy left to fight Forty-five off, having survived by drinking an unknown fluid dripping from a leaky pipe. I still can't really keep food down after that. The Doc would have slaughtered me.

I heard he wasn't even captured? Probably right to leave Mandar a registered *Dead Planet* then, even better to nuke it from orbit.

So that's it. There you go. I'm fucking done. Take your story and do what you want with it. I don't need any help. Just leave me alone, I'm done.

The screen faded into a close up of Doctor Parker in his office. 'I hope you realise the seriousness of all this.'

'We may need to take some action,' said the small alien hybrid who spoke earlier. 'Perhaps a psych evaluation every month or so?'

'Perhaps only in the quadrants where we hear reports or issues?' added the red lipped woman.

'No!' A vein in Doctor Parker's forehead was throbbing. He leant into his camera and whispered, 'This calls for a full-scale investigation, better yet, an extermination.'

'Out of the question.'

'But the tech's there for us to repeat the Doc program and do it right this time, without putting lives at risk. If we can get the bugs worked out of the genetic process of their creation—'

'The science may be here, Reginald, but the money is not. We have... We have to be economical about this.'

'We have to be humane about this. This can't stand.'

'It has and it will!' the woman snapped shrilly.

The board went quiet. They were all too weak to pick a side, a common trait amongst the spineless.

'Perhaps it's because I know things you don't,' Doctor Parker said, 'that I understand these creatures I helped to create. I'm begging you, you can't be so passive. I've seen the look in their eyes when they lose a patient, no matter how legitimate their practice had been. This can't be your final decision.'

'I'm afraid it is. Isn't it?'

All the other board members nodded in agreement. Most were reluctant, but the chances of objection were nil. Doctor Parker could see it in the pathetically flash decorations each member layered over their pampered, squishy frames. Money would always come before men.

She continued, 'You can't convince us to lose sleep over the general public. There were always going to be bumps along the way, best to just smooth them out. Given all of the laws that were bent to make the Medi program a success, you will never get a full vote. Mr Toffman's testimony is tragic but—'

The eyes of Doctor Parker went dark and he interrupted. 'So be it, it's your company.'

The woman smiled hesitantly and resettled her blouse that was rising up during the argument. Silently, she and the rest of the board made to leave, only to be cut off by another shaky announcement from Doctor Parker.

'Coincidentally, today is the first day of the company's mandatory medical check. I've just notified the board's private Doc and he's on his way to meet you now. I wish you all the best with the tests and that hopefully the next time this topic is put up for discussion, you will approach it with a more open heart...'

The monitor faded to black.

The sound of a clicking throat and a locking of the boardroom door echoed behind the board members. 'Good morning. I am Doc Two-Zero-Six, how may I be of service today?'

TIME AND SPACE

Within an inescapable tautness, a man's binds gripped hard at his wrists. They were so tight he felt blood trickling over his palms and onto the wood they grasped. Wriggling helplessly, his nails dug deep into the splintered arms of a chair, he tried to plant his feet on the ground but found a numbness to them. There was a burning at his knees and his soles were nowhere close to reaching the stone floor on which his seat rocked. Calling out wasn't an option, the inside of his throat throbbed as if hounded by acid. Somebody wanted him here, and they wanted him still. The last blurs he remembered before falling unconscious were just that, vivid, washed colours mashed with the sounds of thumping bass. Even if he was to shout, those screams would only do to attract the malefactor who stole him from last night. The back of his head ached dully as it searched for a memory prior to his abduction, but even his name remained lost to him.

'Ah, Jacob,' a hollowed voice spoke behind chiming cutlery, 'awake at last.'

Jacob? Jacob! Suddenly, the man's entire life fit neatly beneath the heading of that name, released by that drained tone sat opposite him.

It was no surprise to the young businessman that his evening hedonism, in battle against such a dull existence, would lead him into a situation such as this. Drunken, drug fuelled searches for something to give his life edge had become his modus operandi as of late. Last night had led him to the sharpest edge imaginable. Wearing the most expensive suit in his collection, its fine cuffs laced with hidden nano-luminance, Jacob attended one such establishment that no map knew the address of. It was so far below the bustling levels of his home city that no satellite could see it and was in such a dark corner the eyes of the law could only squint at and then wisely ignore.

His exuberant suit had been quick to catch the attention of a figure bathed in the detail diminishing red light of the club. Jacob tried to picture the man's face, but only the drinks in his leathery hands were clear. With his judgement already impaired, Jacob wasn't shy in his sharing of them. As they danced and consumed the bar's seediest extravagances, the rest of the night erupted into a whirl of confusion and colour. In the end, that brightness became so overbearing that his vision desaturated completely in an attempt to escape it, until the world matched the haunting grey wheeze of a stranger with far darker pleasures in mind.

Jacob had awoken in unideal places before, but none that deepened the pit in his stomach so far south. And none, surprisingly, came bearing this level of nausea, a level that kept a throat full of vomit primed behind his teeth. But he had questions for the man chomping loudly in the room with him. Swallowing his sickness, Jacob forced, 'You were there last night, weren't you?'

The voice did not answer straight away but gave a chuckle that basked in the scraping of Jacob's vocal chords. Eventually, it said, 'I was. We had a good time.'

The butterflies within Jacob's intestines felt like mouldy moths as he prepared to hear what depraved acts the two had gotten up to whilst he wasn't conscious. *Oh, please no!* he thought. *I'm strapped to this chair because of some sick sex game, aren't I!?*

'Don't be so vulgar,' the man replied, reading Jacob's thoughts on his scrunched face. 'What kind of monster do you think I am?' Jacob was ready to breathe a sigh of relief. 'I've only removed your legs.'

Jacob wasn't sure he had heard right and re-scrunched his face appropriately. He tried swinging his limbs at the knee but still found his feet numb.

'Look at his stumps wiggle, Master,' another sickly voice chortled beside him. Jacob jumped. This voice was deeper, and if the confused businessman had to imagine what a goblin sounded like, that would have been it.

The other man tutted. 'Don't mock him, Orix. Things are going to become increasingly uncomfortable for our guest, best not to add insult to inju—'

'Have you actually cut off my legs!?' Jacob screamed, caring little for the creature mocking him and more the dripping sounds coming from below his chair.

'Only up to the knee.'

'Only up to—' That vomit Jacob had forced down before was building again. There was pain around his knees for sure, a searing sting, but this wasn't the level he would have expected from something so extreme. Maybe the voice was lying?

'Can we remove his blinder, Master?' Orix asked, feet tapping in rhythmic excitement.

His master thought for a moment, then said, 'Yes. I don't see why not. It's going to be difficult for him no matter when he sees himself.'

'No!' Jacob bawled. 'Please.'

He didn't want to see. He didn't want it to be true. A pair of crusty fingers tugged at the rag that covered his eyes. After it slipped below his chin, Jacob tentatively took in his surroundings.

Sat before him, shining gloriously, was a kingly feast. Extravagant meats and fruits piled high upon golden plates that almost spilt onto the floor for lack of space. The wooden table housing the spread must have been ten feet long and just as wide. The details carved into its dark, shimmering varnish depicted many of the animals Jacob imagined had been cooked and strewn atop it. The rest of the room was pitch black. The harsh light beaming upon the food, from a low swinging chandelier, was so bold that it refused sight past the table's edge. Given how his coughs echoed, however, Jacob imagined the room to be hopelessly large. Jacob couldn't have guessed the horrors it housed, as his total view was limited only to the food in front of him, and the ugly goblin creature to his left.

Jacob had worked with Ruglets before, at his father's offices. They were always skulking about, fulfilling the most unfulfilling jobs that no self-respecting member of the company would be caught dead doing. Most were engineers or plumbers because they were the only ones who could fit into the unpleasant nooks of the building and, to the relief of the more reputable employees, remain for the most part unseen. Whenever one came onto an office floor and Jacob saw their grey, scabbed skin wobbling upon their flabby, midget frames, it became difficult to hide a snort of detestation. He was bursting with anger to see one skipping next to him while he was strapped down. But Jacob wasn't stupid, he wasn't prepared to invoke the wrath of someone with free hands while his were cuffed. All he could do was turn away to save himself from saying something he would regret.

In doing so, his gaze fell upon the dried blood covering every inch of his chair. Jacob gulped; how many had sat in that seat before him? After much inner struggle, he forced himself to face the horror he had so far avoided: his leg stumps. They protruded like gnawed, strawberry lollipops from beneath his haggard suit trousers, and he immediately recoiled. It was true; from the knee down, he was legless. His head felt loose upon the uppermost joint of his spine, the onset of vertigo forcing his head to flop and take in the mangled flesh. A multitude of needles plunged into his thighs, dripping with anaesthetic, could not hide the pain. Jacob wheeled his face to the sky and screamed for a God he didn't believe in.

'Why, God? Why!?'

His voice echoed and any further shouts were muffled by the tears and mucus that dribbled into his mouth. The attachment one has to their limbs, regardless of how useless they appear on paper, had never been so painfully apparent to Jacob than then. He knew that he didn't need his legs for work, and, aside from being nothing more than a stain on the city's night culture, he hardly had an active social life. Even to his own perception, he was just another face in the crowd, just making up the dense numbers of his society, neither adding to nor taking away. Now the chance of becoming anything more was dripping away like the blood yet to clot on his sharp, broken femurs tucked below the table. *What can half a man do!?* he moaned to himself.

The origin of the meat sat before him, adorned with its fruitful dressings, became clear. What further torments did Orix and his master have planned? There was no way all the food on the table had been stripped from his calves alone. Had others befallen a similar fate? Would the torture continue while he was awake? He knew he should have cursed out the leathery visage of the man he had met last night, but again God took the full brunt of his rage. He hated the deity more than himself, more than even Orix or his master. And so he blamed and goaded the most powerful being in the cosmos, hoping to lure him from his non-existence:

'Argh! There is no God!'

'Don't be so foolish. Of course there's a God,' snapped that cold, dead voice Jacob had so far refused to look to.

Jacob blinked his eyes tear-free and finally saw the gaunt being to which that voice belonged. He sat upright at the other end of the table draped in a blood red cloak of deep, gold linings. A nightmarishly pulled face, struck harshly by the chandelier's ambient light, poked from a hood, stark against the surrounding darkness. Jacob remembered who his fury should be aimed at now. The leathery one, who had drugged and plucked him from the club last night.

'You? You believe in God? Don't insult me,' Jacob spat across the table.

The creature, although similar in shape, was not altogether human and almost choked on his mouthful.

'Insult you? My dear boy, how?'

Jacob laughed. 'How? I don't even know your name and yet, after chaining me to a chair, you feign hospitality? Then spout nonsense about a God as you chow down on my fucking legs!?' He hawked the built up saliva in his mouth as far across the table as he could, the bulk of it landing in a bowl of punch. A closed fist socked his jaw.

'How dare you insult Master!' Orix squealed. 'Now who's being insulting?'

For Jacob, the time for tact was over. As his head sprung back from the Ruglet's strike he spat again, right into the sorry alien's face.

'Come on then you toad!' Jacob shouted, presenting Orix with his chin for another punch.

Orix's grey face dropped in shock at the word *toad*. His brows contorted and he shook with anger before his scabby hands splayed out, claw-like, and Jacob flinched away, believing rightly that he was about to have his face ripped off.

'Uh uh ah,' the master tutted loudly. Orix held his hand back an inch from Jacob's face. Jacob could hear those claws singing. 'What else would you expect, Orix? Our guest is right, we haven't been particularly well-mannered hosts. Now, be gone for a moment, you appear to be all too much of a distraction for poor Jacob.'

The Ruglet kept eye contact with the equally irate Jacob as he shuffled out of the room.

When he was gone, his master continued, 'Of course, spouting nonsense like, *there is no God*, is hardly necessary either.'

Jacob was dumbfounded. Here he sat, disfigured, sick, in tremendous pain, and in fear of things about to get a lot worse, and the being responsible for all of it can't understand why he doesn't believe in God?

'Are you out of your mind?' Jacob said, infuriated, mouth unable to close due to the obscurity of the man's position.

'In a sense, but trust that I am in complete control of my functions when it comes to traversing the realms of logic. I'm also surprised you're still badgering the person who holds the key to your inevitable, lifelong torture. Most who have sat in your seat try to soften me with words. You haven't even asked my name.'

Jacob flung his head back laughing. He didn't understand, he couldn't understand. Why would he exchange pleasantries with someone threatening him with eternal pain? It was a snapping within his mind that made him go along with it.

'Fine, what is your name?'

'How nice of you to ask. I am Dreaden, the Master.'

Jacob looked down at his knees.

'The Master? Well, it lacks poeticism, but I suppose it's difficult for me to argue. Not much I can do but sit here and agree with you.'

'I never claimed to be a master of words.'

'Yeah right, only logic, huh? Where in the fuck is the logic in this?'

'Logic has nothing to do with torture. Torture is an action, logic applied to the usefulness of the action has nothing to do with actually going through with said action, that's down to the individual's choice.'

'What?'

'I see that confusion on simple matters such as these run parallel with your disbelief in God.'

'God, by his universal definition, wouldn't allow this.'

'A universal definition often bears little resemblance to reality, Jacob. Many widespread falsities have been dismissed when given over to enough individual thought. Logically, God sees no sense or usefulness to what I do, but it his choice not to interfere. Whether you believe him wrong or right for taking such an action, doesn't dictate his existence, or whether he is wrong or right for doing so.'

'So what does?'

'Logic.'

Jacob paused, not through confusion, or to reflect on what Dreaden was saying, but purely because he didn't understand why he was speaking at all. He shouldn't be giving Dreaden the time of day. To discuss matters as philosophical as the existence of God, during such a time of turmoil, was insulting. *You're going to take my legs and threaten to do worse and then call me out when I express how screwed up my situation is?* He could see Dreaden's sunken eyes reading his mind.

'Of course I, by applying of logic, know that a benevolent God exists,' Dreaden said.

'Despite the fact you've mutilated me and others and this *benevolent God* has done nothing to stop you?'

'Countless others.'

Jacob was almost sick again. The needles protruding from his severed limbs were running short of their anaesthetic. He felt a tremendous stretching pain where his knee caps should have been. A sudden, quiet, sniff and gasp echoed out of the blackness to both his left and right. He turned his head sharply to find the cause but strained his neck. Dreaden smiled a thin and curled smile. *Who was that?* Jacob asked the voices in his head, the same voices screaming out mercy but who Jacob was too proud to let speak aloud.

'Fear not. You will join them shortly, Jacob. Like I said, your time with me will last as long as time itself, you will be brought to the edge of your sanity, and past the very thresholds of pain. You will be preserved, kept from death, and your suffering will continue, on and on until the universe's end.'

Jacob didn't know what to say. He looked over at Dreaden's squashed, pig-like nose, and saw it sniff the air, a true connoisseur of suffering. Jacob didn't want to join those who hung in the black beyond his eyesight, too mutilated to behold. He had to think of something. He had to get out. The knife and fork held by the spindly digits of his captor clanged against the plate for the last time, which meant that was it for him, the feast was over. *What can I possibly do?* he called out to those voices again.

'Persuade me,' Jacob said, his lips moving without him realising.

Dreaden delicately patted his blood stained mouth with a soft napkin, then raised a hairless brow in Jacob's direction. 'Pardon?'

'Persuade me... of God.'

'My dear boy, there will be endless life times for that. Although colour me concerned, are you stalling for time?'

Jacob was quiet again. He was indeed stalling for time.

'Should it matter?' Jacob's mouth began again without him. 'If I'm going to be here with you forever, you can take a moment to explain your so called *logic*.'

Jacob knew it wouldn't work; as cruel as he was, Dreaden was no fool. The master of this gore house wouldn't be taken in by the offer of conversation when screams were the alternative. And yet, Dreaden leant back in his throne-like chair and his face lifted into a ponder.

'I do not believe in God,' Jacob continued, 'especially not a good one. I can't possibly, not after hearing what you've promised, not after what I've seen you eat and do to me. You seem to be an intellectual—' Jacob's mouth quivered reluctantly as he offered the compliment '-and nothing would pain me more than to watch you try and convince me a benevolent Lord and Saviour is out there. So, I say to you again, with the hope that you will engage my claim: There is no God.'

'Of course there's a God,' Dreaden replied, smoothly, salivating at the coming conversation and drinking in the pre-storm silence before the battle of wits commenced. Jacob's plan had worked, although he knew little of what he would do once they had finished speaking.

Regardless, Jacob drew breath in preparation for his rant. His voice was shaky at first, but his confidence grew with every layer of fact he spat in Dreaden's direction.

'Science has come a long, long way since those archaic times when we worshipped *Gods*,' he began. 'We know exactly how the Universe came to be and where it's going. The universe has expanded and expanded and countless different worlds and races have merged together with countless others, and we've all pulled together our countless experiences and histories, and every intellectual race spread across the Universe knows for a, pardon the pun, God-given fact, that it was not created in seven days at the swish of some mighty overlord's whim. It came to fruition with a bang!' Jacob let that last word echo over the table. He knew he should not have gone so hard and heavy straight away, at the risk of insulting Dreaden, at the risk of proving him wrong in the first statement, but he couldn't stop his adrenaline and anger building as he spoke. Dreaden did not look flustered, if anything he appeared bored and rolled his eyes.

'Time and Space, Jacob. Time and Space.'

Apparently Dreaden thought these two words were enough.

'Time and Space?' Jacob repeated.

'Yes. Time and Space. You've spoken many words, Jacob, but not actually said much at all. Time and Space is the easiest and simplest rebuttal to the easiest and simplest *argument* against God with which to rebuke.'

'How!?' Jacob asked, furious that his speech should be so easily cast aside by an unsubstantiated, throw away comment such as *Time and Space*.

'Clearly, it appears that one wishes me to expand?'

'One clearly does,' Jacob said, stropping in his chair.

'You're right; science has come a long way since the days of the space travelling Black Christians; of the Salarks who conquered multiple worlds with their doctrine; even the passive, but immensely persuasive, Ori had their spiritual ways *humiliated* by science. In turn, however, all that science and its explorations into Time and Space did, which of course is an exploration into all things, was help prove that without the spirit, a physical realm cannot exist.'

'Those two realms are separated by the fact that one doesn't.'

'That's a baseless statement, Jacob, not an argument. Let's begin with what we know. First off, *Space*. We can break down everything that exists physically into blocks. For example: We can smash a brick into pieces; then crush those pieces into dust; then separate every flake of dust into the atoms that comprise them; then we can go even further and examine the subatomic particles of those atoms; and so on and so forth until we reach the smallest block, which, when patched together with an incomprehensible multitude of others, would comprise our original brick. And so there it is; the very end of space and the bare bones of what we know about it. *Time,* however, is slightly different, and many, even the greatest minds, struggle to understand it. Which is laughable, because it still uses the exact same principals as space, hence their affiliation.

'Time is also made of blocks, but instead of atoms and sub-atoms, the blocks of time are comprised of a series of actions and reactions. Let's look at the brick again. You pick up that brick because someone told you to do it; because someone told them that they needed it; because that someone was given a lot of money to build a skyscraper; with money they stole from someone else; who earned it working. Now, we can break down those blocks of actions and reactions far smaller: When you pick up that brick an electric impulse travels from your brain to your fingertips, telling it to pick up the brick, which was of course brought on by the external action of being told to pick up that brick, after having witnessed, via the travel of light, an example of how to pick it up, which entered the eye, then reached the brain and so on. Tiny, tiny actions that can be traced all the way back, much like a brick can be broken down to its atoms and further, to the very beginning where we can go no further, to the beginning of time itself.'

'Which was the Big Bang.'

'A-ha,' Dreaden clapped. 'No. Because unlike say, the argument of which came first, the chicken or the egg, the fact of time being made up of a long standing series of actions and reactions is that actions and reactions do not go around in circles. The action comes first, otherwise the re-action is obsolete and non-existent. There was an action, made by something beyond our physical world. If we place our brick on the floor and we do not push it; we do not touch it; we do not attempt to manipulate the temperature or gravity or environment surrounding it; and it remains unaffected by outer or inner influences, then that brick will not move or change. Ever. Neither can a universe just spring into life. Rules, like Time and Space, need to be set. The rules of physics need to be written, written by an unrestrained hand that does not follow, and existed before, those rules. Enter, the Spirit, an infinite power beyond the limitations of Time and Space. The Spirit, by its very definition and our understanding, can create and manipulate the physical, but it certainly doesn't work the other way around. A Big Bang is all well and good, but with nothing omnipotent preceding it, how could it possibly exist? This universe follows scientific rules, but rules must be written by the rule-maker.'

Jacob was silent. He was still in so much pain and so unwell that he found the argument difficult to process. He knew there were arguments against this theory. *But why can't I think of anything to say back!?* he thought to himself. He blamed it on his physical distractions, as well as Dreaden's smug face. If only he had a Bible, or some kind of text, with which to pull quotes from and tear his abductor's faith apart.

'It won't help you, you know,' Dreaden said. 'You can take all the damning evidence you want from scripture, but that will do little to trump logic.'

Wait a minute. Can this guy actually read minds!? The question spiked in Jacob's head.

'No, but I can read facial expressions, and I know every argument that can be thrown at God and that's normally the route these conversations take.'

'So you converse often with your prey?'

'Never, which is why I'm enjoying you so much. As you know after our night on the town, I don't confine myself solely to my home and my subjects. Occasionally, I'm offered the chance to speak with intellectuals.'

'You consider me an intellectual?'

'That depends on how quickly I can change your mind. I know you work for your father, and that it takes a lot of trust for greedy men to put their faith in fools, so you must have some sense.'

'Go on then.'

'Go on?'

'Why wouldn't me tearing apart the inconsistencies of an ancient book not disprove the book's subject? Why wouldn't you yourself use it to knock back my claims?'

'Because, logically speaking, the inconsistencies of said books are rather difficult to defend for they mirror the hands and minds of the men who wrote them.'

'So, you don't believe in the God of which the Bible speaks?'

'Of course I believe in the God of which the Bible speaks.'

'What!? How?'

Jacob wanted to laugh but was struggling against his own irritableness, caused by Dreaden's constant flip-flopping. Was this the Master's way of torturing him?

Dreaden answered after savouring the flavour of Jacob's confusion. 'The Bible of the ancient Black Christians, is probably the closest any religion has come to recording the one true God. As the human species evolved, over time you will notice, and often mock the fact, that the Bible becomes lighter in theme. There's far more talk of love and tolerance than death and punishment. Clearly, it takes a long time for the mortal beings of the universe to realise that helping, rather the hurting others, was God's plan all along.

'Slowly, but surely, your species was figuring this out, whilst others on far off worlds were evolving similarly. It's easy to imagine, in the first few millennia of your people's existence, God banging his head against the wall as humans preached hate in his name. You can imagine more so, God's dizzying eye rolls as the men of the time gathered together his word, sealed it, marketed it, and claimed it as the be all and end all, and in doing so stunted his word, rather than allowing it to evolve naturally as it had been doing. The battle between God and Man is an arduous one, and the only truth that can be taken from the scriptures are those that do nothing to convey cruelty and pain as a positive.'

'That's not an argument. I could say to you, "Why would God send angry bears to kill misbehaving children?" And you would simply claim that God didn't want that and the story is an embellishment made by man, and then preach to me from the same book that God wants you to turn the other cheek. Who's to say that we didn't simply evolve into better people and left the archaic, brutal God in the dust?'

Jacob didn't know where he was pulling these examples from. Some long forgotten memory of a history class had no doubt been unearthed by his own brain trying to save itself.

'I am to say it, because an archaic and brutal God would have quashed out that kind of rebellion long ago. Too long has God taken the blame when it was men and women doing the deeds of evil.'

'But he's God! Why not stop the evil? If he truly cared, why would he let war streak across the universe? A benevolent God would act.'

'Who says he isn't?'

'I say he isn't!'

'You do not know the facts or apply logic. If the men who came closest to God do not understand him, how can someone so vehemently against the idea of him understand?'

'And you do understand?'

'Of course, because I apply logic!'

For the first time, Dreaden was beginning to lose patience. Not in a frustrated, losing the battle kind of way, but similar to that of a parent trying to convince a child that they need to bathe.

'God is not mortal. He does not play by the same rules. I understand that no one can possibly understand how or why God does what he does because he is infinite. He does not concern himself with Time and Space as we do; he is concerned with the everlasting. He places far more stock in our souls than our lives. Even then, would you think it fair that he strip the happiness of those unaffected by the woes of the universe because you or others are suffering, or cease their existence altogether? Occasionally God will need to interfere with the balance of things in order for the universe to run smoothly, but rarely, or never, in a way that we perceive as benevolent. He places stock in all of us, and so he has to stand back lest he rupture the very point of free choice and life altogether. He has to let the horrors unfold in order for us to learn and be free, to make the right choices. It is choice that sets us apart from the mechanical existences of the insects.'

'*His ways are not our ways* is a cop out answer.'

'It is the only answer! You think an ant could understand our logic? Of course not. God has supplied us with feelings and sympathies and we continue to blame him for our own misgivings. Call them sins, call them wrong doings, call it laziness or ignorance or selfishness, but we constantly choose to ignore the twang of our moral bows. God loves us, and yet when he preaches to do good to *all*—not just ourselves, not just heterosexuals, not just men or humans, but to *all*—we ignore him. Bend this world he made to our own agenda and then blame God for it.'

'How can you sit there and say such things?' Jacob seethed, the needles poking from his stumped legs running out of fluid completely. A horrific pain was mounting within them.

'Orix!' Dreaden called. 'Our guest is hurting. Relieve him would you.'

From the darkness, Orix called back with a grunt, 'With shock or more anaesthetic?'

'Anaesthetic again I think, we still have much to discuss it seems.'

'My pleasure, Master.'

Orix hobbled back into the light with a bent syringe. He stopped right beside Jacob, breathing so heavily that Jacob could smell the stink of his scabby mouth spreading mistily over his skin.

Jacob was ready to spit on the ruglet again but remembered Dreaden's words: "*He preaches to do good to all*". But surely God wasn't talking about this monster? Or the one sitting across from him. Jacob quickly decided that the pain must be making him delirious; why would he apply the word of God when that word was inconsistent and untrue? If speciesism was a sin then Jacob decided that it was a far lesser one than whatever these two intended to perpetrate against him. He looked down at the Ruglet, and whatever Dreaden was, and was sickened by the sight of them, and didn't care who knew. He would not be preached to, no matter how enlightening the words, not when he felt like this. Naturally, Jacob indeed spat in Orix's face once more.

The retaliation came in the form of a violent stabbing from Orix, who plunged his needle into Jacob's already torn leg flesh repeatedly. In and out, in and out. There was no rhyme or reason, and the mutilated meat of Jacob's legs flaked off and peeled away as his screams were muted by squelches. Soon, shouting out in pain became an impossibility. His vocal chords were wrecked from the strain of it, and Jacob scowled purple faced. He followed the spraying blood with his eyes as it mixed with a fountain of green anaesthetic, which had long lost its effect. Orix laughed along with every jab.

'Enough, Orix,' Dreaden said.

The Ruglet obeyed, but not before making one final gash.

'There you are. Feeling better?' Orix asked Jacob.

Jacob didn't reply. He couldn't. All he could do was huff as Orix bowed out of the light and into hiding.

'The anaesthetic should kick in after a couple of minutes. Would you like to wait before continuing our conversation?' Dreaden asked.

'No,' Jacob growled, the word rumbling in his throat. 'You fucking answer me right now, truthfully, and don't bend shit. How can you defend God, when you do the complete opposite of his teachings? What are you trying to prove? If God was going to step in, he would have stepped in by now. Nothing is so good in the world, not even free choice, that he would allow this to continue.'

'That's your opinion Jacob, not an argument. It's clear you can't understand the complexity of God's work; of what it takes to run an entire universe and the infinity that comes after.'

'No, I don't. But that's because I know that God doesn't do anything and the world just exists without him.'

'We wouldn't be here discussing him if he didn't exist. There would be no universal theological obsession, no thought of anything at all. We wouldn't be clinging to hope as we all do.'

'So you're clinging to hope too?'

'Well, when I say we...'

'Why are you even doing this!?' Jacob erupted, deviating from the conversation, unable to hold back the question.

He had been struggling so hard that his binds looked ready to rupture the veins in his arms and Dreaden looked over him with a bored expression. Jacob had forgotten that the longer he kept

Dreaden talking, the longer he would forego his torture. He tried to settle but knew his captor could see through his pained guise.

'I'll show you...' Dreaden said.

Below the table, the Master clunked a switch and the lights of the chandelier lifted. Nothing could have prepared Jacob for the sight. He slunk into his chair. He so desperately wanted to escape through it.

Countless bodies decorated the reaching metal walls, no space left between floor and ceiling. The dank colour of the steel couldn't desaturate the bright red scars, burns, and injuries, adorning each person as they lay malnourished against tube-tangled wire canvases, crisscrossing in and out of each tortured soul, pumping them with unknown fluids. Their twisted frames were reminiscent of ancient, torturous paintings, the brush strokes laid by a poisonous hand. Each person groaned silently, whatever broken parts left of them shaking in the reveal of the light. Some had been so stripped of their flesh they were nothing more than a head and a heartbeat, kept alive and conscious by Dreaden's sordid life support.

'For centuries I have sought to bait the one true God,' Dreaden said. 'He will only intervene in this universe if the scales of its existence are tipped. By wreaking havoc upon his creation for as long as I live, which, as a being who does not bow to senescence, is forever, I hope to pull on the heart strings of The Lord and lure him into confrontation. Like I explained in the very beginning of our conversation, I know and understand his rules but I do not follow them. It is my choice to take an action that defies his good logic.'

'But what will you do?' Jacob asked, shaking. 'What reason could you have to meet with him?'

'Pride, Jacob! All these shallow atheists, blind to the real world, constantly call on God in a mocking tone to show himself.

But by believing, and being more vile and heinous than any of them could imagine this Godless world to be, I will do exactly what they are asking. I will reveal the true extent of Godlessness as his polar opposite. And I will draw him out.

'I am not a being of compassion, or mercy, sympathy or empathy. I knew many millennia ago that I cannot love as he loves, but can match that emotion and become just as great. All I need him to do is recognise my accomplishments, and I will truly become immortal.'

'He will destroy you,' Jacob said, suddenly sympathising with Dreaden's imaginary enemy. 'He will wipe you off the face of existence. He will reach into time itself, latch onto those *blocks* that you hold in such high regard, and rip the very memory of you from history!'

'But *he* will remember. And I will sit within him a festering parasite.'

Jacob didn't know what to say. He couldn't shake the faces looking down at him from the walls. He could feel their worry laid upon him like a cloak.

'I do believe we have exhausted this conversation,' Dreaden said. 'Sadly, you have not provided me with the excitement I originally thought. You have al—'

'No,' Jacob whispered.

'Excuse me?'

'No,' he said louder. 'You still haven't changed my mind. God does not exist. Your speech, your last point before it; you opened many holes in your argument. We will discuss it until I'm sure that what you say is true. Then, and only then, will I join your collection.'

'Are you lying to preserve yourself, Jacob?'

'No. If you can live forever, and you can hook me up to one of these hideous machines and keep me alive too, then we have time to fucking talk. When all is said and done, God will be revealed to one of us, but he will appear as nothing more than the sham I know him to be and the very realisation that you have wasted your time.'

Dreaden twiddled a bone in his hand, considering the request. The bone reflected his own pale features and a grin twisted his skin. Jacob heard it squeaking.

'Then let's continue...'

THE FOLLOWING

The following is a transcribed publication of voice recordings carried out by Gov. Chief Intelligence Officer Meghan Salamans and are one of a kind. The tapes were recovered from a Pre-UH Gov. Research Facility (Neross) following its departmental transfer from Earth, preceding the planet's nova consumption, to Antra. By order of the Universal Repartum, the contents of this manuscript are to be destroyed following the reading and acknowledgement of Gov. Senate Officials, the Jury, the Witnesses, and other State Officials. The State dubbed *"Great War Crimes Hearing"* will commence immediately and without delay.

This is *Exhibit Q.2*, of Forty-Four total examples of logged Heavy Evidence, and is scheduled to be presented on the nineteenth day of said trial.

Day One: Fifty Dollars.

I'm going to start by telling you all right now; fifty dollars says this isn't going to work. Seeing as bluntness is the aim of this entire mockery of an exercise, I have no qualms boasting its absurdities through this recorder, as instructed. It's backwards, thoughtless, and its premise better suited within the realms of a children's party magic act. But, before I lather your ears with the same foam drenched words I have saved for the end of this immensely expensive failure, I would do well to bring any uninformed listeners up to speed on the concept.

Sat before me right this second, on the other side of what I'm assuming is a two-way mirror, is a man. He is stark bollock naked and alone, with his eyelids pinned to his forehead and cheeks. He might have been good looking once, before being stripped and beaten and starved. Credit where credits due, I suppose. I digress, most people's attractions, as mine have, would quickly dissipate when they learn this man is a serial child molester; a necessity for the experiment, by the way. And isn't that always the most frightening thing? How good looking these monsters can be?

This man was offered two options by the Kingdom: Die, or take part in this experiment. One so cowardly and conniving as him, it wouldn't take an Intelligence Officer of my standing to guess which he chose.

Every day he's injected with a serum that keeps him awake permanently, the aim to—and I'm quoting here—"Slowly open his eyes to the next world and gaze upon Beings beyond us." I'm genuinely not making this up. From paedophile to spiritual peeping tom, I don't know what's more pathetic. I'd have much rather he chose death. Now I'm stuck staring into those dead eyes for hours on end and reporting the findings, or lack thereof.

[*repeated banging on window*]

Hey, you!

Nothing; he's just sitting there.

Ever since esteemed Captain, and philosophical lunatic, Sova Portalo took the reigns as Chief of War, it's been demanded that a sizeable chunk of the planet's military budget be spent on occult research.

151

On this, the silver anniversary of Earth's first contact with extraterrestrial life, Sova fears that the only way to potentially combat the ramifications of recent mistranslated communications is through an alliance with the Spirit World.

These are his words! I've heard him say them in meetings, in front of me, in front of his entire cabinet! Fear will make you do retarded things apparently because the whole project was greenlit suspiciously quickly by Ministers. I'll admit he has a way with words but you've got to draw the line somewhere; when he explained that these Beings would need to feed on that which is *"Beyond the flesh"* in order to survive, perhaps? Yes, that would have been an opportune moment.

The only reason I'm even taking part is because it would look bad on my husband if I didn't. I'm certain he believes it nonsense too but be damned if that's going to get in the way of his career. He's been acting like such an arsehole recently. What ever happened to that man of charming stone, who would never have put up with this absurdity seven years ago? That son of a bitch is long gone.

I'm allowed to say these things by the way. I'm *encouraged* to say these things, to criticise. My role is outlined as such: Be brutally honest and passionate within these walls, and stoic and cold towards everything and everyone outside of them. My job is basically to be a 24/7 bitch, just a different kind of bitch depending on where I am.

I can't imagine my mood improving much over these coming months either; only being allowed to vent for five minutes or so every week into this recorder is not nearly enough time to unleash my frustrations when I'm in here for three hours every day. My work and family life is bound to suffer, and I risk Court Martial by the hands of my own husband if I refuse to comply. Bloody brilliant.

Staring through this mirror, it's tough to say who has it worse, me or the child molesting Vessel of the Spirit World next door. For the benefit of the tape, please note that I'm raising my middle finger at said Vessel, and symbolically at everyone who thinks this is a good idea.

This has been Meghan Salamans' report on Day 1 of Project: Who Gives a Damn?

Day 8: I'm tired.

You can't see them, but be sure that the bags under my eyes are fit to burst with the heavy load of fucks I've not given this past week.

It could also have something to do with sleep deprivation. Since my last recording, I've moved house and it's been a struggle settling. Husband and I got a raise you see. Yay! Now we can be depressed in an even bigger home! If there's one thing a combustible relationship needs, it's more wood to burn.

My son's taken the move the worst, though. Every day I return to an absolute pig sty; crumbs from the lunch I left him all over the floor, chalk drawings cover the walls and floors, he's acting positively neanderthalic.

I shouldn't be surprised, he is still quite young. I forget exactly how young, but I still see him wobbling a bit too much when he walks sometimes, if that's any indication. I can't leave him with my mother anymore because we live too far away and, as per the request of this experiment, I have to be even colder than I usually am with him, so I can't hire a nanny.

It's not that I don't love him. I do, I think. It's just that serving my planet has always been so much more exhilarating. To be perfectly frank, looking after children just gets in the way.

Another thing I can blame my husband for I suppose. Not that any of this matters now. Now this job is the complete opposite of exhilarating, it's positively grunt work.

You may be wondering why I haven't reported on the Vessel yet. It's because there's nothing to report. Literally nothing. He hasn't deteriorated any further, he hasn't moved, changed appearance, he isn't any more hideous or bruised, I'm not even certain he's breathing. He's thinned a little, I think. I'm not entirely sure what food counts as "Beyond the Flesh", but apparently sarcastic comments aren't as viable a substitute as I would have hoped. He's more akin to a poorly executed taxidermy project than a person who needs monitoring. And yet the experiment continues.

Not to worry, I'm sure the gateway to the Spirit World will open soon and I'll be chin wagging with Apollyon or Zeus in the coming weeks. After that, it won't take us long to figure out the best counter attack to a potential alien invasion. Never thought you'd hear those two sentences strung together, did you?

The war seems to be escalating and there are a million and one things I should be doing instead of babysitting a vegetable. Today, I had to stop mid-intel meeting to resume where I left off yesterday: sipping on a cold green tea, with my feet up on a wonky table, leaning back on my wheel-less wheely chair, trying to make out shapes in the ceiling cracks. The planet's doomed if we keep this up.

Occasionally, I check the monitor in the corner of the room and rewind the image to see if the Vessel does anything during the hours I'm not watching him. Spoiler alert, he doesn't. The only time anything interesting happens is when the nurses administer his injections.

Those guys are funny. They always do little dances and skip around him before Mexican waving out of the room. They probably know we're watching and are attempting to make the whole situation less painful.

Reminiscing over their happy jigs will not do however, I have a busy afternoon of ceiling gazing ahead of me, and one such stain appears to be leading into a Picasso-like rendition of a cartoon dog that my great grandfather used to be obsessed with.

As you can see, I'm going to have to cut this recording short. This has been Meghan Salamans' report on Day 8 of Project: Gromit?

Day 15: Delirium.

They say that in any confrontation, whether it be against a person, thing, or subject, it's always best to take the high road. The air up there is much thinner and the lack of oxygen makes it far easier to sleep at night. Well, I'm afraid sleep has been lost to me for four days now, so excuse me while I rattle the walls of this room with the offensive back firings of my haggard Renault that can barely reach second gear, let alone struggle up the hill to a preferred moral high ground. The fumes from those cracks and bangs are making me delirious in quite a different way, and the forces of heaven and hell can't stop me from what I'm about to do...

[*shuffling*]
[*loud bang*]
[*glass cracking*]
[*huffing*]
Shit.

Sorry. I genuinely thought I'd get a reaction if I smashed through the glass. For the benefit of the tape, let it be known the mirror didn't fully smash as intended, and the Vessel didn't react at all. I'll probably get a reprimand for breaking the objective parameters and he didn't even flinch. I've been planning this all week, ready for my recording.

You prick! Just die already so I can go home!

[*prolonged silence*]

I'm scared for my son...

I hear footsteps in the house, dragging feet. I'm starting to think it has something to do with this experiment.

[*prolonged silence*]

No. That's stupid. So fucking stupid.

I said stupid! Do you hear me!? You have a stupid bloody face!

I need a holiday. I need a break away from all the pandemonium sewn together into these hours of dullness. It's maddening. How many more months will it be before the drugs kill him? Or I kill him?

I've been involved in battle before, taken a life. I can take another. Especially one that actually deserves to be cut short, rather than one who was just unfortunate enough to be on the wrong side of war.

The sad thing is I could have gotten away with it had I not just admitted it on tape, quite easily in fact. These words will no doubt be dissected by whatever witch's coven Sova is receiving his new intel from.

I wonder if my husband listens to my tapes? Maybe that's why I haven't seen him in a while, why my house smells so funny in his absence. He's no doubt off gallivanting with some of those same bitches I see Sova being trailed by in the hallways, frolicking naked in the forests on the weekend in some wild blood orgy, committing satanic rituals with the purpose of casting curses that fill my nose with the constant stink of bleach.

Wait... No... I'm Meghan Salamans; why am I even thinking like this? My perspective has been distorted by those vacant eyes staring back at me from the other side of the mirror. Sometimes I feel like I'm the experiment.

With the glass broken, I'm not going to lie, I feel a little exposed, and I still have two hours left to observe the Vessel. There's a small hole in the mirror now. I'm going to get closer. Let me just move this...

[*table legs dragging*]

His skin looks so dry, like it's layered with a thin pattering of chalk. The room smells too, like... Oh fuck... It's revolting! I can feel it seeping into the room with me. These two hours are going to be unbearable.

What an idiot. No, I can't be this close to him, I just can't. I guess that's why the nurses wear masks when they give him the injections. Are we really sure he's not dead?

I may have to leave early, this won't stand. If the experiment doesn't work, which it won't, we can always weaponise whatever gasses a permanently awake body produces. I'm offended by it. I want him to turn and look at me to apologise but he's still just facing forwards, his jaws clenched together. I can see the striations in his cheeks now that the tint of the mirror is gone. I suppose I should be grateful his true face was slightly distorted. I'm... I'm going to go and find someone to fix the mirror, I can't bear this.

This has been Meghan Salamans' report on Day 15 of Project: Date with a Corpse.

Day 22. It's over.

[*hurried footsteps*]
[*crowds of voices in background*]

It's over. It's fucking done! I'm not in the observation room yet, I'm headed through bustling corridors and... Move out of my way!

[*thump*]

[*stacks of papers flapping in the air*]

These people... I'm trying to be poetic here.

I'm headed through bustling corridors and reporting early because I'm not staying for long. The war has very much begun.

Implants, our own people, our own species, have seemingly struck a deal with the Anthrans and are blowing up landmarks across the globe. Worst of all, they're targeting key military officer homes, officers like me. That's where I'm headed now: Home. I'm grabbing my baby boy and leaving before any of their grubby traitor bullets can get close to him.

It's only for the sake of duty that I commit one last look in on the Vessel. Also, the holding room is on the way to the car park and I was caught by Sova on my way to the exit. What a twat. It's insane that he's still pushing this bollocks even now. I was seconds away from putting a dent in his obnoxious jawline, and shoving that compass he's always twiddling right up his arse before I was carried away by a crowd of nervous admin interns.

I'm going to look in, tell you what I see, leave. To be honest, I can't wait to wear the smuggest face I can muster when I see that the experiment has achieved fuck all. I don't think my soul would let me stay in there for another ball-achingly dull three hours anyway, not while my son's at home alone. Here we are...

[*keys insert*]

[*door unlocks*]

[*door creaks*]

[*door closes*]

See. Nothing.

My tea is here on the desk from yesterday; the remnants of the chair I broke against the mirror last week are untouched in the corner; the Vessel is still just standing there; and the mural of cracked paint on the ceiling is as beautiful as ever. I am out of here!

Wait. The Vessel is standing there? Standing?

This... This is new.

[*Megan Salamans is now whispering*]

He looks different. His eyes are focused. They're on me. His body looks fuller, strong; it's still beaten and coated in a green tinge, but thick. I recognise his face as his but it doesn't belong to him. I can't describe it.

I... I should get someone.

[*door handle turning rapidly*]

The door's locked.

[*door handle turns again*]

No...

[*random screaming, incoherence*]

[*static*]

He's by the window, inches from the glass, it's fogging up.

I didn't see him move. My eyes were on him the whole time but for a second when I tried the door. Let me check the video feed. My fingers are barely moving, I can't read the buttons on the video player, the symbols are jumbling up. Gah! Where's that rewind button?

[*rewinding of video tape*]

There, got it.

[*heavy breaths*]

Am I dreaming? It shows him still sitting. Even now, it's in real time. But he's there. I swear to you he's... I can... I can barely talk. I can't breathe. Someone, get help. Get-

[*gasping*]

[*incoherent babbling*]

[*static*]

[*enter new speaker(s), male*]

The White A-a-agent. Victorious.

Ye-e-es. It begins.

Bring me your doubt.

Bring me your panic, your confu-sion.

Bring me more-ore-ore. I see it.

I see-ee-ee you.

All of you.

Always.

More.

Here ends the transcription of Megan Salamans' tapes. No other words or sounds were recorded despite an extra fifty-five minutes of silent content, which enhanced produce faint, reversed fragments of the above recording.

Once read, this document must be destroyed, in accordance with the Universal Repartum and its Higher Court's Laws on Extreme Privacy and Classification. The penalty for forfeiting said duty will result in the handler's immediate incarceration, without bail or appeal, and investigations of the utmost intrusion will be issued.

DEAD FLOWERS

The bow of the Serabim waned beneath the pressure of battle. Human jet troopers, deployed from a comparatively minuscule enemy cruiser, had landed within its shallow maze of white spires, turrets and exhaust vents. They were charging the Serabim's quarterdeck and the control room within. The howls and flashing lights of death coloured laser-fire painted the air between warring cruisers and the dwarf planet above.

Two Generals, adorned in a full lapel's worth of medals, stared back at the troopers through the quarterdeck's thick glass. They were Homo-Nox; a cruel and incomprehensibly perfect branch of mankind. Or at least, that was how they appeared to the humans who charged them. But even those higher beings on the evolutionary scale felt their heartstrings tug with the strain of their current mission: The extermination of the human race.

It was uncomfortable, watching the humans scramble over their own dead to reach the quarterdeck with nothing but doom to greet them. They were picked off so casually by the Serabim's turrets. One by one, from their safe cocoon, the Generals saw their limp bodies drifting through space like fire and blood stricken dolls. It was enough to bring even the most hardened soldier to their knees. Space battles were perilous at the best of times, and to deploy vessel-less soldiers into the fray was deemed madness in any age of civilisation, but with their entire fleet on the brink of

161

collapse, the humans charged with taking the Serabim's control room had no choice but to embrace their suicidal mission. One last hurrah.

The two Generals, who commanded the Serabim in guilt ridden awe of the carnage they were perpetrating, had spent over a century in the heat of war and had barely reached middle-age. Youth and experience made them powerful leaders, but they were not strong enough for this. Their grey suits matched their skin tone and white, featureless eyes, bore holes in the souls of the first human soldiers encroaching on their position. Catching the sorrowful glint in those eyes was the closest the humans got before the quarterdeck's gunfire tore them to shreds, as expected. The two Nox recoiled as much as their military upbringing allowed. Even for these veterans, it was nigh impossible to watch the blood of their fragile predecessors splatter across the deep black backdrop of space. One General nodded to the other, a nod that didn't need words. It demanded an immediate halt to the madness. The time had come to strike back, swiftly and without mercy; the next hour would be the nail in mankind's coffin.

Before the next wave of jet troopers made an attempt on the quarterdeck, the Generals punched a plinth mounted control panel. Defence shutters slammed tight around the deck's panoramic view, blocking the massacre outside. Behind the Generals, a crowd of battle focused officers made last moment checks on holographic desktops before pulling away from their duties. They retreated further into the vessel and were replaced with six heavily armed soldiers: the NEGs.

The Nox Elite Guards were a last resort, an anvil designed specifically to sway the pendulum of war. Even the extinction of the human race was below their rank—it would have happened with or without their help. The insult was apparent as the band of nonpareil warriors made a slow approach to their superiors.

Their battle armour, which placed each soldier well over seven feet tall, filled out the deck with hostile silhouettes. Faces hidden behind crystal visors with frowns carved into the sheen purveyed the control room with disinterest.

'You know what to do,' the sterner of the two Generals said.

'But not why, General Dorez,' replied the least objectionable of the NEGs through a speaker on his helmet. His name was Number One, he was their captain, their brother, and he did not take kindly to his family wasting their time. He grazed a gloved hand over the etching he had made in his forearm plate, a leafless tree whose roots and branches spread further into his armour, waiting for an answer.

The rest of his squad ranged from Zero to Five, distinguishable by their own bespoke markings, carved into once pristine white armour. They corralled around their leader.

Dorez wasn't taken aback, he had dealt with NEGs before. 'Because we owe the humans more than a slow death,' he said.

'We owe them little,' One said. 'In fact, we hardly owe them death at all.'

'On the contrary, we owe them everything.'

'General, the NEGs are wasted on this. This is child's play and a blasphemy against all we have trained to be.'

'Your very manner of existence has hardened you to the reality of this situation. All of you.' Dorez aimed that comment at a particular NEG with a plethora of circles cut into his armoured back plates. He had yet to face the two Generals. 'We are wiping out our very history.'

'That doesn't excuse the breaking of protocol,' One said. 'Should our Royal Family be attacked, or a terrorist threat emerge on one of our colonies, who would you send instead?'

'One of the other nine NEG squads of course. Don't go thinking yourselves too highly now, there's a reason you were given numbers and not names. I think you're all understating the importance of this mission.'

The other General stepped in before Dorez lost face. The name *A. Norridge* gleamed on the name tag sewn into his shoulder pad and he spoke in a softer manner.

'This is an act of mercy and compassion. The power of God hangs within the barrel of your guns.'

'And yet I hardly feel the weight of it,' One said, shrugging the canon sized weapon attached to his left arm momentarily off of the floor. 'How many humans are even left? One hundred? Fifty? We aren't needed here.'

'Never underestimate a dying flower, Captain,' Norridge said. 'They may appear withered on the surface, but their scent is always strongest before the final wilt. Good men have a knack for overcoming the most perilous of situations, and evil men will sink lower than you can imagine to survive. Rest assured, the human race is home to both sorts and it will take more than the power of God to put an end to them completely.'

'So if you feel you're above it...' Dorez added. He held out a hand and gestured for the NEGs to leave the way they came.

The Elite Guards stood in silence for a moment before One said, 'Nice speech. NEGs! On me...'

A focused ruckus of clanging weapons and butting shoulders echoed as the NEGs spread about the quarterdeck. Zero, the NEG covered in circles, approached the plinth that had closed the defence shutters.

'You'll need a code,' Norridge said.

Zero cocked his head in reply, then withdrew a pistol and shot the plinth. The bullet shattered the control panel and pinged about the room.

'Zero!' One said. 'Cut that shit out.'

Zero shrugged.

The shutters lifted slowly, Zero's handy work causing them to shriek. Once fully open, the sound was replaced with One's barking commands.

'Two, Three, left!'

Two of the NEGs, one male, the other female, both covered in similar chequered patterns, took stance a few feet away from the left side window, their rifles focussed on the corners of the pane.

'Four, Five, right!' The last two soldiers initiated a sprinter's position on top of a large table that was busy rendering star map projections. The light from the maps danced delicately over the various animals carved into their armour.

'Zero, you're on me.'

Number One crouched, his head up and focused on the window at the very centre of the control room.

Outside, the battle had grown tremendously. The NEGs' visors displayed complex diagrams of the carnage; predictive trackers, heart beats, ally positions, heat signatures, best routes of action, intel lists, shock waves, an endless smorgasbord of information that would have whirled most minds into bouts of vertigo. Only a Homo-Nox could have followed them on top of the real life visuals.

'Hostile report?' One said.

'Forty-six jet troopers,' Two replied, her voice muffled by an explosion that rocked the Serabim. She twisted a knob on the side of her helmet and her volume increased. 'Enemy cruisers abandoned... Destroyed!'

The Generals behind them flinched as a flaming exhaust from one of the human vessels, taller than a skyscraper, barrelled across the Serabim's bow.

'The last wilt indeed,' Five said, turning to the Generals. 'That explosion came from inside their own ship.'

'We warned you,' Dorez said. 'Remember, failure in this is to fail all beings. Good luck.'

'Keep your luck,' growled the deep voiced Four, overly aggressive considering the smiling cartoon ponies and cuddly teddy bears pictured on his armour.

A subtle, respectful nod was all the General's got from One before they left the NEGs to their mission. The air tight doors hissed behind them. They were safe now, the bowels of the Serabim more than enough to withstand any level of human onslaught, especially one so weak as this. It was left to the greatest soldiers in the galaxy to do what they always did.

'Zero... Now!' One yelled.

Zero took the charge like a relay runner handed a baton. The other four flanked him with precise laser fire that cracked the reinforced window at the end of his path. Splinters of light scorched Zero's armour, the heat spurring him on. Behind the glass, the last remnants of the human forces were mounting. Using the custom blade attached to the barrel of his rifle, he rammed his way through the window. The shards of glass bounced off his suit.

A lone human jet trooper, who had somehow made it past the turrets, was unlucky enough to meet him head on. Zero's crystalline visor shattered the human's helmet and his blood veined into the endlessness of space. Back on the quarterdeck, the air pressure flipped. There was a sudden whoosh and all sound dissipated. The five remaining NEGs were sucked out, thrown at their enemies like canon-wielding canon fire.

Zero had already landed in the white maze of the Serabim's outer shell by the time One touched down behind him. Gravity enhancers in their boots pulled them towards the ship, and while the humans floated, the NEGs charged.

The numbers were astronomically disproportionate; six NEGs against nearly fifty humans was immensely unfair, for the humans. However, as predicted by Norridge and Dorez, the humans fought with unparalleled bravado. Their gunfire fell like rain and was so numerous and intense that the numbers and calculations displayed by One's visor almost blotted his vision entirely. In theory, these were the last humans left in the universe, and in being so must be the best when it came to surviving. They certainly weren't going down without a fight. Despite his earlier trepidation, One was now eager for the coming battle; or at least he should have been. Something was wrong.

He felt uncharacteristically shaky in his stride, and for the first time in his life his heart rate picked up speed. He watched Two and Three lob flash grenades at the jet troopers and disappear into a flare of white, whilst Zero, Four, and Five avalanched into the lines of humans before them.

Meanwhile, One's finger seized up against the trigger of his gun, unable to pull, the power of God apparently too much for him to bear after all. The diagrams flashing in front of his eyes were unreadable. Claustrophobia gripped him. It was all too much.

He slammed his back against a thin transmissions tower as bullets pounded the other side. He breathed heavily and gripped at his suit's collar. Everything within him wanted to escape it. He gawked up at the dwarf planet and felt its cloud systems creeping towards him. The planet called to him. He would not answer. He needed out.

'One? Where are you?' Four's voice called over the headset.

Number One ignored him, he didn't know why. Fear was a whole new beast within him and he was struggling to tame it.

'I can see your position on the scanner. I'm coming!' Four called again.

One didn't want rescuing. He didn't want to be there at all. His hands moved shakily towards his helmet, the tips of his fingers primed against the clips that would unleash his head to the unforgiving atmosphere of space. Nox battle jets rainbowed overhead, following the clumsy evasions of their human prey. Training and instinct told One to follow them, to shoot down the human ships and use his pulse cannon to send the wreckage careening into the enemy jet troopers encroaching on his position. But all One could see was the planet above, a planet that loomed over him and crushed his soul. A twinkle caught his eye, just below the sphere's thick, green mists. *Click*.

He lifted his helmet. He was free.

Number One's angelic face, usually chiselled and without imperfection, had pulled into a constrictive grimace. All Four could do when he found him was push him away.

'What the fuck was he doing!?'

He withdrew his flamethrower. Huffing heavily, his finger rattling against the trigger, he prepared to scorch his leader's body for the betrayal, then lowered the flame. Memories were the only force that held him back. Four left the icy corpse to drift.

'What the fuck happened?' Two said.

'He took off his helmet!'

'What!?' Three chimed in, his voice high pitched and scathing.

None of them knew how to process the news that their unwavering, always focussed, always prepared captain had just committed suicide.

'Thirty fucking years of service together,' Four said, 'not a single fatality between us, all gone for nothing!'

'Focus, team,' Five said. 'Oh shi—!'

Another eruption shook the Serabim, close to its horizon. The last few humans left alive were mounting.

'We're going to have to sit back and pop them off,' Five continued, 'the Serabim can't take much more of this—'

'Fuck the humans, what about One?' Four said.

'He ain't much use to us now, is he,' Three called.

'We can grieve later,' Five said. 'The humans have one last ship and she's changing trajectory. If I was a betting Nox I'd say they're planning to cut the Serabim in half.'

'We still gotta get closer than this. Four's the only one with a sniper,' Three said.

'We can get closer, but if we split too far in the open the Serabim will draw fire from too many sides.'

'Why don't we just jet to another Nox ship?' Two said. 'Let the Serabim go down, we have an entire fleet waiting on the other side of the galaxy.'

'The personnel on board are too important,' Five said.

'They're as good as dead anyway,' Two moaned.

'Shut the fuck up, Two!' Three said. 'Five's second in command. No discussions, only actions. What's the plan?'

As the others argued, Four was busy picking off any human within range, the trails of his shots careening across the sky. It wouldn't be long before he put down the entire human race by himself. Something within him had snapped.

Five issued his first orders as captain. 'Four, keep doing what you're doing. Myself and Three will tackle any human you don't; Three, time for a *Light Shower*, don't you think?'

Three clenched his fists. 'Oh, hell yeah!'

'With their jet troopers distracted, Two, you head to that last human cruiser. My readings indicate that she's only manned by three hostiles. If you can commandeer her before she gets in position for a jump you'll save us all.'

'Just commandeer it? You do realise that's the Bastion? The most destructive ship in humankind's history?' Two said, in a strop. 'Not to mention it's going to take me five minutes to get there.'

'Then be quick!'

She took off, a streak of blue light erupting from her boots. The display immediately grabbed the attention of a band of human jet troopers. Four put them down quickly.

'Now, where's Zero?' Five said.

Zero answered the call by saddling a smoking human space fighter and riding it like a cowboy back into the bulk of the action. Its previous pilot hung limply from the cockpit, his head twisted all the way around. Zero pushed off and let the fighter bowl into a pin-like formation of enemy troopers. The explosion was catastrophic.

'That's my boy!' Three cheered.

He and Five joined Zero in the charge. They ducked under the flames caused by Zero's latest massacre masterpiece and hurdled various vents and exhausts. Their weapons were trained on every human in sight. Any bullet headed for them was pre-empted by the calculations made by their visors.

'Zero, move ahead,' Five said.

'We've got you, buddy,' came Three.

They moved like phantoms, untouchable, and armed to the teeth with weapons the humans could only imagine wielding. The NEGs mowed through them, their own passions to avenge One and save the Serabim almost enough to match the vigour of those battling for their species' existence.

'I'm loving these new audio readings,' Three said, after casually driving the barrels of his chain gun into the chest of a human trooper and blasting a gaping hole through his sternum.

Ears popped on both sides of the battle, the sound all fluff produced by the NEGs' headsets. There is no sound in space, not as it would appear in a planet's atmosphere. Depending on what their visors recorded, their headsets could calculate and produce what the actions should sound like, in order to help the wearer avoid and predict oncoming attack. The rumbles and screeches of twisting, burning balls of wreckage gave the NEGs a sense of purpose. It always had done. The pops of bullets against flesh were music to their ears, the act of battle an art form. With Four covering them, Zero, Three, and Five danced through the enemy lines.

'Don't become too enamoured with the sound of death,' Five warned. 'We don't need two Zeros in our squad.'

Zero had adopted a plasma shield, which ignited from a thin pole and covered him from head to toe. A fan of a more personal style of combat, he enjoyed nothing more than feeling the thud of an enemy against his wrist joints. Three and Five used him as cover, cutting down enemies whenever the shield dropped.

Three unleashed a storm of plasma chain gun rounds over the white desert of the Serabim as Five bowled flash grenades over its surface: the *Light Shower*. Able to read heart signatures through the haze of blinding colour, the NEGs were quick to eradicate any enemies taken aback by the blaze.

'How are you getting on, Four?' Five called.

Four replied with a hefty grunt.

'Good, lad,' Three said.

It wasn't long before the forty-six humans detected by Two had been whittled down to thirty, then twenty. Soon it became difficult to spot any humans at all. After the glare of the *Light Shower* had faded, all that remained of the humans was a small contingent of jet troopers who had banded together at the tip of the Serabim. There couldn't have been more than ten; a rag tag collection of men and women, their different origins apparent by differing uniforms. It wouldn't be long now.

Zero, Three, and Five approached slowly, the shaky silhouettes of the humans pressured by Nox space fighters flanking the

NEGs. Four joined them, a friendly shoulder barge past Zero put him at the front of the unit.

The humans weren't firing, for they had neither the ammo nor will left to give. They let their rifles go. The final remnants of an entire species had buckled. Surrender wasn't an option, death was the only escape now.

The pressure of the moment weighed heavily on Five, and he was happy to let Four go ahead of him. In the shadow of its end, he had personally never understood this bloody campaign. He was too smart to let any mission's details become more than an endless series of variables, let alone one so important as this. Five had spent hours combing over the details of what it meant to destroy the humans; calculating the odds, entering the philosophical realms of his mind and getting lost in the ethics of every moment of existence. An acceptable state of being for one who was second in command. Alas, that time had passed.

Now he was the keeper of this garden of mayhem, and as he knelt down to pull those last weeds free, he couldn't help but feel they didn't look like weeds at all.

Perhaps that's why One killed himself? Five thought. *He didn't understand either... No, that couldn't have been it.* Five himself wasn't even close to contemplating suicide, and he didn't fear the humans, or that they may somehow emerge victorious. This was just another complex scenario that the new captain was having difficulty processing. But he was the leader now. It would be up to him to make the call.

Not that Four needed it. The brute of their unit was already standing toe-to-toe with the lead human, dwarfing him. The human stood with his head held high in helpless response. His arms were outstretched, a small knife in his left hand, one that wouldn't have even pierced Fours armour. Humans were an intriguing bunch, and Five would have loved to ponder them further, in the same way a human might take interest in how monkeys used twigs as tools.

The humans could have easily attempted to flee, although not so easily have fled, yet they stood like the Old Saints, with a nobility so bold it would one day put them in stain glass windows, their heads haloed by the green planet behind them. Five wondered if he might honour these humans with a similar gesture one day. *Humans,* he thought. *Victims of their own destructive nature, their demise a horrific necessity.* Before him was a sight both uplifting and heart breaking. Either way, it was also an unwise stance when faced with a Nox who specialised in using both sniper rifles and flamethrowers.

Four did not look to honour this last stand and pointed his sniper rifle square in the face of the lead human. The rim of the barrel left a smudge of war residue on the man's helmet. Five, Three, and Zero, re-equipped their weapons, unable to believe this would end so simply at the hands of Four. It just couldn't.

It didn't.

The fight didn't come from the humans in front of them, but rather the three manning the Bastion. A violent shattering mounted in the NEGs' headsets before giving way to complete silence. They grasped their helmets and whipped around to see the human cruiser erupt into a million glimmering pieces. It didn't take them long to conclude they had just lost Number Two.

'Two?' Five called in vain. 'Two!?'

Molten metal rained over the Serabim. Taken off guard, the human leader kicked forwards and stuck his knife in between the Four's neck plates.

The mighty Four shrugged him off and stumbled away. He pulled the knife free expecting to see blood. Through pure dumb luck, it hadn't pierced his inner suit. The knife looked ancient in his palm, its wrappings mouldy, with a glint of gold poking through from beneath. It felt heavy. It had a gravity to it; it shouldn't have had a gravity to it.

The debris of the Bastion clobbered the Serabim, causing the NEGs to lose footing. The humans, on the other hand, looked upon the storm of hellfire and smiled. Their jetpacks ignited and they set forth for the mounting supernova.

They must be mad, Five thought.

'Are they fucking crazy?' Three shouted.

'They're as dead as we are if they stay here,' Five said, although even he was struggling to understand the humans' course of action. They would be swallowed up by the destruction, surely.

But as they flew, the last men and women left in the entire universe were untouched by the flame. The debris flipped and skirted past them, sparing them from what should have been a most uncomfortable fate.

'There's got to be a better way than that,' Three said. 'What the fuck are we supposed to do?'

'Follow them?' Five asked.

'What!?'

'Follow them.'

Five had never come to a decision that quickly before, but every book he had ever read, every calculation he had ever made, and every battle he had been at the forefront of, told him that the humans wouldn't smile at death the way they did if they were actually going to die. Unfortunately, that meant the best course of action was their action.

'They know something we don't, and I'm going to find out what.'

His gravity boots switched to thrusters and blue flame kicked him away from the Serabim, a ship now cut like Swiss cheese and ready to blow. The bulk of the Bastion's hull had broken away and was just seconds away from colliding with the quarterdeck.

'What about Two?' Three said.

'If she's alive we'll pick her up on the way!' Four called, who followed Five's example and launched himself at the great fire ball of death that stood between them and the green planet.

Three looked at Zero. The silent soldier shrugged and joined them.

'Y'all are messed up,' Three said. His boots ignited too.

The NEGs grouped up to make a smaller target of themselves. Three sat reluctantly at the rear, humming a shaky song to himself, one that got louder as their headsets took liberties with the sound effects. The outlandish whizzes and clattering zaps of the Bastion exploding weren't far off what could have been the actual noise. Even the dark matter of space rumbled in the face of it.

Breaking past the first wave of fragments did nothing to quiet their fear, but it was too late to turn back now. The Serabim below had morphed into a blue blaze that sandwiched the NEGs between it and the Bastion with white hot fire that latched onto their suits. Beneath their armour, the NEGs seethed, the protection of their advanced shielding nothing but paper to the sun. Five kept his eyes fixed on the group of humans, concentrating hard to blot out the pain of his sizzling flesh. If the NEGs could keep pace with them, they may just survive.

The heart of the Bastion broke open to a reveal a small arch of empty space; the humans disappeared through it. The cool green of the planet behind beckoned the NEGs forwards and their spirits rose, for a moment. Without warning a skeletal foundation of girders pinged away from the main bulk of the wreckage. 'Evasive action!' Five called. Each Elite Guard took a different manoeuvre.

Zero swerved sideways and landed on a flapping sheet of metal headed in the same direction. He used it to surf atop the girders. Sparks flew before the pressure got too much and he was forced to kick away and thread himself through a perilous gap.

Four and Three shoved each other, allowing the structure to pass between them, both angrily cursing each other once they were free from the danger. Five just held his arms close and hoped for the best, praying that the trajectory of the human his thrusters had locked onto would hold true. It did, just, but at the cost of his right shoulder that collided with a steel beam and ripped free from the socket. 'No!' he growled, furiously.

'Fi-you-go-w...' The others were calling out to him, but their words chopped in and out due to the damage his suit had sustained.

He spun away, almost blacking out, helplessly headed for the main blaze of the Bastion. The new NEG captain's right boot thruster was malfunctioning so badly he had to kick it free. There was no heading back now, no chance to reach that gap in the Bastion wreckage leading to the dwarf planet. It was too dangerous for the others to attempt a rescue. He knew that he wouldn't have tried.

As he approached the ship he pulled his limbs in close, shutting his eyes to block out the vertiginous whirls brought on by the spin of his single thrusting boot. He fell into horror. He could hear electric crackling, vents unleashing rushes of hot air, walls tearing themselves down and melting into others. The fact he wasn't dead yet nudged Five's curiosity and he opened his eyes. He was still spinning, the Bastion sharp and pointed and more menacing than ever in the blur of his visor's intel. Then he heard something he did not expect, a sound that simultaneously gave him hope and lit a fire of irate disbelief within him.

He called over the intercom, 'You morons! No!'

He couldn't believe the other NEGs had been so stupid as to attempt a rescue. He tried to focus on the incoming whiz of NEG thrusters, but they didn't belong to Three, Four, or Zero. They belonged to Two.

Her once chequered armour had been warped by the black hands of flame but she was still very much alive. She grabbed Five, careful to punch him in the arm as she did so, and ploughed them both through a thin wall using her concussion rifle.

Freedom.

It was empty out in the gloom above the green planet. It was refreshing. Five felt weightless as Two carried him, and he didn't look back at the storm of death still raging behind them.

Every Nox aboard the *Seraphim,* and many more in its accompanying space fighters, would have fallen to that last desperate act of the humans. All that loss and yet it only stung to think of One. The Nox Elite Guards had been a family, one that thrived on the game of war, but now that One was gone it no longer felt like a game. All of a sudden war was real. Five couldn't even revel in the fact that Two had survived. *How had she survived?*

It was difficult to imagine any further action at all. Out in the expanse of space, where the battle had yet to touch. Five took a moment to bask in a moment's silence. To his left he saw Zero, Three, and Four, headed in the same direction, still snapping at the humans' heels. Then they were swallowed by the haze of the green planet. The light of a final, all-encompassing explosion flashed over their decorated armour and together, Five and Two plunged into the atmosphere after them.

'Good to see you, Two,' Three said, as Two and Five got within communication range.

'Likewise. Not a fan of how this played out though,' Two said, thumping Five in the shoulder again, knocking it back into place.

'Argh!' Five moaned. 'We're all still here aren't we?'

'Barely.'

'Forget the pleasantries, what are we going to do now?' Four said.

Five contemplated this and quickly decided he had no idea. They were already being buffeted by the low cloud, which meant it wouldn't be long before the Guards touched down and the battle against the humans undoubtedly resumed.

'We land,' he said. 'We regroup. We complete the mission.'

'We're already grouped. Let's land and finish them,' Four said.

'No, we need to take a moment to strategise. We headed into hell the last time we didn't.'

'Oh yeah, *that's* why we headed into hell,' Three said. 'How in the fuck were we supposed to strategise for One taking his helmet off? We can strategise now. Then land and yeah, kill them.'

Five's head was spinning with too many variables. He conceded. 'Fine, but we go in light. Discard the heavy artillery. Stick close, we sport leapfrog tactics; two of us forward, three back. Two, what do we know about this planet?'

'Nothing,' Two replied.

'Seriously?'

'It doesn't even have a name and we wouldn't have found it had we not passed nearby. It was uncharted, we presumed the humans were hoping to lay low here and re-colonise without the UR noticing, hence their fleet hanging above the atmosphere.'

'Presumably it's Aldar-like?' Three asked.

'Seems more like Earth,' Five said.

'Where?'

'The actual human home world; they lived much longer down there, or so I read. There are several other colonial planets with similar atmospheres and—'

'Whatever, the thing I'm asking is can we breathe down there?'

'Vis-Intel says, *Yes,*' Two said. 'Although, until we reached this altitude there was too much interference to tell what the bulk of the planet's environment was. Things might change again before we hit the surface.'

'Is our Vis-Intel even trustworthy?' Four asked.

'This is my fear too,' Five said. 'None of us picked up on the explosives riddling the Bastion. There could be a system fault. Space madness brought on by shoddy intel could have driven One to off himself, could have led us into a trap. Maybe there are more humans. What if—'

'Yadda yadda yadda,' Two interrupted. 'Stop thinking for a moment and act. We need to land, get our bearings, hunt, kill, and then find a way off the planet.'

'And if that doesn't work?' Three added. 'Which seems likely considering the unlikeliness of everything that's happened so far.'

'I've always been a fan of going rogue,' Four said.

'Tempting,' Five said, genuinely. 'Two, have you got terrain diagnostics yet?'

'Forest planet,' she replied, 'the whole thing.'

'My favourite,' Four said.

'Try not to burn it down hot head,' Three said. 'How long until we land?'

'We should be breaking the clouds any moment and hitting—'

The side of a chalky cliff face leapt out of the mist. Buffeted by the trees breaking through its rock, the NEGs made a sharp transition through new, murky air. The branch needles broke against their armour, scratching away most of the paintwork left. They flat bottomed just above a treeline that sunk away endlessly into a bowled valley, drowning in an impenetrable smog.

Picking pines from his visor, Five pointed to dancing fires ahead of them. The human Jet Troopers were landing.

'You all ready?'

A commutative 'Ready!' sounded around him.

'Okay, knock your heavies offline and drop them.'

The NEGs let go of their larger weapons; Four's sniper rifle and flamethrower, Three's chain gun, Two's concussion rifle, they all fell away into the pitch black undergrowth. Five had only ever used standard issue, and Zero was busy readying his far smaller energy weapons.

'Okay, circle output, king of the hill, no one breaks the circle, we aren't hunting yet. We ambush, let the humans scatter, ready ourselves for the chase, got it?'

'Got it!'

'Good... On me.'

The synchronised shunt that echoed as their thrusters lurched them into the air and then down into the trees sent an aggressive vibration about the forest. They landed heavy on soft ground. Moss kicked up around them like confetti.

The humans were already shadows hopping away through the green fog. Even the NEG visors struggled to pick out enemy shapes as their "light" artillery tore through the tree lines in an attempt to slaughter anything and everything in the vicinity.

The Nox stood back to back to back, moving forward but keeping a tight diameter.

'We need to get closer, we've got them!' Four said.

'No fuckin' way, keep the damn circle,' Three replied. 'I can't see shit out here... Shit!' The ping of return fire forced him to duck behind a log drenched in dew and moving moss. 'I swear they dropped their weapons back on the Serabim.'

The others took cover as more bullets broke against the bark of shuddering trees.

'Fuck,' Two said. 'And we're surrounded.'

'The shoddy visors strike again,' Five said. 'Shrink the circle.'

Four was furious. 'Two, you should have known they had more numbers!'

'The planet was uncharted!' Two hissed back. 'That's why the humans were stationed above it, not on it. It's suicide setting up camp in a place like this with their numbers. Did you see any human bases when we landed?'

'We couldn't see much of shit, to be honest,' Three said.

'Bite me,' she said, and pointed a pistol at him.

Three dropped as she unloaded. She caught a human, wild in the eyes and barbaric in approach, square in the throat. He gurgled and dropped.

'Thanks.'

'You're welcome.'

But that small victory did little to quell the rest of the humans' counter attack. They seemed to know what they were doing and skipped through the forest more nimbly, and with greater purpose, than the NEGs had done on the bow of the Serabim.

While the overgrown forest provided decent cover for the Guards, it's plethora of pale plants looked venomous. One wrong step could spell disaster.

'Tell me at least one of you refused to follow orders when I said drop the heavy artillery?' Five said. 'Zero, anything up your sleeve?'

A blue wave thundered from Zero's position. It whipped across the floor and then lurched to hip height. The wave slipped over the NEG armour like butter but ruptured all other living things within its climbing ratio. Screams sounded back through the green haze. The NEG visors, which provided a bird's-eye diagram of the battle, showed the red dots of their enemies disappearing out of range as Zero's apocalyptic pulse grenade continued to ebb. Once it had subsided, silence fell over the glade. A sly wind whisked through it with a sad song on its back. They were alone, although it didn't feel like it. They were in a world where the air was as thick as deep water and stunk of gloomy beasts.

What brought the humans to this dreary place? Five wondered. *Dead yet somehow full of life. What did they know?*

A voice cackled behind him.

> *Beneath the sky.*
> *Within the glen.*
> *That is the home of the Barney Men.*

A new red dot flashed alive in the centre of their circle formation. The NEGs spun around.

Sat on a low, mushroom covered tree stump, with fungi growing all the way up onto his soggy red waist coat, was a dwarf, or at least one with the same dimensions as a dwarf. It was more of a squat, toad-like being.

A bent bowler hat hung lopsided over one of its pointy ears. The other was chewed and pierced with mismatching gold rings. Wet black hair, stringy and thin, crawled from beneath the hat and curtained a scrunched face. Whatever it was cracked a thin smile stuffed with multiple rows of spiky teeth.

'Visor reads hostile,' Three whispered.

'What damage could he do even if he was?' Four said, noting the dwarf's knobbly knees, which sprouted from a pair of shabby, buckled shoes and into a pair of threading grey shorts. The pockets were stuffed to the brim with various trinkets; from tiny wooden toys to sparkling treasures. The stout creature twiddled a vial of blood between his heavily ringed fingers.

'What do you think? A local?' Two asked Five.

Five approached slowly. He took extra care with each step as the creature, with his back to the new captain, began a carefree twiddling of his bow tie. The wind began to sing again.

'Who are you?' Five asked.

> *Who am I?*
> *Who are you, who point with flame?*
> *A crooked few who have no names.*

'Drop what you're holding,' Five ordered, ignoring the rhyme, the creature's vial hard in his rifle's sight.

> *I will do with mine what I shall,*
> *And in turn protect my home and vows.*
> *For vowed I have to keep them safe,*
> *The Last of Men from fiery gates.*

'The fuck is he talking about?' Three whispered.

> *What am I talking about?*

The creature stood and the NEGs' weapons buzzed and cocked.

> *You have entered the realm of the Barney Men,*
> *A place that's safe for none but them.*
> *To come was a risky roll of dice,*
> *For our games are played with souls and life.*
> *Let's begin...*

He was gone.

There was no flash, no violent outburst or distraction or desperate sprint away from the tree stump. The self-proclaimed Barney Man was simply gone. It was as though his atoms traded places with thin air. The NEGs felt a tingle down their collective spines, a chill touch made by those who didn't play by the same rules as them.

The Nox as a species were not averse to the idea of the supernatural. In the specific case of the NEGs, they had yet to meet a race that hadn't championed a mystical belief system. The fact that spiritual happenings throughout the universe were rarely seen did little to deter their faith in them. The real problem was deciding exactly what they believed those happenings were.

The theory that something physical could only be created by something spiritual, and not the other way round, had been held a fact of modern understanding for uncountable millennia, but with so many differing experiences, frauds, religions, and ways of thinking, a clear and concise idea of the Other Side was near impossible to define absolutely. There had, however, been a clear theme running in every faith system since the beginning of time: good and evil. At this point, it was difficult for the NEGs to attribute either alignment to the Barney Man. Leapfrogging through the forest, low and slow, the Elite Guards had yet to sway from that conversation.

'He was a demon or something, right?' Three said, signalling for Four to skip ahead of him.

'All I know is that we should've killed him,' Four said.

'No, he had information on the humans,' Two said. 'Didn't you hear him? *For vowed I have to keep them safe.* Why are these Barney Men helping the humans? On the surface it might be a good deed; eliminating an innocent creature for sheltering someone would be barbaric.'

'Whatever he is, he isn't innocent,' Three said.

Five finally piped up after a long silence. 'This is a difficult situation. Magical creatures that are good, per say, wouldn't pick sides at all. Those that are evil, or at their very best selfish and vile, wouldn't hesitate to take advantage of those that could never understand them. They may appear genuine and even act out those allegiances, but the Barney Man also mentioned that his kind are fond of games.'

'And souls,' Four added.

'Exactly. I fear that, even if we tread with caution, each step is going to take us further into the lair of creatures that know no mercy.'

'Kind of like us and the humans,' Two said.

'We're not getting into that here; you know why we have to do this,' Five said, stifling out the brief uprising. 'The humans can't be allowed to survive. These last morsels of their civilisation have shown themselves to be the most desperately inward beings in the universe. In order to survive, they have murdered their own, taken advantage of others, and spread hate throughout the galaxy. Most heinous of all, they rendered their only good men extinct. Maybe the UR wouldn't have turned on them had they retained their honour and bowed out when their time came.'

'We've heard the speech,' Two huffed.

'Then you know the drill.'

Five wasn't fighting in the corner of the Universal Repartum; he actually hated the idea of wiping out the humans. He was doing his duty. They couldn't all be as bad as the Nox government believed, surely. Personally, he pitied them. It was dabbling in the occult that led the humans down that famous dark path of theirs, and it appeared they were making those same mistakes all over again at the end of it. Regardless of his true feelings, he had to feign respect for the campaign. If the Barney Men got in the way, they would need to be eliminated.

'How's the tracking going up there?' Five called, two hours into their trek.

About forty feet ahead, Zero knelt in a puddle of blood, a stark contrast to the pale greens of the forest. Tiny footprints hopped away from it jovially. The silent Guard raised an arm and pointed the others in the direction of a twiggy slope.

'Zero's picked up something,' said Four. 'Down the bank.'

He jogged ahead, flanked by Three. Two and Five took a hard right and paralleled the rest of the team's path.

The air felt colder moving downhill, presumably further into the valley depths.

Four had picked up the blood trail and his visor drew a glowing wisp for him to follow. Images of a different, translucent Barney Man danced into view along the line, as did a ghostly, struggling human chasing after him, arms flailing. The tech in his visor had never shown the ability to paint the past before.

'My intel is showing some weird stuff,' he called.

'Mine too,' said Three. 'Video feed or something. How in the hell are we getting interference out here?'

'Stay true,' came Five. 'Let's find the culprit.'

They hit the base of the hill. The ground was soggy and flat and stretched for a rare twenty metres or so without interruption before fading into mist. It squelched beneath the Elite Guards' boots as they established another defensive circle formation and moved into the clearing, Number Two at the front.

'Red dots are back, at the perimeter edge.'

They waited for signs of movement. Zero knelt to monitor another small pool of blood, of which the footstep trail had led to. It rippled, and Zero cocked his head to a far off chime.

'Do you hear that?' Three said.

'Aye,' Four replied.

'There it is!' Two snapped.

The team put up a walled defence behind her, their sights locked on another Barney Man.

He looked frailer than the first, yet youthful, younger than his ancient aura should have allowed. He stood as though caught in the act of petty theft; an unsure freeze much like a child found pocketing penny sweets. Holding tight to a pair of straps hanging over his shoulders, his beady eyes skirted over each of the NEGs. After a moment's uncertainty, that ominous stare met with the corner of his lips as an enormous grin stretched his swampy features. Bells dangling from his hat rang delicately as he made a careful turn towards them.

'Where's that other dot?' Five whispered.

'Coming up behind this guy,' Two said, dreading the thought of meeting another Barney Man.

'Good, hold your fire, perhaps we can take out both.'

You'll take out neither,
Nox who ought to take a breather.
A thief of lives, will lead the Five,
To a quick and painful just demise.

'I fucking hate these songs,' Four said.

Five agreed but ignored him. 'If anyone looks guilty of taking something that doesn't belong to them, it's you. What's in the bag, Barney Man?'

I take what's mine but what's mine is said
To belong to another who lost his head.

Something shuffled within the Barney Man's long, leather pouch. His grin grew larger.

'What's in the bag?' Five asked again.

Mine.

'You've got to the count three to drop it, or you'll join the person who lost their head.'

It's Mine.

The Barney Man reared his teeth, layered like mountain tips, an angry storm weathered upon them. 'One...'

I wouldn't...

'Two...'

I couldn't...

'Three.'

...You can't.

'Put him down, Four.'

Four didn't hesitate. The rifle clicked and a thunderous crack proceeded it as the bullet whizzed out of the clearing.

It had passed straight through the dwarven creature.

'Fuck.'

Foolish to think you could take the name,
Of one who lives and dies by games.
A child of magic to fall by gun?
For all your gall you owe me fun.
Let's play...

The NEGs weren't sure how to react. That bullet had moved like water through a sieve, it didn't even ruffle the bells on the

Barney Man's hat. They had been, up until that moment, the most effective warriors in the universe, now reduced to nothing but a light breeze in the face of this new enemy. This game the Barney Man wanted to play wouldn't be a physical contest, they could be sure of that. Physical prowess apparently meant nothing in the realm of the glen. They would have done well to massacre the little green man drooling over their confusion but metal wasn't going to stop him. No, they had been challenged to a game with what they could only assume in their short time faced with him, an immortal. An immortal, unless he lost the game?

'Play what?' Five asked, his nerves twanging the air.

In return, he heard the wrinkled features of the Barney Man contort like leather.

The creature made to rhyme again but was cut off by the arrival of that second red hostile location dot.

'No!' the dot yelled before its owner broke the fog.

The NEGs relocked their sights as a human charged into the clearing. He stopped short of the Barney Man, very careful to keep his distance. His clothes were haggard, more like rags. You wouldn't have known that a few hours earlier he had been hard at battle in the thick of space.

He was bleeding from his ear, blood pooling beside him onto the ground. He looked ready to pass out, and would have done were it not for an animalistic anger that kept his shaky self afoot.

Why are you crying? Such a shame,
When one has lost their brother's babe.

'Don't listen to him!' the man begged the NEGs.

It's too late Shane,
They owe me a game.

'Don't play with him. He will cheat. He cheated against my brother, made him play a game he couldn't win.'

'What game?' Three said.

'It doesn't matter. No matter what it is the rat will cheat. The Barney are vermin!'

The Barney Man mocked the human, mouthing the words he spoke with his hands and making overly upset faces.

Another gun shot. It was Three this time. Again, the bullet struck nothing but air. At least it put a stop the childish mockery.

'Hold your fire!' Five ordered.

The Barney Man adopted a snarling tantrum.

> *I do not cheat! That's not the goal*
> *When I want to win your life or soul.*
> *You make the choice*
> *Though the choice is hard*
> *To either die or lose your heart.*

'My brother chose to forfeit his soul. Then this monster killed him anyway!'

> *His brother tried to seek revenge,*
> *For losing the last of baby mens.*

Two's voice quivered. 'Baby?'

A sudden surge of parental chemicals stirred up within the NEGs and, like a contagion, Five's heart rushed with fear.

'Is that a child you have there? In the pack?' He readied his weapon, knowing full well how useless it would be. 'Drop it! Drop it this instant!'

'Do it, you son of a bitch!' came Three, who moved slightly ahead of the NEG pack.

He acted innocent,
Then lost his infant.

'You put that child down right now!'

My child!
For with me was the first time he smiled.

'Liar!' Shane snarled. The human lurched forwards, too afraid to make a full leap onto the tiny kidnapper.

He chose his own soul to shun,
That piece of soul? Of course, his Son.
Now his Son is mine, forever,
Bound by Barney golden tether.

Five was trying to get a better look at the pouch. There was definitely something wriggling inside. The bag's flap ruffled and light vines grew into it from tiny pulsing follicles on the back of the Barney Man's arms. Then the bag wailed. The cry was unmistakable.

Usually, the scream would induce eye rolling, for a human child's cry had evolved to take hold of one's deepest emotions. This time it did as it was designed to do: ignite one's heroism. Every Elite Guard took a step forwards, but the Barney Man raised a finger.

Uh uh ah...
Mine.

'No way,' Three said. 'You can't imprison the kid because he didn't play your game. His soul is not his father's. Trust me, I should know.' Five put a hand on Three's shoulder and pulled him back. Three shrugged him off.

Five sighed, his mind drifting into dark places. 'That child is an innocent,' he said to the Barney Man. 'He is his own being. No one holds jurisdiction over him, not even his father.'

> *There's much debate between Gods and Jinn,*
> *As to when a human's soul begins.*

Three edged forwards with every rhyme. 'And who won that debate, huh? You're making up these rules as you go along.'

'Stand down,' Five said.

'I can't,' Three said quietly. 'What if that was my little girl?'

Five let him go.

Three readdressed the Barney Man. 'So you like games? Alright, I'll play your game, and I'll win, just like everything I've ever done.'

Five had feared this reaction the moment the idea of playing games had been introduced by the Barney Men. When the extra variable of children was added into the mix, he should have counted it as certainty.

Three wasn't as strong as Four, but could out wrestle him; he wasn't as intelligent as Five, but repeatedly beat him in standardised testing; he wasn't as effective when it came to killing as Zero, and yet out on the range there wasn't a soul who could outshoot him; he even managed to outshine Two in diagnostic field assignments, although, there was a reason he honoured her with the same armour carvings. The results were blurry at best. They weren't sure if Three loved winning or hated losing, but he loathed the colour silver. He had eyes for gold, a similar sparkle of which glimmered within the mouth of the Barney Man, a golden tooth that didn't belong to him.

Then what will it be?
Will you trade your soul or life to me?

'Don't be stupid,' Four growled. He took Three by the arm. 'What are you doing?'

But Three just looked him up and down, dropped his rifle on the ground, and shoved past him. Four's huff rang over their headsets and Five feared he may have to hold him back too. Three's rifle was joined shortly by his helmet and upper-body armour. He stood naked from the waist up with a body as pale as one who had never left it and the kind of physique to match such endless duty.

Shane, who the NEGs had almost forgotten about, frowned at Three. There was no human race that matched Three's Nox variant. Although in many ways the two species were similar, it was clear how far apart their species had drifted. He pulled at his wet hair. Three showed no such fear.

'If you win, you can have my soul,' Three said to the Barney Man.

'Please reconsider!' Shane pleaded. 'You can leave. You don't have to fall to the same mistakes as me and my brethren, there's still time to—'

There's no time at all,
You should learn from the Nox
and grow some balls!
Ahaha!
A game then... A game... What game?

'You didn't let me finish,' Three said. The NEGs looked nervously at one another. 'If you win, you can have my soul, but if I win, I get that baby. And your cute little hat too.'

Listen here, you little fool,
The Barney are those who make the rules.

'C'mon, my soul's worth more than that.'

The Barney Man looked uncertain, rumbled in fact. His gaze darted about as if peer pressured into something he didn't want to do, until the glint of a ring on Three's left hand made him bow to it.

So be it.
A soul for a soul, but my hat remains here.
The babe you can have though this Barney lacks fear,
For you still won't win, you won't, you won't,
You'll scream to me, 'Please don't, please don't!'

'Enough. What's the game?'

The other NEGs lowered their weapons, it wouldn't do to try and talk sense into Three now. Besides, it seemed the only way to escape this monster was to play his game. If any of them were going to win, it would be Three. But the shuddering Shane had them on edge. It was clear the human wanted to pipe up, to attack the Barney Man and commit all manner of useless disruption, but his heart was no longer in it. Or his body wasn't, at least. Shane dropped to the ground, defeated. Twiddling the layer of twigs carpeting it, shaking his head, he awaited the inevitable.

A race.

'A race?' Three laughed. 'A race? You can't be serious.'

Indeed, I must seem delirious.

'Those tiny legs won't carry you past me, little man.'

True, true, but I'll give it a bash,
What say you to a hundred yard dash?

'A dash it is. Just to warn you, I still hold the Elite Guard junior and senior records over one hundred metres, and I out-ran Bleary Beasts over the plains of Zatol. I don't even think magic will help you.'

The Barney Man couldn't have appeared more thrilled.

Good,
Good.
But when you lose don't look sour,
A shameful taste when I own that power.

'Whatever, let's do this.'

Another tuneful wind echoed across the clearing as the Barney Man held out a hand infected with popping knuckles. Not a long way off, at the very edge of the clearing's fog, two short pillars rose from the earth. They grew slowly and twisted, their stone cracked and moss ridden. An old ribbon manifested itself across the pair.

The first across the line
Will win what's already mine.

'On your mark,' Three said, drawing a line in the undergrowth with his heel. He crouched behind it and held out a hand for the Barney Man to join him. The Barney Man hopped over.

Ready...

The world couldn't have been more still.

Steady...

Shane managed to pry himself from behind his hands. He didn't want to see what he knew would happen, but couldn't help but watch. The Barney Man made an extra effort to wink in his direction.

Go.

Three exploded from the starting line, kicking up twigs and dirt. Were he a cartoon he would have left behind a smoky rendition of himself. The Barney Man played up to a more literal comic animation, and skipped merrily towards the posts, at about one hundredth of Three's pace. The NEGs couldn't believe it. They knew the Barney Man was no match for them, but this was ludicrous. He wasn't even trying. Five had expected the creature to use magic and teleport to the pillars, to become nothing but a blur. As it happened, his and Three's roles were quite reversed. The all-time NEG assault record holder was even surprising himself. The humid air kept Three refreshed and the race would be over in a matter of seconds. The thuds of his feet were music to the NEG's ears, as was the slither that followed him. *Slither?*

Three looked back over his shoulder and saw the twiggy ground taking shape. A haunting wave of roots rose from the earth and took the form of a hand that snapped around his wrist. It slowed him but he wouldn't stop, he had expected such tricks. Not that he wouldn't have preferred an alternative to possessed undergrowth.

Withdrawing a knife from a holster on his thigh, he slashed at the not so natural formation. It hissed and withdrew. Back at the starting line, Five caught his breath.

'That wasn't so bad,' the captain said.

'Hyuck!'

Before Three could resume the race, another branch had appeared. This time, it spun a noose around his neck. The Barney Man continued to skip, humming a happy tune. He was gaining ground.

The NEGs made to help Three but Shane called them back.

'Don't touch him! Don't get drawn into the game!'

They stalled, their emotions an invisible rope gripped by two giants in a vicious tug of war. So terribly they wanted to help their friend, so terribly they feared the whimsy of the Barney Man. But Three was determined. Even though his eyes bulged and throat veined, he trudged on, stride after stride, the now blurry pillars a fingertip away.

Another vine gripped his knife bearing hand, so swiftly it slit his skin and blood poured into the earth. His other hand wavered. The air its useless wagging produced nudged the ribbon and it swayed away from him. The pain of being so close was so much worse than the constriction. A final thin, thorny bush met his outstretched wrist and latched onto him. It was over.

It pulled him harshly to the ground and dragged him away, along with the other tentacle-like arms of the forest.

'Fuck this!' Four charged after his comrade as the others shrugged off their own trepidation and followed.

But as their feet hit the earth Five felt the soft twigs thud back. They were rippling. He slowed and found the beat beneath his soles subside with his speed.

'It's alive,' he whispered to himself.

He watched the forest's tendrils mount after Two, Four, and Zero, as they continued to pound the ground in their heavy armour.

'It's alive!' He shouted. 'Don't disturb the earth!'

There was a reason no trees grew in this patch of the forest, its soil too violent to sustain them. Zero and Two halted immediately, whip lashing against their own momentum. Four, on the other hand, was already busy tugging at the branches that had begun sucking the paralysed Three underground.

The Barney Man finally reached them. He tipped his jingling hat to the pair as he skipped by and maypole-danced his way around the pillars, twirling the ribbon about himself. He made a bow to end his display.

I win.

The NEGs barely noticed him, their minds far two awhirl with slow paced calamity. Five, Two, and Zero were moving at a snail's pace, and Four was in heavy combat with the glen's hedges and other spindly wooden claws. They tried whipping him clear from Three but the giant Nox was relentless. He knocked back a root with a heavy back hand before unleashing a storm of bullets at his endless enemy.

He roared against it and looked to have swayed the onslaught into retreat, before a huge club, formed of a million tiny thorns, clobbered his chest. Four rag-dolled out of the clearing and into the thick of the forest. Three was left alone. His only company were the cracks of his contorting body. Huffing desperately, he spat teeth from his broken jaw, firing them weakly at the Barney Man who crept towards him.

Goblin like, the dwarf silently jeered at the remaining NEGs, stuck in their restrictive movements. Two took a step too quickly and a thin, unbreakable leaf snatched at her ankle. She paused and the leaf withdrew back into the earth.

'I can't...' she said.

The Barney Man crouched beside Three and sucked on the air, drinking in the soldier's failure. The final touch the NEG felt before his nerves shut down completely was that hideous creature plucking the golden ring from his hand.

Then the cold black swallowed him.

'Talk!'

Shane wheeled away clutching his jaw as Four rubbed his blood soaked knuckles free of the stain.

Tempers had risen in the wake of Three's demise and the immediate vanishing of the Barney Man. The remaining NEGs stood alone in the clearing, still but on the brink of bubbling over with fury, faced with a human and in desperate need of answers.

'Enough,' Five ordered. 'We need to collect ourselves.'

'He's in with them!' Four said.

'He hardly looks it.'

'You heard what that first Barney Man said. This second one even knew him by name.'

Five wasn't so sure; Shane appeared equally flustered by their half-pint adversaries. As he had expected as the new captain, Five was struggling to toe the moral line, or even understand which side of it the ethically positive pastures laid beyond. The only immediate pastures in his vicinity were that of soggy decay, and their rot clogged his mind. The NEGs needed answers after all, and they were still technically charged with the demise of all humans. Perhaps issuing a cold, persuasive hand, or two, wouldn't put too dark a blemish on his soul. Not that any were needed; the human was more than willing to talk.

Shane held a rag to his chin to clot the excess blood from spilling out of his split lip as he spoke. 'What did he say?' he asked. 'What did the first Barney Man say?'

'That his kind would protect yours,' Four said. 'What exactly did you give them to persuade them of that I wonder? What perverse, misguided spiel did you—'

'Of course he said that. They say whatever they like.'

'He must have some reason for saying it,' Two said.

'Yes, to confuse you. Do I look like someone the Barney Men care about? Everything they do is through selfish desire. They protect no one but themselves.'

'Then give us their veiled perspective,' Five said. 'Why would they spin those lies?'

Shane looked unsure of himself. 'This is the problem with the Barney Men: they do, technically, speak the truth. Although most struggle, myself included, to recognise it. Their version of the truth is like water, it runs freely, and takes the shape of whatever its vessel desires. We offered them... We offered them a trade.' Shame was cast over the statement. 'In return, they have to help our people survive.'

'You lost that luxury when you first dabbled in the occult,' Five said. 'You're making the same mistakes your ancestors made. Now there are no good men left in the universe.'

'No good men? I suppose you're right. Very nearly no men at all.'

'And say these last humans perished, what of these creatures then?'

Shane laughed. 'The theory and truth in that answer are quite different.'

'Humour us,' Two said.

The human slapped his hands together and then floated them apart, wiggling his fingers. 'Poof.'

'Then it's settled,' Four said, 'we track down and kill all the humans.' He shoved the barrel of his gun in Shane's face, who by now had adopted a crazed confidence since the Barney Man disappeared.

'You can try, Nox,' he said. 'You can try. But the Barney Men won't be stopped. Not by you. Not by anyone else. They are beyond everything now.'

'Now?' Five asked.

'You saw them. How they play. Be thankful for those extra minutes where they mock you because that's all you'll get. They're fans of suspense. You'll meet one again shortly and we'll see the same story play out; a man sat on a donkey's back with a carrot hung at the end of his fishing line. They will lead you to your doom. They offer nothing but an empty death. Good luck killing us all before then.'

'But why are they beyond everything *now*?' Five asked again, beginning to lose his own patience as the pale hue of the forest began to darken.

The human turned sour. He slapped his own head and poked out his tongue. 'Oh do catch up! Do you remember seeing those shiny things about them? Small toys, bells, coins, jewellery?'

Four grabbed Shane by the collar and shoved him into the ground. 'We saw them. Keep talking.'

Shane quickly pushed himself up, the slight rumble in the earth enough to re-instil a more sustainable level of tension. 'At one point or another those trinkets meant something very special to someone. So special that the items' value expands beyond the confines of currency. They are part of that person's very being.'

'Their soul...' Five said.

'Exactly. The more the Barney Men collect, and the more valued the item, the more powerful the Barney Men become.'

'He took Three's gauntlet ring,' Two said.

'The highest medal of physical prowess within the Nox military. One of a kind,' Five said.

Shane nodded. 'Everything it ever meant to your friend. Everything its symbol stood for, belongs to that Barney Man now.'

'So he's as strong and fast as Three?' Five asked.

'Maybe; but they use what they have stolen in ways that you couldn't imagine.'

'But the Barney Man cheated,' Four growled. 'He said he would let Three live if he lost the race, that he would only take his soul, but he let him die.'

'It was the forest that killed him. At least, that's what that demon would say. He knew exactly what he was doing when he proposed a race across this clearing.'

It was a lot to take in. Naturally, Five reverted back to simpler questions, hoping that his mind would make sense of it all at a later time. 'How many are there?'

'I've seen two or three myself, but there are more. Plenty more. Beneath the hedges, in the trees, forever lurking in your blind spot.'

'How do you know all this?'

'You pick it up, in the songs they sing. When they get in your head it's hard to forget.'

'When does night fall?'

'A few hours.'

'And which way best leads out of this glen?'

'Ten miles to the east, ten to the west; you can go if you want but to stay is best.'

The NEGs gripped their weapons.

'Sorry, like I said, it gets stuck in your head.'

'Ten miles doesn't sound too far,' said Two. 'We can call that Plan A?'

Four was downtrodden. 'I thought killing the humans was Plan A?'

'No, we'll call that Plan B,' Five said. 'Facing off against the Barney Men *and* the humans is an absurd notion at this point. We make to leave the glen, by the sounds of that first song the Barney Men won't follow us out. Their power is here, in their home.'

Shane scoffed. So did Four. Five ignored them.

'I know this is new ground for us,' he said, 'but we enter fall back mode. We head east.'

'The compasses are broken,' Two said slapping the side of her visor. 'Which way even is east?'

'You should drop your masks,' Shane said. 'These devils play tricks on your eyes; I can only imagine what they'll show you with those.'

The NEGs were unsure. They had never gone into battle visor-blind before, and the intel they provided had saved their lives more than once. Five watched red dots in the corner of his navigation diagram flit on and off, notes and predictions wrote themselves across his eyesight in a language he couldn't read.

'Five?' Two asked.

'He's right, we lose the helmets.'

Begrudgingly, Five unclipped his visor and pulled his pale face free. On the back of his helmet, he grazed the carving of a ruffled, bird like creature he had studied on his first deployment. The bird had been noted for its intelligence, despite its ramshackle appearance, something he would need buckets of in the coming hours. He threw the helmet down, beside Three's armour. Shane noted how similar Five looked to his fallen brethren. Four and Two followed suit, although their faces were entirely different to Five's, and certainly unlike any human's.

Before throwing hers down, Two tried to rub away the burnt scarring that covered her helmet. She failed but smiled a half smile anyway, just happy to have survived the explosion of the

Bastion at all. It was difficult for her to lose the visor, she knew more about its intricate technologies than those who invented them. She may as well have thrown aside her own eyes. A baby without her comforter, she needed a distraction. She placed a lock of her hair in her mouth and chewed it. That would have to do.

Four pressed his face against his visor, muttering a silent, intensely irate prayer as the cuddly bear carved into it stared happily back.

Zero refused to lose his visor, and the others weren't going to argue with him. Nobody but the NEGs had seen him without it, and none of them expected him to reveal it now. Besides, if any of them were immune to the tricks of the Barney Men it was Zero.

Five decided they would at least keep a hold of their communication headsets. If they got separated, those earpieces might be the only way to find each other, and any mischievous activity or sounds may alert them to a coming Barney Man.

'What about him?' Four asked Five.

'I'll come with you,' Shane said.

'Yeah, no.'

'When your Plan A fails, you're going to need a guide to help you find the remaining humans.'

'And you'll just help us hunt them down? Lead your friends to the slaughter? What happens when there's just one left?'

'Like you all keep saying; there are no good men left in the universe. I'd like to change that. I'd at least like the last man in the universe to be a good one.'

'Bullshit.'

'Fair, but what choice do you have?'

'I can think of one...'

But Five had already made it. 'He stays.'

'Fucking ludicrous!' said Four.

'We're dead either way. I'll let you keep an eye on him, and you have my word, one wrong move and you can make his demise as painful as you like.'

'Fucking right.'

'There's something I'd like to know though.' Five got close to Shane. 'What could you have possibly given the Barney Men to convince them to help you?'

'Us,' Shane said.

'You?'

Shane smiled, his cheeks pushing tears over the lids of his eyes. 'The last remnant of viable human DNA. You all know the story; germ warfare had rendered us infertile, and when cut from us, our blood and flesh dies instantly; an opportune moment for the RU to launch their extinction plan. With what little resources we had we managed to clone one child, the one you saw being carried away by the Barney Man. Before we had a chance to create more, the Nox began their hunt. That child is dead now, or worse, and the single vial of blood we used to clone him is all that remains of our legacy. It belongs to the Barney Man.'

The NEGs remembered the first Barney Man they met, the vial he carried around his neck. *That's quite the trinket*, thought Five. *One that holds the fate of an entire species within it. That kind of power would almost make one—*

'—a God,' Five said out loud.

'Who?' said Shane. 'The one that carries the vial? In a sense, but all the others share in that power.'

'Well, good,' Two said.

'What?'

'Just this morning we were also gifted that power, and I don't know about you boys, but I don't fancy giving it up.'

Their march after they left the clearing was long, and the NEGs were grateful, initially. The longer they went without meeting a

Barney Man the better. But as the hours slipped away so too did the light, and the once fluorescent moss took a muggy turn.

A sharp glare, cast by a moon the fog wouldn't yield, fell over the forest. It did not glow with a colour known to the human spectrum but rather a mouldy lack of light only a few beings in the universe could recognise. And yet each of the party saw it, and it filled them with a sickness. Visor-less, the NEGs felt the wet air against their skin and it brought a sweat out of them despite the cold. With their heads in such a vulnerable state, their ears twitched nervously. They couldn't shake the rustling that accompanied them, the feeling of being followed. It was a fidgeting sound that hovered below the waist, footsteps merrily skipping in mockery to the beat of their trudge.

The higher they climbed towards the glen's edge the more jovial that skipping became. Here the ground became difficult to traverse. It slurried and turned to marshland with every step. *Maybe One knew*, Five thought. *Maybe that's why he offed himself, to escape facing these creatures, to avoid stepping foot in their world.* Doubtful. One, like any of the NEGs, would have enjoyed the challenge of facing such a foe, having read about them on paper, at least. *Perhaps the Barney Men filled him with a sickness; but why? Why would they do that when they could take his soul, become stronger? Unless One had no soul?* Five tried to shake the thought off. *No, that's unfair. But then again, what would One have to offer?* Number One had lived for the Nox people, the NEGs, but that's all he lived for, all he was. The most well-rounded and heroic soldier Five had ever witnessed. *But how could such traits be traded? They are not values valued by the Barney Men.* Despite an all-around aptitude, there was nothing Number One had mastered that another NEG couldn't have bested him at. *Maybe the Barney Men knew they would meet us, and decided to kill One before he could become a factor?*

They don't seem like the kind to barter with the jack. I wonder what trinket they could take from me?

Five decided he had probably taken hold of an endless tangent and discarded it, on the surface at least, it still stained the back of his mind. More important matters, such as how to kill such creatures, were far more pressing right now.

The trees grew thinner and curled angrily. As time moved on they bunched less and less, like they feared even each other. Soon the NEGs made it past the forest's swampy landscape and reached the edge of a lake, or a river, or an ocean for all they knew. Twenty feet either way along its bank the shores faded into nothing. The still water stretched unperturbed until it merged with a muggy horizon. It was eerily quiet and stunk of carcasses.

Four took a deep sniff of the air. 'What is this?'

'The edge of the glen to the east,' Shane said. 'I'd heard them sing of a loch but—'

'Then why didn't you tell us!?'

'Because they also sang of a swamp and puddles; I was hoping we'd already passed it. They sang of far worse things to the west I can assure you. You could try to swim—'

'Oh yeah, good idea. You can't even run in this place without the plants getting testy. I can only imagine how their lakes will react to my doggy paddle.'

'How about we take the ferry then?' Two said.

She knelt close to the water's edge, using the butt of her rifle to batter thick mould from a chain whirled around two small gears. After one harsh knock, the chain spun and tugged itself from the mud. Now free, the rusted, flaking metal links clunked their way out of the loch.

'There, across the water,' Two said, stumbling back from the bank's edge, knowing full well not to trust any movement while they were still in the glen.

No larger or more imposing than a crate, square and unreasonably buoyant for a vessel so full of holes, the ferry floated towards them. It was impossible to see clearly from the bank. Far away and shrouded in dusk, the shape of a loan captain poked above the ferry's rim; the NEGs knew all too well what creature the shape belonged to.

'We should go back,' Four said.

'Agreed,' Shane said, taking a nervous step behind him.

'Shut up.'

Two grabbed Shame's arm. 'And what, face a similar fate to the west? Is there no way around?'

'How well do you think I know this glen? I spent as much time away from here as possible before our little battle began. I know as much as you about this loch. It could take days to skirt around it, probably forever if the Barney Men have any power over it.'

Two let him go and look to Five. 'We can't face another Barney Man, Five. It's suicide.'

Five was unsure and too fixated on the ferry that had run aground to answer. It clunked against a rock below the shallow water, about ten feet from beaching. Now he could see its driver he decided that anywhere was better than here.

'We go around. The long march isn't so foreign to us.'

Why so shy?
Come, my boat has room for five.

The rhyme was sung from a hoarse throat, and the singer's hideousness kept the NEGs rooted in place.

This Barney Man was covered in mildew, so much so his face was dark green and coated with crust. A crown of twigs and weeds weaved through his greasy hair. It trailed off down his lumpy back until it provided a soggy cushion for his bony rump.

The jangle of keys resonated from him as he leant over the edge of the ferry. He was scouring the bank for a better look at the NEGs and their human guest.

'No thanks,' Four said, 'we'll get the next one.'

Where will they go, to best the glen?
There's no way out but death for them.

'Whatever.'

Wary in their steps, they began along the bank.

I hear him screaming, you know...

They halted.

...beneath the soil where flowers grow.

Four turned hatefully towards the ferry master.

'Four?' Five said.

'You'd better stop before you say what I think you're going to say,' Four whispered at the Barney Man, knowing full well he would hear it.

Alive in the mud,
Heart pounding, thud thud thud.
He breathes dirt.

Four stormed over to the ferry's chain, followed by Zero. The silent NEG ran around his brother in arms and pushed against the massive soldier's chest, back towards to the others.

'Ignore him, Four!' Two shouted, wrapping her arms around his. Five took the other.

Four took a deep breath, but he could feel the Barney Man's sharp little claws reach into his head, pulling at the strands of his temper, willing them to snap.

'How can I!?' the goliathan Elite Guard boomed back at her.

The Barney Man rocked his boat with laughter, water sloshing about it.

Oh how tragic,
You think you can kill me without any magic?

'You know what?' Four said. 'I was *this* close to leaving.' He pinched his thumb and forefinger together so tightly his gauntlet cracked. 'But you've gone and crossed the fucking line!' Four broke free from the six arms holding him back.

'No!' the others all called at once.

But it was too late; Four entered the water up past his shins. He straddled the chain connected to the ferry and started to pull. The loch looked fit to boil.

Uh oh, he's in the water, what a frown!
It'll furl like the waves as his body drowns.

'I'm not drowning,' Four said, mad eyed. 'You say it takes magic to kill you? Well, I've always found the most magical moments in a NEG's life are those where he beats someone to death with his bare hands!'

'Four, we're leaving!' Five said.

He and the others were too apprehensive to enter the water and retrieve their giant comrade. As Four tugged at the chain the water lashed and stained his armour, bleaching and sizzling it. It was an acid that corroded everything but his determined face, taught and irate.

The Barney Man had stopped laughing. He tried turning his own wheel to reverse the direction of his ferry. He wasn't going anywhere.

'Looks like the magic's working!' Four roared.

The NEGs couldn't believe it. The Barney Man was in full panic mode. As the boat drew closer, all the creature could do was lean over and splash more water. The burning only spurred Four on. Before long, he had hold of the ferry. He tipped it sideways and the forest ghoul tumbled out. The confused Barney Man surfaced, gasping for air, his crown ruined and trailing as Four dragged him back to shore. Everyone else tossed their weapons aside, glad to see a chink in the Barney Man's armour; who would have thought Four's brutality would reveal it?

They scanned the immediate area, ready to put this revelation to the test. Zero cracked his knuckles, Two her back, Five his neck, and the trio readied themselves for a more physical ride than they had expected.

Even Shane, shaking his head and muttering nervously, felt a sudden rush of hope. He held back, silently cheering the NEGs on. This was the first he had seen of the Barney Men in trouble. Five, Zero, and Two gathered around Four as he pounded the Barney Man's face into the mushy bank. The creature's mangled visage was little comfort when remembering what happened to Three, but it was a start. *Crunch! Crack!* The Barney Man would have sung to the beat had the tables been turned. Four was in control now.

'You can join him in the earth!'

It would have been uncomfortable to watch had the Barney Man not deserved it. But he did, they all did. Every strike rang with a vengeance for those the goblins had stolen from. The creature twitched, unable to escape, unable to cry for a mouth filled with blood and bone and mush. His slushy remains married the grime of the bank. Four wound up for the killing blow and time slowed. The Barney Man looked much more the victim than he should have done, and why was he smiling? No matter how hard the NEG had hit him, the corner of those lips remained curled.

In those stretched seconds Four became intently aware of everything around him, of his emotions bubbling over, all the memories of the past, and every squalid detail of his present. He hesitated for another half a moment. In that gap of time, he caught the Barney Man subtly twiddle a set of slender silver keys in his left hand. They inserted themselves into the tiniest of padlocks, which slid from the prankster's sleeve. When it clinked, the face of the Barney Man transformed into that of a Nox woman, pale and fair, if not aged with the lines of a tired mother.

Four gasped and let his fist miss. It pounded against the bank and the other NEGs leapt back as Four clambered away. By the time he regained his feet, the Barney Man had morphed back into its usual hideousness, otherwise unscathed.

'Who in the hell was that!?' Two quivered, but none of them could recall. None but Four. A new fire had been lit within him, and he dived back onto the Barney Man. The other NEGs didn't follow this time.

The Barney Man tried to wiggle his way free but Four's bear hug was too strong. It would have been a morale boost, to see Four unleash such power, but this new rage felt uncontrolled and reckless. The upper hand was no longer clear. Five scanned the area, feeling the approach of an eerie presence. A pointless endeavour in such mists.

He was so expectant to see the image of murderous dwarves crawling out of the fog that he didn't notice the ferry creeping back towards the bank at the call of its master's outstretched hand.

Four hadn't noticed either, far too preoccupied with the strangling. Unlike Five, he was also blind to the growing dread. The only thing that stopped the other NEGs intervening was the morsel of blood coloured hope pooling in the battered Barney Man's cheeks.

Those worries climaxed as Four flipped the comparably doll sized Barney Man over his shoulder towards the loch. The ferry cradled him harshly. That should have been the moment to flee, to take this as a victory and leave a message for the other Barney Men, but Four could not let it lie.

'It's over, Four!' Five grabbed his arm as he made towards the ferry. Zero grabbed the other but Four just used their heels to plough the earth.

'Why won't he die!? I can't let him live!' Four screamed, his eyes fading into a dangerous shade of red.

'Fool! The longer you fight the more it favours the monster!' Shane shouted, running alongside them.

'Snap out of it, Four!' Two said, grabbing the back of his collar plate. 'Or we'll put you down ourselves!'

Disobeying a direct command from their captain was indeed a court martial offence. Five wouldn't have gone through with it, but he was glad Two had the fortitude to at least threaten it. But Four was nothing but rage now. Five and Zero let him go, and Two's fingers slipped off his armour. Four pounced into the ferry.

It rocked and kicked up a wave before sailing out into the loch. Four's grunts echoed over the water until the clouds consumed him. His final silhouette, in full desperate realisation that he was beating on nothing but rags, clasped the remaining NEGs' hearts. Four was lost in his own fury, his target no longer in the boat.

'Where is he! Where is he!?' Four screamed over and over, stranded on his island of inner turmoil.

A naked Barney Man had joined the NEGs beside the chain and gears on the bank. Five and Zero retreated behind Two and Shane, Shane somehow now a part of their formation.

A pity...
That he should be so strong but not so witty.

It was, of course, the same Barney Man, stood remarkably proud for one without any clothes, short of his twiggy crown. He twiddled a strand of it between his fingers. Zero, Two, and Five raised their weapons again. Shane was on the verge of an insane *I told you so* sort of laughter.

Three soldiers down, three to go.
A lock filled with blood begins to flow.

Four was still cursing away in the distance.

'What's happened to him?' Two asked, shakily pointing her gun, her scowl a damn for her tears.

Stuck forever.
The water will burn
As his anger boils,
The chain won't turn
No matter his toils.

They watched the chain that once connected to the ferry rebury itself. Four was floating alone in the cold now, locked in the asylum of his mind.

Five wanted to go after him, to dig the chain out of the mud and pull his friend to safety. The hissing waves held him back.

'What now?' Shane laughed.

Death.
I'm always honest.
Before next light, you'll all be gone,
This is the dark you can't run from.

'Always honest, huh?' Five said, 'Then tell us truthfully; how do we kill you? How do we survive?'

I'm always honest,
Never stupid.

'It... It can be a game,' Five stuttered, as Four's cries rang over the loch. 'Make the song as hard as you can. See if I can't decipher this Barney Man.' The Barney Man's teeth sparkled.

I like you.
I really do.
A shame that your soul will be sucked out too.
But if it's a game you want, then a game you'll get,
As for riddles, this one you'll enjoy I bet:
A soul's a soul,
But a voice a voice,
It's in a name,
And it's in a choice.
But you won't know what the choice will be,
Until you're faced with names the Barneys see.
Know your name.
Know your trade.
Know your price.
Know you're right.

The Barney Man was gone.

'Did you get that?' Five asked.

'Got it,' Two replied, clicking the flashing red light on her earpiece back to a neutral grey.

'So, what did that mean?' Shane asked. 'Do you know what it means?'

Five looked at him with the first grin he had managed to muster all day.

'It means Plan B.'

Searching for humans to kill was difficult. Seeing five feet in front of your face was difficult. Not worrying about the human travelling with you was most difficult of all. But the human leading Zero, Two, and Five had yet to reveal a treacherous side, despite having the complete right to do so.

Shane had been silent since the team left the loch and Four's wailing behind. He was forced to march ahead so he could be watched and seemed lost in prideful contemplation. Indeed, he was doing the right thing; the humans had caused far too many major universal disasters to be allowed to live, but would that stop his instinctive urges to survive? Five understood his pain, felt sorry for him. To betray your very kin, even if it was for the sake of the universe, was a heavy cross to bear. Five knew if he was asked to hunt down the NEGs, even if it was to save innocent lives, he would not have done it. So although he was impressed with Shane's commitment to the cause, he kept an ever watchful eye over the man leading them back down into the heart of the glen.

Two was behind him, replaying the Barney Man's riddle through her earpiece. Five didn't need to, he remembered every word. Zero was quiet as ever at the back of the pack, his head twitching with every sound made by the forest.

Five was proud of the way he had manipulated the Barney Man, but he would be a liar if he said the riddle wasn't troubling him. *You won't know what the choice will be until you're faced with names the Barneys see.* Probably meant he wouldn't be able to figure it out until the right moment anyway. By then it could be too late.

'Shane, isn't it?' Five asked, joining the human. Shane was taken aback. 'Sorry, the Barney Man that killed Three, he said that name. I assumed it belonged to you.'

'No use getting to know me now.'

'I should at least acknowledge the name of the man giving his life for mine.'

'I don't give it for you. I give it so that the humans might bow out with dignity.'

'Sorry.'

'It's fine. You *should* be thankful.'

'I am, and look, if the time comes, I don't want to be the one to put you down.'

'How brave of you.'

'I don't want any of us to put you down. Here, take this.'

Five handed Shane a pistol and one bullet.

Shane couldn't help but smile. 'Braver than you look.'

'I want you to make the choice, and I won't judge either way. But don't be surprised that if you turn the gun on us, we'll turn ours on you.' Shane nodded an unsure *thank you* and a subtle tension mounted between them. Five decided to steer the conversation away. 'So, what do you really know about these Barney Men? How did you find them?'

'We stumbled across them, as you did us, shortly after we fled the Heavy Systems. We came across this planet that wasn't on any map, or in the orbit of any star. It wouldn't give off any readings of any kind. We guessed it was some uncharted rogue planet. We stationed the Bastion inside its orbit and hoped it would carry us away with it.'

'That's when the Barney Men showed up?'

'Yes. We had yet to explore the planet, but for a few weeks we heard things at night; high pitched gusts through the air conditioning; singing when none of us knew how; the clank of small metal things. I heard it too, and for a number of days I kept catching a gold sparkle in the corner of my eye. It's like they were calling to us. Enough to drive you mad, and very nearly did.

'Tempers rose when we learned that in a matter of days the Nox would reach us, to finish off the RU's extinction plan. There was in-fighting, a food shortage, we were going to wipe ourselves out. Then the Barney Man showed, without warning, on a tree stump in our central control room. He offered us the trade; that his kind would protect ours if we gave them our last hope.'

'The blood vial?'

'The blood vial.'

'Did this Barney Man have a hat, and mushrooms growing up his back?'

'I'll never forget.'

'He has to be their leader.'

Five wondered if a new plan, one where he took that particular Barney Man captive and used him as a bargaining chip off the planet, might be more fruitful than trying to figure out the riddle. He was wrong of course, and he knew it.

'He's certainly the most cunning,' Shane said, 'and the best with words. He kept going on about how he owed the humans, how it would be an honour to serve them in exchange for their blood.'

'So they knew about you? About humans?'

'I think. Perhaps. They used the word human anyway, but the men they spoke of sounded a far different people. And they know nothing of the greater universe, aside from the little they picked up from us. It's like they'd been stuck in a time vacuum. Not that they were in awe, or surprised, or afraid of anything we showed them. Rather indifferent, in fact.

'The rest is history. We made the trade, and they invited us into their home. They said we should abandon our ships and live with them. You can guess we didn't like the idea; told them only as a last resort. The relationship has been a little rocky since then.'

'They sound like one of the ancient human myths,' Five said, 'like fairies or—'

'Goblins.'

'Yes, yes you mentioned that.'

'We don't know what they are, but of all the stories that I've been told, that seems to fit the closest. Evil little forest sprites. The only thing that's certain is their greed. The faster we can get through this the better.'

'Agreed.'

'Gentlemen,' Two interrupted over the headset.

Shane and Five went quiet and a faint call, somewhere deep in the forest, became apparent. It was human, or so they presumed, the speaker certainly wasn't rhyming. The dwindling team paused behind Five's raised fist. His two lead fingers made a subtle dash to the right and Zero followed them. The hunt was on.

Zero stayed low, floating over the undergrowth with such finesse that the leaves beneath his boots hardly crunched. The humans' calls grew louder. There was more than one, perhaps three or four, arguing. Zero took base behind a fallen log and peered over it into a shallow quarry of poorly cut stone.

Four human men and a woman were huddled around a fire, shifting uncomfortably on their sharp seats. Zero was glad for the light.

'Still can't believe it,' the fattest of the group said, his podge poking through the creases of his armour. 'Just asked his name and bang! Bled out.'

'I didn't see such nonsense,' the woman said.

'Well, we all saw it, didn't we?' the fat man said. The other men stayed quiet, as if afraid to speak. They could not look at each other. 'See!'

The woman waved a hand over the quiet men. 'These idiots didn't see a thing.' The men didn't argue.

'You weren't even there,' the fat man stropped.

'They were hired to protect us, not kill us.'

'Well, if you were offended by someone that hired you, wouldn't you want to teach them a lesson? They're the ones with the powers after all.'

'So he was offended?'

'Little goblin looked like the guy had cussed out his mum! Just asked his name.'

'Then the poor sod should have kept his mouth shut.'

'You're too cold... Part of The Reason.'

'Shut your mouth!'

Zero had heard that term before. *The Reason* was an incredibly offensive term in human circles. It was a phrase that placed the doom of the human race upon the shoulders of the person being offended. On the cusp of extinction, it grew more offensive with every lost human life.

'Well, you are a bitch sometimes, someone has to say it, right?' The fat man slapped the smallest man next to him.

'Yuh,' the small man said, who then cradled himself.

'And where's Shane, and Dumi? That little'uns gotta be hungry by now.'

'They'll be back shortly,' the woman said. 'It's getting late and the Barney Men claim that this campaign against the Nox ends tonight. They'll want us close to the Horx Stone. They'll want us here to fight.'

'Ain't we done enough fighting? Dropped a whole damn spaceship on them for crying out loud.'

'Didn't you see the Nox following us? Those aren't regular soldiers, how we made it back to the planet was a miracle in itself.'

'Suppose we can thank the Barney Men for that. Don't much like it here though. Can't imagine they'd let us leave even if we had a way to.'

'There may be a way...' The woman looked over her shoulders. 'Oh?'

Zero had been moments away from leaping into the quarry. He was quickly growing tired of the babble. His finger itched on the switch to his plasma shield, and he struggled to fight his better instincts to hear the woman out. He crept a little closer, turning up the microphone volume on his visor and switching it to record, knowing full well how important this revelation could be.

'We beat them at one of their games, of course,' the woman said.

The fat man was fit to burst with laughter. 'Oh of course! Good luck with that. A few of us have already died playing their games.'

'Then we goad them into playing one of ours. I think they take a lot of pride in playing and wouldn't be able to resist the challenge. Besides, it's not like they can kill us all, otherwise they forfeit their original trade and die with us.'

'As long as that baby lives, so do we. And they have that vial. They could use it to clone more. They couldn't care less about us.'

'Clone more? With what?'

'Urgh, magic.'

'Pfft!'

Zero's eyes were rolling behind his visor. He wondered how the humans could be so stupid. He never gave them a second thought before this campaign, but presumed, having existed for so long in such dangerous parts of the galaxy, that they would have more sense than this. Speaking so openly of your plan, in the home of creatures that quite clearly were magical, and quite clearly willing to crush you into dust, was suicide.

'Well, what would you propose?' she conceded.

'I don't know. We could learn their names? They don't seem to like that.' He chuckled a little. Zero, however, liked the idea of ruffling the feathers of the Barney Men. Such a tactic might also prove more useful than its surface result. *It's in a name.*

'Don't be stupid,' the woman said. 'They aren't as magical as you think. My plan will work.'

'You'll die.'

'Shut up. Now I'm hungry.'

'Buh, I'm not,' another one of the quieter men said, looking deathly pale.

'Oh sure, they pipe up when the topic changes to food,' said the woman. 'What have we got anyway?'

The fat man pulled a small rodent out of the fire, the gaunt creature attached crookedly to a lop-sided spit. 'I don't know, but this thing's taking years to cook.'

'What even is it?'

Zero's attention had completely dissipated. He had recorded what he needed to hear; now it was time for action.

He stood tall and cracked his back. A sharp buzz echoed over the quarry as he ignited his light shield, silencing the mundane dinner talk. Like a phantom, he fell from the mist into the human circle. His feet set down hard, kicking up sparks from the camp fire. The humans fell over themselves. They made to grab their guns but Zero was too fast. His boots lit blue and he cascaded into the fat man. The human's face squashed up against his translucent plasma shield before Zero sandwiched him against a jagged rock. The crack of the man's spine was so loud Zero could barely hear the gunfire behind him.

He spun as the fat man rolled aside and took immediate cover behind the shield. It took all his strength to keep the impact at bay, and with every fiery crack against the shield his knee sunk deeper into the earth. Thankfully, Zero knew guns. He counted every bullet that pinged off his barricade; it wouldn't be long before it was time to reload. Silence.

The Elite Guard stood and readied himself, unafraid as he watched green dots creep into the diameter of his visor's scanner.

The humans were fumbling. They swore and growled at each other as they dropped magazines and their fingers got caught in their guns' mechanisms. If they could have seen Zero's face, they would have turned scarlet from embarrassment. The Nox shook his head at their military incompetence. But, as he looked closer, he could see the medals that adorned them, their shine unhindered by the fog. Zero wondered who they had stolen those medals from.

Frustrated, the humans dropped their guns, withdrawing short swords instead. They tried to compose themselves but were clearly rattled.

'I don't know what the fuck's going on here,' the woman screamed, the three men readying behind her, 'but you're insane if you think you can kill all of us from behind that shield.'

Zero was glad she said that.

He twisted the handle of his shield and watched the wall of energy morph into a double ended glaive. The humans' robbed him of his reaping as they turned to ghosts by their own accord.

223

Then, four anticlimactic pops from Two's rifle robbed him further.

She, Five, and Shane had skirted around the human base and burst onto the scene expecting a much larger scuffle.

'Oh, that's it?' Five asked. 'How many are left?'

Zero sheathed his glaive handle irritably and shrugged.

'This was it,' Shane said. 'This was my squad. Just getting ready to eat.'

'You don't seem too upset,' Two said.

'Cowards, slobs, what would I be upset over? They would have headed back to the Horx Stone soon; it's later than I thought. The others must already be there.'

'Then that's where we go,' Five said.

'The Horx Stone? I'm not sure we should go there.'

'Not getting stage fright are we?' Two said. 'Your time will come either way, no use skipping out on us now.'

'The Barney Men draw power from the stone. Or at least they're far more ruthless in its presence.'

'Those things don't get any more ruthless. Stop trying to avoid this.'

'That's enough,' Five said. 'She's right, Shane. That Barney Man by the loch said we would have to make a choice. I've no doubt it starts and ends with another confrontation. Maybe the extra magic will work in our favour.'

Shane turned his nose up at the NEGs. 'I don't fear death. I fear them taking my soul. If we go to the Horx Stone and she brings this unhelpful, tactless attitude with her we may as well just slit our own throats now. It would be a more pleasant way to go I can assure you.'

'Oh, I'll show you tactless!' Two took Shane by the scruff of his collar.

Five shoved a pistol beneath both their chins. 'Enough!'

Two had not expected this. Neither had Five.

'This is serious, everyone here needs to wake up.'

Two held up her hands and conceded, Shane's nostrils returned parallel to the ground.

'Shane will lead the way,' Five said. 'He's led us true thus far. Two, you and I will continue to work on this riddle, and Zero stop slouching would you. You want a fight, you'll get one. Did you hear what the humans were saying before the fight? Any useful info?'

Zero shrugged again. He flicked a switch on his visor and the line he recorded by the fat human played for Five to hear; "*I don't know. We could learn their names? They don't seem to like that.*"

Five paused then nodded. 'Just make sure that energy, multi purpose, death contraption of yours is ready and charged. I don't expect negotiations to go smoothly.'

The deepest realms of the glen did not boast smooth paths. Shane, although more familiar with the forest than the NEGs, was about as useful given the lack of light. The Elite Guards' armour torches threw up walls of white against the mist. Shane carried a torch forged from the human campfire with him, which seemed to sit better in the environment, but was hardly an improvement. The shapes of the forest were still lost. It was impossible to pinpoint a location by the rogue branch or vine that appeared suddenly along their path.

Occasionally a leaf or shrub would catch the flame, and like a fairy tale concerning lost children, a trail of small fires lagged behind them, begging for a hero to follow and save them.

But no one would follow, no one could. The team were alone with nothing but thoughts and fears. Five was still wrestling with the riddle, but at least Zero's new insight from the human conversation gave his mind direction. He had heard the Barney Men mention *names* in regards to one's life, and even the NEGs themselves. *We have no names, only numbers, could it have something to do with that? But what has that got to do with choices, or rights? Price? Would the Barney Men put a price on their names? Or their lives? Voices? These things could well be traded with the Barney Men, but how?* He was going to have to put every word that came out of his mouth under a microscope if they were going to survive.

Watching the others didn't fill him with confidence. Shane had turned his nose up again, and had quietly been shaking the entire trek; Two was cursing not-so-subtly under her breath at herself for being, as she so poetically put, *such an ass hat*; and Zero walked with the swag accompanied by one who wasn't going to let the trading of words take place before the trading of punches.

None of them were ready for this.

The once tight knit unit of the NEGs were, without their true leader, a ragtag team of opposite personalities and at the end of their collective tethers. However, as is often the case with doom, those tethers are quick to bind themselves back together when faced with it. Soon enough, doom loomed over them in the form of a gaping cave mouth. It swallowed the fog, cleared it, and bared its rocky fangs. Against all rationality, they had stumbled upon it and were now faced with the abyss. Five would rather have stayed lost.

Drips of water echoed sweetly from its innards like notes plucked from a harp. The NEGs had learned to be wary of such serene sounds. No music, cheery or otherwise, could soothe the holes carved into their bellies, now a match for the endless black facing them.

'After you, human,' Two said.

'Obviously,' said Shane. 'The Horx Stone sits on a mound at the cave system's centre. You wouldn't make it halfway without me.'

'So what's your point? Just show us the way.'

'The point is you can give him more respect,' Five said. Two cut herself off before saying something she would regret. 'That's as close as you'll get to an apology, Shane. Are you ready?'

'As ready as I can be. What's the plan?'

'Is it wise to say out loud?' Two asked.

'They can read our hearts, listen to our thoughts, no harm in speaking it out loud,' Shane said.

'We talk to them,' Five said.

'And say what exactly?'

'I don't really know.'

'That's good I suppose,' Shane sighed. 'If you don't know, they don't know. That almost puts us on a level playing field.'

'And if talking fails?' Two asked.

'Kill all humans,' Five said. Zero's glaive sparked into life. 'Except for Shane. The choice to die a hero lies with him.'

'No pressure,' Two said.

Shane walked in.

The others followed in a line, Zero at the back, letting his glaive's tip crackle against the surface of a stream. Other streams petered down in shallow, miniature waterfalls along the crevices of the cave's grey walls. When the red shade of Shane's flame hit them, the light splintered into various greens.

'This isn't natural,' Two said.

Five ran his hand along a moist wall and said, 'If you spend enough time in this universe you'll realise that anything's natural somewhere. Then when you add magic into the mix...'

'That won't stop me from pointing it out. Being able to determine the real from not is the only thing keeping me sane at the moment.'

'I suppose if one of us can keep our heads then maybe we can, well, end up keeping our heads,' Five said, rubbing his neck.

'It's times like this I wonder if it would have been best if our parents could have chosen what happened to us.'

'When have we ever faced times like this?' Five said. 'We've always come out on top, never lost a man. In a matter of hours we've lost three.'

'Don't lose yourself to semantics, Five, you know what I mean. Whenever we face any real hardship I wish that maybe life was simpler.'

'There's nothing simpler than war, unfortunately. At least it's where we seem most at home.'

'And yet, without my visor, I feel more lost than ever.'

'Your footing is still surer than mine. My head's all over the place. These tunnels can barely contain my thoughts.'

'Oh please, we would be long dead by now if I was calling the shots. You're doing better than you think, all things considered. I'm grateful one of us is thinking for a change. Don't worry, One put up with a lot more shit from me. I'm just scared.'

Five knew that was difficult for her to admit.

'I'm scared,' she continued. 'I can't track, I can't navigate, I can't fight these Barney things. My specialities are wasted in this place, and when I think of the pain I've already been through—' Two tugged a bent shoulder plate free from her arm and rubbed the black markings before discarding it. Five got a flashback of that nuclear-sized blast she somehow survived. '-I wonder if a name, rather than a number, would have been better.'

'What name would you choose?'

'I don't know. You?'

'No. No idea.'

Shane stopped walking up ahead at a crossroads. One tunnel forked away and down, the other up. Both looked as menacing as the other. 'Do you think this is the *choice* that Barney Man spoke of?' he asked.

Five looked down at him. 'Why? Don't you know the way?'

'This wasn't here before.'

'Maybe then.'

'So, down or up?'

'Down.'

'Really?'

Five had already worked out hundreds of different outcomes depending on which direction they chose, all of them ending in rather gruesome fashion. Down seemed the most dangerous option, down is where this nightmare would end, for better or for worse.

'Down.'

The labyrinth swirled over and under itself. Vegetation clogged the way. Vines and bushes, moss and flowers, all bunched together in a mass of non-uniformity. The threat of trapping themselves in a blazing inferno became too great, so Shane extinguished his torch and left it behind. The NEGs' armour lights would have to do. A staircase hewn from the rock, bent and out of shape, sparkled under the glow.

A familiar musical wind ebbed towards them.

'Getting close,' Five said.

Two joined him. 'Still sure we should have gone down?'

'No. Are you all ready?' Silence. 'Good.'

As they lost their bearings further, and the humidity reached new levels, drums joined the melodic gusts and the floor vibrated. The stems of plants and different grasses rustled until the increasingly claustrophobic caves opened out into a wide cavern. The drumming stopped.

The cavern was tall, and a huge hole in its ceiling provided a window to the natural outside light, somehow unimpeded by the mists of the forest surface. Silver moonlight trickled in and focussed on a towering boulder that stuck out from the

229

top of a mound of toys, jewels, clothes, and bones, as well as any number of random object that meant something special to someone once upon a time. It was all rotting and caked in mould, and completely covered the ground. Several toys took pride of place within the chamber, hanging from its roof by way of ropes or thin string.

There wasn't a square inch of the chamber that didn't appear somewhat odd or out of place. The history of these lost souls created an unsettling collage, and the artists had yet to show themselves.

Opulence had been attempted, and unachieved by any standard throughout the universe, with bouquets of flowers that intertwined with the cavescape on uprooted tree trunk pedestals. Their roots stuck out haphazardly and created natural walls and fences. Each NEG made a note of the potential cover.

'This is it,' Shane said.

His eyes trembled in the light of the Horx Stone, flitting between that and the dark corners of the cavern.

'Where are they?' Five stepped tentatively into what he would describe as an arena. The various items littering the floor crunched underfoot. 'Maybe we beat them to their own climax.'

'No,' Two said, remembering the slow demise of her comrades, 'they're just fans of tension.'

'Aye.'

Tonight...
The Dying Flowers must earn their hours.

The cave's carpet of trinkets rattled beneath the echo and the NEGs whipped this way and that. Then those dying flowers rose. The humans, just as General Norridge had warned, burst from the hills of foreign objects with an enthusiasm their race had failed to exhibit in centuries. They were of limited ammo but potent in spirit, and there were far more than Five had expected.

Fumbling into action, he made to cut down the man closest to him, charging maniacally into the NEGs' stream of bullets. Despite Five hitting his mark, the human barrelled on into him regardless.

As they rolled and battered one another across a hill of lost souls, Five saw Shane dive head first into cover. Satisfied, marginally, that he was safe, the NEG captain slammed his foot into the ground and stood, flipping the human over his shoulder and into an unforgiving rock. A moment's reprieve let him scan the area for Zero and Two.

They weren't difficult to miss. They had taken cover behind Zero's energy shield, which he had jammed into a lop-sided tree root. Two held the onslaught of human guns at bay with more precise return fire. But her ammo was wearing thin, and somehow she had yet to hit anything; an old NEG trick.

With the humans edging closer, their confidence building, Zero twiddled a pulse grenade behind his back. When the humans had satisfactorily bunched up, and Two's rifle clicked rather than boomed, he let the grenade loose. Five saw the blue twinkle of the grenade from the corner of his eye. Utilising the distraction, he bolted past the approaching humans and leapt onto a terrified Shane.

The blue wave of death cut through the air and the humans, rendering any too slow to react into dust. Their ashes washed against the cavern walls. The Horx Stone rocked and fell and crushed the men who had taken shelter behind it, steamrolling their bodies into the base of the mound. Moss, water, and souls, kicked into the air. The sound of the explosion reverberated without pause and grew stronger with every wall it bounced off. It was as sharp as the energy that had torn through the humans. When Five was certain the bulk of the damage had subsided, he pushed himself off of a trembling Shane and held his own head. The ringing was so loud he felt like it might break in two.

As he groaned, a group of unarmed humans collided into him, wailing their fists like desperate animals. Five had seen lower primates battle this way, pounding their prey until they turned to juice. He would have laughed off the primitive assault had it not proven so effective.

The strikes vibrated straight through his armour and bruised his skin. All he could do was cover his head and pray it would hold out. He peered through broken fingers to see what had happened to Two and Zero.

Two was busy assassinating the other groggy human survivors as Zero took to the top of the mound of trinkets, where the Horx Stone once sat, and beckoned the last few men and women to attack him. He looked more like bait than a warrior, stood with arms open and his visor focussed on the moonlight streaming in from the hole above. But Zero had a skill that was rare even in Nox circles.

A human woman rounded on him.

'Die!' she screamed, popping off shots at the NEG.

Zero drew his energy glaive and, with an unfaltering swish, parried the bullet straight back at her. Her ribs shattered, blood spurted, and before she had even hit the ground, Zero whipped his glaive in one huge arc, sending her comrades' semi-automatic encore hailing back at them. Although less accurate, the men were cut down at the knees as Two swooped in. Their necks snapped quickly, and Two looked up at Zero with the same face she made every time he pulled that trick. 'You're ridiculous,' she said. Then, as she always did, she smiled. Now there was only one band of humans left. Five would have smiled too, were he not busy swallowing teeth by way of their boots.

He tried calling out but the beating was too relentless. He could hear the Barney Men laughing, as if the further he slipped into death the easier they became to hear. Two and Zero would surely help him now. Whether or not they would reach him in time was another matter. As the world began to blot, and the sounds of fists faded, all he could do was hope that Two and Zero found a way off the planet without him.

A gunshot split Five's ear drum; he was sure that had been the killing blow. Then why was he still breathing?

Five craned an eye open and watched a man hit the ground beside him, bullet hole in his forehead. The reaching figures above him were focussed on another shaking black outline. Five focussed and he saw Shane stood aquiver behind an outstretched arm, empty gun in his hands.

'Traitor!' shouted one of the human men.

'How could you!?' volleyed a woman.

'This has to stop,' Shane pleaded. 'Stay back, I'll shoot!'

But the humans could see two zeros on the side of the gun. His magazine was empty.

'You're as cruel as them,' the woman said. 'You'd massacre your own people?'

'Our people's fate was sealed when we handed it to the Barney Men. Who knows what more horrors we'll unleash on the universe? We're nothing but poisonous weeds, and we've outstayed our welcome.'

'You've outstayed yours!'

The gang of humans leapt at him. Against any hope, Shane pulled the trigger again, to no avail. The men and women throttled and battered him with twice the venom Five had received.

'Zero!' Five called.

Zero and Two were already on the scene. With a slash of his glaive, Zero clove every one of the humans into soaring pieces. Whatever still breathing parts were left, Two tackled like a bull into a tower of playing cards. To Five's surprise, she was the first to drop to Shane's side.

'You idiot,' Five heard her say. He crawled over to them.

Shane didn't have the durability of a Nox Elite Guard, and the pool of blood he lay in reached out into the cave's own silver puddles. His jaw was broken, his windpipe crushed, but Shane looked proud. He had a choice to make and he made the right the one.

Three tears carved clear rivers into his dirty cheeks; one for his brother and nephew, one for every human that ever tried to live right, and one for the NEGs who, if they had any sense, should have killed him hours earlier. In that state, his soul slipped out of this world and into the next; the last human in the universe. A good man.

The NEGs bowed to his sacrifice.

'Does this mean the Barney Men are defeated?' Two asked.

They scanned the blood soaked cavern. There wasn't a human left alive. Five wanted to believe it.

'If they are, why do I feel so on edge?'

Because the man misheard what the Barney said.

The familiar voice cut through the chamber and slit their hearts. It was the voice of that first Barney Man, a nightmare they didn't want to believe but found all too easy to do so.

'They didn't mishear a thing,' Five said, being helped to his feet by Two.

The trio of NEGs eyed every corner of the cave but saw no sign of that first Barney Man.

'You just used loose words, a coward's ploy.'

A coward?
That I would bathe myself in boiling showers?
Invite the strongest to my home,
With a chance to overthrow my throne?

'You offer no chance. Your games favour you and you alone.'

No matter the plight,
No matter how slight,
You've still a chance at life if right.
But so far you're wrong,
That's the name of the song,
Which is why the Barney keep singing along.

'Bullshit. You're demons. You exist to torture. Why even bother lying about it?'

There's more to us than demon kind,
Who care nil for either soul or mind.
We are just men who like to win,
And we win a lot, and so we grin.

'You cheat a lot,' Two said.

We don't cheat.
We can't cheat.
We won't because we love souls to eat.

'Then why are you breathing, and the humans not?'

Don't forget,
The vial that hangs around my neck.

Five could have sworn he saw a twinkle away in the dark of the chamber.

The blood of the humans remain,
But of course, you'll hark the same guff,
That in our game we cheated again
And try but fail to shame us.
We know we're right.

'You're wrong!' Two shouted, her hair slapping her face as she sought a glimpse of the Barney Man.

'No,' Five said, 'he's right.'

Two looked betrayed, even Zero took a double take.

'You can't be serious?' she said.

'I didn't say I like it. But they are always right.'

'Their very existence is wrong!'

'But even spiritual things follow rules, and if they're right then that... Then that means I'm right.'

Five held up a hand. It was coming together.

The separate parts of the riddle were clicking in his head. It was still a jumbled puzzle, but he had started work on the corners and was busy bundling together all the various shapes that comprised his long history of philosophical research. '*Know you're right*,' he said to himself. The games they played, they were Barney games, and they were completely and one hundred percent in command of every vague rule. But he remembered that for the past few hours they had been playing *his* game, they had accepted *his* challenge. A magical contract was afoot.

Two screwed her face at Five who was holding his head. 'I need time,' he said. 'It's a good job they like dragging these things out.'

> *And yet we quickly tire of larking about.*
> *If it's time you need then time will quiver,*
> *As Two plays with Styx down by the river.*

'Wait...' Five was quick to put the wording together. Two not so much.

'What?' She looked at him cluelessly. He returned a look of horror. Her eyes were bleeding.

'No, please. I need time!' Five called into the darkness.

Time that wasn't defined?

'I define it!'

'What's happening?' Two said.

Zero got right in Two's face, trying to figure out what was happening. Two then saw herself reflected in his visor and put a hand to her once white eyes, now a flood of red. She teetered on her feet and put a hand to her cheeks, dabbing the clots between her fingers.

'Show yourselves!' Five roared.

All he got in return were the hidden scuttles of tiny feet. A nauseating chorus of giggles joined them and Two grew more and more upset.

'I feel sick...' she said.

'You're going to be fine... Stop this now!' Five called out again.

'Really, really sick.' Two ran shaky fingers through her hair and coughed.

'I said you'll be fine.'

'Can't I challenge them?' she said desperately, attempting and failing a weak pull away from Zero, who caught her before she fell. 'Put my soul on the line? It will stop the pain, won't it? I don't need a soul.'

'Shut up, just breathe,' Five snapped. He got right in her face, beside Zero.

'I can't, there's something in my throat.'

'No there isn't. Focus on me. Look into my eyes.'

She did. It was horrible.

'Okay...' she whimpered.

'There. Feeling better already right?'

'Yes. Yeah...'

Then she burst into tears. Her voice croaked and strained against a scream that she was holding back.

'You said *yes*, Two. They can't hurt you. You don't belong to them.'

But she does... Five suddenly realised he was lying to her. Two should have been long dead, back when the Bastion blew. She couldn't have denied the Barney Men any more than a puppet its master.

'My throat. I'm going to be sick.'

Her cheeks ebbed with air that she swallowed back. Five put his hands on her shoulders and stared harder as she tried turning her head away.

'Don't let them, Two!'

He had to dodge her chest, which was hyperventilating so violently it almost pushed him and Zero away from her.

'I... can't...'

'Don't let them! Don't let them!'

'I...'

She stopped. It was a haunting stillness. Two looked Five in the eyes with a face so sad the farewell smile masking it was more glass than flesh, brittle and transparent. Five stopped breathing. Two's neck cracked.

Her head writhed and she finally screamed. Five and Zero stepped away, unable to watch her cheeks shake as the slobber and blood from within showered them. They wanted to help but her arms leapt about in a fit they had never seen. Five was ready to put her out of her misery before eight sharp talons tore their way out of her throat. Five and Zero leapt back further down the mound of trinkets. The rip of her skin strained their ears.

Then a Barney Man, decrepit and burnt and naked, crawled out of her neck stump. Her innards slopped about his person as he crawled over her armour's collar. Like an insect he scurried down her body, racing her decapitated head to the ground.

Two's face bounced away and out of sight as Zero hurled his glaive like a javelin at her goblin parasite. It missed. The first enemy Zero had ever missed. The Barney Man was gone. Two's rigid frame remained standing, blackened and now bloodied, a testament to those who dare to challenge the Barney Men. Five stormed over to the corpse and shoved it over, he would not let her stand as an insult.

He was silent as the scene replayed over and over in his head. But that wasn't the only terrible thing that collaged his thoughts; Four's battle-mad distant hollering, the cracks of Three's contorting body, and the harrowing unresponsiveness of Number One, all rang about his head to the backdrops of Two's own outbursts of fear as the Barney Man burrowed its way from within her.

The NEGs were destined for death and had been lucky to survive this long. That is why they were given numbers, undoubtedly, to make it easier on those they protected when news broke of their demise.

Had Two considered her own name before the end? Five wondered. Then he remembered the last thing to go through her mind were the claws of the Barney Man. She was brought back from death by them, only to be slaughtered once more. Him watching her die a second time would have paled next to the worry and confusion she must have felt.

The dishonour of her demise made Five furious. He cleared his head and readied his lips to argue his answer to the riddle. That was the only way to get even. Death would not be enough for them. He wanted their souls too.

Then, they came.

As a swarm of jeering insects, they snuck from the cracks and crevices of the cave; some running, some skipping, others hobbling on three stumps, all covered in varying amounts of tat and clothing long forgotten. Shane said he had only seen a handful of Barney Men, yet they rose like an army, squeezing into the chamber, snapping at each other to get a better look at the giant Nox soldiers. They were far more rowdy as a group than they were alone. That so many sharp claws and teeth belonged to creatures below Zero and Five's waists caused the two NEGs to stoop and press their knees together. Stood back to back as the Barney Men circled them, there was nowhere they could turn to feel comfortable.

The younger looking Barney Men edged closer and barked, only to return to their peers and laugh at Zero and Five's reaction. To them, the NEGs' fear was theatre. But as the Nox stood taller in defiance, their laughs turned to scowls. Then spoke their leader.

I sit on this Stone I won,
From a man who lost his thumb.
The man's name was Horx,
And with this rock he'd wrought
The first weapon that killed for fun.

A Barney Man was indeed sat on the toppled Horx Stone.

It was the same one who had introduced the NEGs to the glen all those hours ago, still dressed in his crooked hat and fungi infested clothing. His underlings danced a crooked dance to his song and he was flanked by two other familiar Barney Men, the one from the loch with the crown of lumpy twigs, and the one with a dead human baby strapped to his back. Those two generals watched intently over the crowd as the lead Barney Man continued.

Now the stone has rolled away,
And a messiah has risen to play my game.
So we play with Nox who angrily say
That playing and killing are one and the same.
But I say to them who the Barney slays,
That prayers are saved for ones with names.
Doomed are you who play to slumber,
And that the next to go is not a number.

'Zero,' Five mouthed. 'No!'

You do not choose who lives and dies,
No number at all? Was he really alive?
Beneath the stars,
Within the glen,
We choose the fate of silent men.

'Then you will die,' Five said, sternly.
He was met with a broken smile, one not sure it should exist.

Oh come now NEG, with what dice do you bet,
That are loaded full with heart to threat?

'The ones used in my game.'

This is our game.

241

'No. No, it's not.'

Then I'm sure that proof you've got?

'Zero is still alive.'

Until I call for his demise.

'Then you call for your own because Zero is part of *my* game. And if you kill him you break *my* rules. And you lose.'

Your rules?

'My rules.'

The Barney Man wasn't sure how to respond. His froggy face twitched and he scratched a mushroom free from his neck. His agitation spread throughout the rest of the hoard.

Zero nudged Five, who tried his best to give a reassuring look, but the evidence that his captain was winging it was clear. Nevertheless, Five took a deep breath and readied himself for the Barney Man's response.

Explain.

'The game I've been playing began with him.'

Five pointed at the loch dwelling Barney Man, who couldn't help but grin when the spotlight fell on him. The others of his kind spat curses in his direction. He drank in the attention, wiggling on the spot with anticipation. His master was not so thrilled.

Explain!

'I asked him how to kill you. He told me in the form of a riddle. In order to answer it, I need both myself and Zero to stay alive, as we are both integral to your deaths. This is my game, my riddle to decipher, and you can't kill us. Not like you did to Two and One.'

He waited for an inevitable rushing of irate dwarven hell spawn but it never came. In fact, their once cocky demeanour took a turn for the opposite. The masses looked back at their seething master for an order.

Then what is your answer to the riddle?
Speak quickly, I long for a requiem fiddle.

'My answer is a trade.'
A murmur waved through the crowd.

A trade?
Why waste a light that begins to fade?
A trade?
That is not an answer to the riddle made.

'Says who?'

Says me.

'Says you?'

Yes, me.

'You have no say at all. It's my game and my riddle and I'll answer however I please.'
The Barney Man did not like this role reversal.

Why would I accept a trade
That lays a path towards my grave?
You threaten me with death,
Should I take the step?
This trade, I do not accept.

'Or maybe I expected you to deny the trade and, in your denial, I'm one step closer to winning?'

The squirm on the Barney Man's face was wonderful.

'What if through the trade I only hope to leave this glen and never return, leaving you alive and well. Either way, I win.'

Shut it!
Speak your trade so I might snuff it!

'That vial around your neck.'

Your number must be off,
If you think I'd trade the strength of Gods.

'Then let me offer the one thing even a God lacks: the power of the paradox.'

This had the Barney Man intrigued. It had Zero intrigued. It even had Five intrigued as he was making this up as he went along.

'I offer you a voice of the voiceless.'

Another murmur waved through the hideous crowd. The Barney Man licked his thin, scabby lips. Five's insides were rattling.

As intriguing as that sounds,
I'm more attached to the strength of Gods abound.

'Really? Attached to rules and structure?'

'Tis our nature.

'But imagine the Barney Men free from their own shackles. Able to unleash the power they have gathered from a thousand souls without restraint. Every impossibility will be yours. To speak without a voice, frightening don't you think?'

Some of the Barney Men in the front row were drooling, but they weren't the ones with the human blood vial.

And what then?
With the vial you hope to escape the glen?

'With your help I hope to leave, yes.'

Our help?
We'd sooner see you yelp.
You ask for two things in exchange of one,
You ask for blood as well as sun?
No deal.

'Then you give up on infinity.'

I...

The Barney Man was speechless. Five was surprised at how long he had managed to string the goblin along; now he just had to hope Zero was willing to co-operate with the next phase of the plan.

Where is this voice?
Or is this all just noise?

245

'I'll ask him...'

Five turned to his last breathing comrade. Zero could barely look at him. The moment voices had been mentioned he had skulked, and a battle raged within. Zero knew what his captain was going to ask of him, to speak when no word had passed his lips before. Through introverted defiance, his communication had been nought his whole life. He painted himself as a being of war, yet quivered at the thought of stumbling over words.

'It's in a voice,' Five repeated.

Five didn't know what that voice would say, if anything at all, and he couldn't outright prescribe the words he wanted to hear. All he could do was pray, to every God he had read about, that Zero's first words would be powerful enough to get them out of this mess.

Five handed him his earpiece, flicked on a small red light, and waited.

A buzz hissed over a far off voice that spoke quietly through the NEG communications gear, then Zero switched the red light off. He didn't look away, or stand tall, just fixated on Five and handed the earpiece back.

Five couldn't tell if Zero was outraged or quietly liberated. Neither reality mattered now. All that was left was the trade.

'The voice of a mute,' Five said, as he dangled the headset over the crowd at the Barney Man with the bowler hat. 'Amongst all the treasures you've stashed in this cave, I doubt you'll find a purer addition.'

No trade.

Five didn't know what to say. The rest of his plan was hazy at best, now it was scattered to the wind.

'No?'

No. I am still bound to man,
As long as time still deals in sand.

'And?'

And you know what happens if the vial breaks.
The Barney succumb to mortal fate.

'Death?'

As good as.

'Look, I don't want you dead. I don't want the humans dead.'

Despite that being your charge?
You would save them and lose your right to march?

'I would. I met a man in the glen, a good man, I wish to honour that legacy. Mankind's flower will bloom again. Besides, you still have that baby; as long as one human survives...'

Piffle.
This soldier speaks nought but wiffle.

The younger Barney clutched his pack. 'I tell the truth. Now trade, or lose your chance at becoming the kings of pandemonium, masters of an upside down, Barney universe.'

Titles mean nothing...

'Then shed them, keep playing your games as you see fit, but never lose again.'

The crowd was growing agitated. Half wanted to trade, half gurgled furiously at the mention of games without any real stakes. A sick stink rose with their growls until the chief Barney Man snapped his fingers with insatiable lust in his eyes.

No more skulking in the glen,
Instead, the hills will fill with Barney Men!
Monuments will be erected.
Your trade? This Barney Man's accepted.
Quiet!

The Barney Man screamed at his lessers, who had broken into infighting. They did as they were told, though agitated rumbles hovered just below the surface.

Five was about to give them an infinite power, in return for a species who before today he never truly cared for beyond an intriguing history. The Barney Men will have to let them leave, but with this new found part of Zero's soul, would it be so out of the question that the Barney Men would follow?

Five tried to catch the eye of the Barney Man from the loch, hoping for a giveaway that he was on the right track with his riddle. The Barney Man with the thorned crown did nothing but giggle silently to himself as he watched the other deformed members of his society snap at each other, awaiting the trade. The younger Barney Man, the one with the baby strapped to his back, had so far been quiet and expressionless. However, the longer the conversation went, the harder he gripped the straps of his pack. Five saw his discomfort as a positive.

Five threw the earpiece. He threw it badly, on purpose, hoping to bring those monsters down a peg or two. Somehow it landed flat in their leader's scabby hand. The Barney Man looked upon it as though it were gold. To see one of the Barney

Men so happy was hollowing, the lust for the sound that trinket carried tangible.

It was so consuming that the Barney Man cast his vial aside without looking. Now it belonged to Five. He picked it up after it rolled over the mossy rocks to his feet.

'And the second part of our trade? The part where we get to leave?'

Zero was agitated beside him. He was watching anxiously as the Barney Man forced Five's earpiece over his long, pointed ear.

No deal.

'You can't!'

He can.

Interjected the Barney Man from the loch.

Because you failed to kill a single Barney Man,
The aim of your initial plan.
So dies your game.
So dies you the same.
You failed to answer, 'What's in a name?'

The goblin looked disappointed if anything. The younger Barney Man was ecstatic with relief. The crowd before them was riotous. Five and Zero drew back to back again as the Barney Men's crooked teeth gnashed.

Five watched closely as the Barney Man covered in fungi played the recording to himself, ignorant of everything else.

This is it, Five thought. *It's up to Zero's words now.*

You dare...

The Barney Man growled, on the verge of explosion.

You Dare!
I will string you from the roof by hair!

The gods must have had their reasons for keeping Zero silent.

You will suffer and I will not care!

Five desperately wanted to hear what Zero had said, but the floor began to shake beneath the Barney Man's wrath. It shook at his very will, and the mists that plagued the glen drew into the cave through its gaping ceiling in a smoky waterfall. It was heavy and thick, thicker than any mist should be, and Five regretted ever offering the creature such power.

It was a power they had barely glimpsed, a power so vast and terrible the Barney Man didn't know where to start with it. He could turn back time, breathe life into death, turn water into running gold and still winds into razors, he could flip all of creation upside down and now that power was aimed directly at Five and Zero.

In his panicked state, Five said aloud and proud, 'It's in a name!'

The storm brewing in the chamber was limitless, endless, filled with the blood and screams and faces of every soul the Barney Men had ever taken, yet it softened to make a platform for Five's bluff.

He looked around for it, hoping it would fall into his hand from the heavens. Alas, all he held was a vial filled with human blood. His bluff clicked into place.

'Five!'

Just a number!
I'll watch you slumber!

The other Barney Men, who were attempting to scurry away from the madness were sucked back into the chamber. Their eyes were awash with mind control, their mouths trembling with drool.

Don't leave!
Stay! Kill! Feed!

'No number! It's my name!' Five shouted over the chaos.

What of it?

'Five and Zero. We know who we are and are proud of our strengths, our souls. We are Elite Guards, soldiers, bred for battle and to follow orders. That our names are numbers is your downfall, because we still have an order left unfulfilled and my promises are not as magically binding as yours; we came to destroy all humans.'

Five punched Zero in the arm and Zero withdrew a pistol. Without pause, he shot the younger Barney Man. The army of Barney Men went silent. They let the storm ruffle and buffet them for a moment whilst they pondered the attack. As expected, the bullet sailed straight through the Barney Man and the shrug the goblin returned made Zero and Five's victory ever sweeter, because Zero wasn't aiming at the Barney Man. The baby, once sat snugly in the Barney Man's pack, fell through a torn seam, bullet hole in its head. It's pale, dead body, slid off of the Horx stone. The Barney Man wailed and chased after it. Then Five smashed the blood vial.

Its contents blackened against thick dirt and murky waters, and the storm subsided. In a mighty, instant swoop, the mist left; the rumbles of pandemonium rolled back into nothing; and all that was left was a collection of squat, pimply men, pointy and hunched, naked and frightened. Not a coin, toy, or faded photograph remained, the cavern as bare as its masters.

A foul hatred replaced it. The Barney Men had been tricked into mortals, and none of them looked ready to die. If the humans had been likened to dying flowers, the Barney Men were surely weeds, ready to fight death stubbornly and strangulate the universe's beauty in the crossfire.

Facing a Barney Man strapped with the power of an anti-God was actually a more pleasant alternative to the cold, murderous stares of those naked monsters. They were mortal now, but Five and Zero were weak, and nothing compared to this new batch of goblins.

Their leader smushed down his thin, greasy hair proudly. In the face of his undoing, he stood unashamed.

Feed.
Strangle them with weeds!

The high pitched war cries of the Barney Men were as piercing as the first clawed hands that gripped the two NEGs, a tsunami of evil that poured over them.

Five's legs gave out immediately. The bruises on his face were like honey to a horde of bees, their stingers replaced with a thousand dirt coated finger nails. He couldn't see Zero, he couldn't hear his cries, he was too busy clenching every orifice as those spindly Barney Man hands started ripping new ones. It was no surprise that winning a game against those underhanded beasts would lead to death regardless.

He instinctively started to calculate an old mathematics problem in his head, one that had eluded him all his life. He was going to be him until the very end, Number Five, soldier, thinker. The pain was nothing but a reminder that his thinking had thwarted the Barney Men.

A hot blue glazed over his arms and the flesh of his exposed face began to peel away. It was so bright it pushed open his eye lids and the familiar blazing light of a pulse grenade, no doubt set off by Zero as a last hoorah, rocked him violently into the next life.

The heat didn't dissipate fully. It just changed. It was no longer a scold but a tepid breeze that bounded over the tiny hairs on Five's skin. He was comfortable in it, his aches soothed. *Is this heaven?* he wondered. Five cracked his eyelids apart to get a glimpse of those fabled pearly gates. There was no such decor, and he couldn't understand why heaven would need three suns. He sat up lazily on his elbows. The trio of stars were small, but together packed a heat strong enough to cook the sand he was laid on.

It was a welcome change to the damp, mouldy confines of the glen. A well-deserved polar opposite for someone who had helped rid the universe of the Barney Men. He bathed in the heat a while longer, too tired to move or think for the first time in years.

He was sat in a desert of endless soft dunes and light winds. The sky was an overly saturated blue, and the desert as equally orange. He pushed sand between his toes and drew lines in it. He wasn't wearing any armour, just a pair of thin leggings that warmed or cooled the wearer depending on the environment. They no longer worked of course. They were torn and loose upon him, and through them he saw deep cuts that had yet to heal. They covered him in fact. He prodded and pushed himself, to see if the cuts and bruises were still fresh. Running blood probably meant they were. He found it strange that in the next life he would still feel pain. He also thought it odd that Zero, his visor still secure, would join him.

Not a few feet away, sat in the same confused slump as Five, Zero was pouring sand through his fingers. He nodded at Five, who nodded back, and then they both stood. Without saying a word, they scanned the area more thoroughly. This was no heaven. Neither was it hell. Just a half way point that most people call reality.

Congratulations Nox,
You killed the Barneys, believe it or not.

Five wasn't sure he could; he was staring at one of them in the flesh that very moment. It was the crowned Barney Man from the loch, old and weathered and wet as he had always looked. Thankfully he was clothed this time, not that his usual rags were much of an improvement.

Although like a slide that's greasy,
To follow my riddle was rather easy.

'It was vague,' Five said, plainly, too tired to attack or seek retribution. 'You wanted us to win; you wanted us to use endless possibilities to our advantage, just like you and the other Barney Men would. Why?'

It shouldn't matter all the same,
But perhaps you were part of a bigger game.

He winked.

Zero and Five just stared.

Then the Barney Man hobbled away. He looked impossibly small against the desert.

> *Regardless, you win your freedom from the glen.*
> *I'll let you rest before we play again.*

A number of galaxies away, back in the cave where the Barney Men met their end at Zero's pulse grenade, a broken glass vial dripped its remaining contents into a small stream.

Shallow water carried the clotted red downhill, into the sightless crevices of the chamber, swirling past pebbles and rocks. It passed by tiny, torn limbs and rustling shreds of flesh. Though dead, the fingers of those hands twitched as the blood sailed by. But the blood swam with a mind of its own, petering side to side and downward until it disappeared into a mound of thick mud that had mounted in the lowest most corner of the cave. There, beside the remnants of a brown satchel, half a young Barney face without a body, singed and cloven in two, sunk to meet it.

In its place a flower grew, tiny and frail, but defiantly beautiful against its dank surroundings. It didn't stop growing and continued to break ground until another head followed it, a human baby's head. The new born cried as the flower, whose roots tunnelled into her forehead, withered and died. As the last petal fell, that cry became a surly laugh. She opened her eyes for the first time, the slightest of twinkles within them.

THE TRAGEDY OF KORR AND BANI

The smile of an impossibly confident man is so wide that when he dies his body splits from his soul still holding it. But let it be clear, that man is dead, and he's never coming back. The final moment of one so fearless often comes harder and faster than they or anyone else expects. When one is so sure that they can cling to life for as long as they see fit, Death is sure to bear an extra sting in her strike. This, however, is the unfortunate tale of when Death fell for a confident man, and in doing so landed hardest of all.

Death's name was Vaern Bani. She was not Death in the traditional sense, a skeletal spectre in a hooded black cloak, but she bore all the reaping tools and traits of Death incarnate. At this point in her career however, she loomed over only one prize in particular.

His name was Dredrick Korr, and he was a warrior. To most, he was a hero. He was valiant, gallant, too handsome for his own good, and in possession of every adjective one would use to describe the *"perfect"* man, but that was not why Death loved him. She, in fact, loved that she could see through those theatrics, at the man who hid behind them. She lusted after his truth, and after chasing him across galaxies, it was no surprise that he fell for her in turn.

Beauty would not do well to define Bani, for she shone with a light greater than that cast over natural things. It was Korr's infatuation, his ultimate weakness, in which Bani first saw those cracks in his once pristine armour. Soon, surviving her or capturing him became secondary to the pair's mutual longing for the bloody taste of each confrontation. For years they dragged out their twisted games, far longer than sense dictated.

Tragically, the allure of the chase was too great for either to admit their feelings, and so the eternal fight went on, ever violent, ever deranged, and it was during one heated, unexpected showdown that Death finally bagged her man. Sealing his fate, however, would not come easy. For although Korr laid prostrated below the guillotine swing of Bani's blade, for the first time in her long history of carving people from existence, she chose mercy.

Bani wrapped Korr in chains, which she could not bear to fully lock, and slapped a bow on his head, deciding that she would offer him as a gift to the Rung'h, an off galaxy super race. They would decide his fate. Or he would decide there's, and Korr and Bani would meet again, as they always did. It was a hollow hope, one that she barely believed in, and even now, at the end of their personal war, she could not say she loved him. She did not know how. It was a far too unfamiliar and uncomfortable thing.

'Are we going to talk about last night?' Korr asked, smirking. Despite his shackled ankles and the worn away soles of his boots, he was surprisingly perky as he and Bani made their way over the rocky desert terrain of Mos Daf, the Rung'h home world.

Existing beyond the reach of star light, Mos Daf had evolved its own fluorescence, which grew in the form of a neon mould. It plagued an otherwise pitch black, crumbling landscape. Anything those lights didn't touch was coarse and broke easily underfoot, like charcoal. Bani bemoaned the hours it took to lead her prisoner across it but there was no faster way. If she flew too close to the Magna Dortha, the Rung'h parliamentary stronghold, her shuttle would be under serious threat from immediate and remorseless cannon fire.

'What's there to talk about?' she said, rolling her eyes.

'Oh, I don't know, maybe the noises you made? Or the noises I made when I realised what kind of freaky talents you've been hiding from me all these years. Someone's been taking their flexibility training seriously, haven't they?'

'Stop it.'

'Come on, Bani. That thing you did with your legs? You know the thing. Bani? The thing?'

'Stop it.'

'I'm sorry, I guess I didn't expect you to be so nimble. I can't even imagine where I'd start wi—'

Korr's voice suddenly caught in his throat, his gullet squashed by the flat of Bani's Black Scimitar.

'I said, stop it.'

Korr went red holding back a grin. Bani melted at his gall. Of course, that only made her press the blade harder. Korr gulped and said, 'So you don't want to talk about it?'

'What do you think?'

'Fine, just walk on ahead in silence. Better view from back here anyway.'

Bani would have slapped the head clean from his shoulders, but Korr would have loved that.

'Look, if it'll shut you up,' she said, 'last night was just me celebrating.'

'Celebrating?'

'Yes. It's taken me a decade to capture you, so last night was simply me congratulating myself on a job well done.'

'I wish you'd have told me this sooner; I'd have let you catch me straight away.'

'Look you!'

She drew her scimitar and spun around again. Korr was saved from an early end when the air erupted and the black clouds above split a path for two Rung'h infantry jets. They were thin but heavily armoured, thickened by layers of metallic scales that rattled against monstrous rotator blades flanking either side of the crafts. The pilots circled the pair before one stopped and hovered a few feet above the ground in front of Bani. She batted her wailing hair out of her eyes so they could see her scowl.

Korr looked on in mild disinterest as the jet addressed them both behind a giant spotlight.

'Dork gra'dok g'taraark!' an aggressive voice roared, invisible behind the tinted window of its driver's cockpit. A pair of turrets ascended from the jet's top and centred on Bani.

'Common tongue, idiot!' she shouted back over the immense whirr of the jets' blades.

There was a pause and then, in a language she could understand, the pilot growled, 'What business?'

'A gift,' Bani replied.

'Oh, that explains the bow,' said Korr. 'If I'm honest I was hoping it was for some kinky game you had planned.'

'What gift?' asked the pilot.

'I am Vaern Bani, my gift for the Magna Dortha is Dredrick Korr.'

Riotous conferring filled the air between the two jets before the one hovering said, 'You will follow us.'

'I know the way,' Bani called.

'The mighty Rung'h race, the lords of Hell Space and the Defilers of Light...'

'Give me a break,' Korr moaned.

'Shut up!' Bani hissed.

'...the Grand Jury of the Magna Dortha demands it. You will yield and you will follow.'

259

'I will pull you and your partner out of the sky before I yield to anything. Now, out of my way.' She twisted the hilt of her Black Scimitar and the ancient runes carved into its metal began to smoulder.

'I'm crushed that you don't reserve that kind of talk for me anymore,' Korr said.

The turrets atop the jet cocked and duplicated, their buzz a clear warning for Bani to stand down. She would not. Behind her, Korr was eyeing up his own Sword of the West Nova, which was strapped to Bani's back. To their surprise, the fight they expected never came. The jet withdrew its weapons and spun away with its partner over a mountainous ridge ahead of them.

'Must have recognised your knife,' Korr said.

'Scimitar. And probably, but I doubt that's why they moved on. Not like a Rung'h to back down from anything.'

'Couldn't blame them for running from you though.'

'Shut up. And hurry up. The Rung'h won't like the idea of me threatening their guards and being late in the same day.'

'If you uncuffed my legs I could move a lot faster.'

'Yeah, right.'

'Come on, I'm going to escape anyway.'

'Not this time, great hero.'

'I love it when you call me that.'

The two continued at a snail's pace for another two hours before they saw the gothic silhouette of the Magna Dortha. It was a bold, iron forged castle larger than any planetary skyline. Its metal walls were fused with a hyper durable compound native to Mos Daf, one that ebbed with the same dull glow dotted about the planet's landscape, intent on absorbing the hope of those brought to it. Not that Korr had shown any sign of fear in the two hours it took for him to stumble there.

Bani had to restrain herself on multiple occasions from either killing or kissing him, as he prattled on relentlessly about all of the fun they had the evening prior. Beneath the shadow of Magna Dortha she quickened their pace, impatient to hand him off to the Rung'h Warlords, if only so that she could finally gain reprieve from the constant stir of her emotions. Stood before the colossal gates, the butterflies in her stomach lurched against her spine, eager to pull her back. Hunting, killing, war; none of those things had caused her heart to skip in her chest as it did at the thought of pawning off someone who on the surface she found so frustrating.

It was too late to change her mind now. With an earth bending crack the spiked gates opened. Turning back was not an option. The Rung'h knew she was there and who she had brought. She may have stood against two infantry jets without so much as a quiver, but if their Warlords received news that she had departed with their gift, she would not have made it off their doorstep. Bani and Korr entered.

There was no welcome or escorting, the Rung'h believing the sheer scale of the Magna Dortha, combined with the race's reputation, would be enough to police any potentially disruptive visitors. Bani already knew the way to the High Council Chamber. It was impossible to forget, the walls so sharp they bore holes in her memory. As they walked, eyes loomed over them from branching corridors that hung in the dark. The halls were as cold and winding as the trails of Mos Daf itself, and the heavy breaths of the lurking Rung'h made the short journey uncomfortable. Statues of broken heroes, carved from recycled space ships, lined the walkways.

Korr snarled. He had never owned a famous ship but knew that would not stop the Rung'h from adding his image to their morbid collection. They would no doubt melt down his Blade of the West Nova and re-forge it into their latest cowering statuette.

Korr was never one to be easily riled, but as he recognised some of the heroes he had idolised as a child, deformed and weeping, he grew a further distaste for the Rung'h, if that were possible. Any further thoughts on the matter were broken as Bani kicked in the triangular double doors of the High Chamber. She strolled in first with her chin held proud.

Such confidence was necessary when dealing with the Warlords, lest they perceive your complete compliance as weakness. It was a thin line to walk, as one wrong word in the High Chamber would lead to a swift and bloody execution. She didn't have to worry about Korr, he would have walked up to the Devil himself and cracked jokes were he given the opportunity.

The chamber was vast, its walls laden with the same broken statues that filled the corridors. The figures were a crumpled mural of defeated warriors, their bodies the foundations of the towering hall. Their sorrowful forms piled all the way from floor to overarching canopy and were held together by that shining mould, strengthening the shadows they cast. At the very back of the hall the Rung'h throne, sharp and rusted and built with six seats, housed the closest thing the mega species had to a government. They were the Warlords.

The Super Races of the universe were defined simply: by their inability to be conquered and their prowess when it came to conquering others, whether through physical out-evolution, or a history cemented in more than this world. Everything about the Rung'h reeked of power unimaginable. They were strong, intelligent, and propelled by a code of ferocity, and the six bodies making up the figurehead of the Magna Dortha were the most dangerous beings the sordid race had ever produced. They were adorned in ancient armour that clanked heavily with every subtle movement of the wearer, and four bulging arms sprouted from wide and sharp shoulder guards. Their muscles were so large that they strained against the colourless skin containing them, forcing brighter tissues to poke through the tears. Two eyes, tiny and shining with the twinkle of fading stars, hovered in the middle of their abyss like faces, hidden by heavy helms.

A multitude of claws tapped impatiently on the throne arms as Bani and Korr approached along a red carpet. On their way the pair circled a wide pit cut into the floor. They were careful to ignore the hole's hollow bleakness, knowing that everything about the Magna Dortha's architecture had been designed to unsettle visitors.

Once clear, Bani stopped a few meters short of the throne and folded her arms before the council. She waited for them to address her. Korr stood behind her like a bored child. Confident and cool, this was the image she had to portray; one equal to the Rung'h, one ready to do verbal battle. Unfortunately, her folly was short lived.

Behind her, Korr whispered, 'What, in God's name, is that thing?'

Bani wanted to ignore him but the alarm in his tone caused her to lose concentration. She darted an eye behind the Warlord throne and upon the most soul sucking sight the High Council, with all its wretched imagery, could have produced. It was the Rung'h Queen, mounted on the wall behind the Warlords in a position of comatose.

Tales had been told of the Super Race's Queen in hushed tones throughout the universe. The Mother of all Rung'h, Spouse of Tortured Souls. She was a horror story used to sway naughty children from tarnishing their reputation, lest their eventual corpses become ideal incubators for her macabre offspring. Now the twisted words from those story books had manifested themselves before Bani far beyond what her childhood mind could have painted.

The Queen was four armed like the Warlords, but each limb was thin and delicate, her skin as white as the eyes of her children. She would have stuck out like sunlight had the statues pasting the walls not crowded everything south of her waist and stuck forward of her outstretched arms. She looked dead, frozen in a state of rage, but Bani could feel an eerie awareness looming behind her closed lids.

'You fear our Queen?' the Chief Warlord, Mog Borton, asked, his words booming from a deep cave in his belly.

The other Warlords sat quietly as Mog rose from his chair and descended the stairs. His two war hammers were tied in an X across his back and shook as though alive with the lust for death.

'You needn't worry,' he continued, 'she rarely reacts to such lower beings.'

'And yet here you are parading her before us,' Bani said. 'The last time I entered this chamber without Korr she was nowhere to be seen. A little nervous are we? Going to do all the talking for her as well as your underlings, I see.'

She looked past him at the rest of the council members, praying she hadn't come on too strong. The insult garnered little reaction, although that did little to settle the nerves pulsing through her fingertips.

'It's a pleasure to see you again, Bani,' Mog said. 'Although late was not the frame of time in which I expected you.'

'No time frame was expected at all,' she snapped back, careful to look him dead in the eyes as he circled her and Korr. The idea of the giant Mog hovering between them and that pit did not help her uneasiness.

Korr looked the warlord up and down, holding back childish sniggers.

'As bold as they say,' Mog said, his layered teeth snarling to match Korr's grin. 'It's no surprise you fell for him, Bani.'

He returned to her, pacing backwards and forwards before the throne. 'I did no such thing,' Bani said.

'Well, you did,' Korr whispered.

'Stop it.'

'Our spies see further than the surface, human,' Mog said. 'Do not be ashamed, love is a common weakness of your kind.'

'Like the inability to capture Dredrick Korr was yours?'

'Be careful. We did not catch him through inability; we had more important matters to attend to. You think we would bother chasing down one human when we had the Jan on our doorstep? Or the issues of heading a Mogel Beast extinction?'

'A Mogel Beast extinction?' Korr scoffed. 'Good luck with that.'

'Keep your luck. We did not need it.'

'Why so desperate for Korr then?' Bani asked.

'By freeing the Kangtru, Dredrick Korr ruined an already perfectly formed Rung'h nursery, an unimaginable crime, and unforgivable. But with so many campaigns to deal with, we found it more fitting to send another human to take care of him.'

'You're welcome, by the way,' Bani said.

'Enough. I wanted him dead, Bani, not alive. I'd rather not stain the Magna Dortha with his presence.'

'Stain the Magna Dortha?' Korr exclaimed. 'With this bow?' He flicked the glimmering pink wrappings stuck to his forehead. 'I like to think I've classed the place up a bit.'

Mog was unsure how to react to Korr's humour, and looked uncomfortable trying to forge a worthy retort. He chose the safer option of addressing Bani.

'And yet I can't say I won't enjoy his suffering; our next generation yearns for flesh.'

'So you found a nursery in the end?' Korr said, rolling his eyes before Bani could reply. 'See, you didn't even need the Kangtru, did you.'

Bani was almost firmly back in the *Let's kill Dredrick Korr* camp; he was going too far. The Rung'h could deal with her straight insults, but Korr was talking to them like they were children. Mog moved in close to the great hero, his breath volcanic on Korr's cheek.

'This is our Royal Nursery, Master Korr.' Mog waved an arm over the large hole in the centre of the chamber. 'It contains our most elite offspring. Like every generation before them, they have evolved into far more impressive specimens. Even in infancy, they are ready to be tested against the likes of you; not that it will be a test.'

Mog's bulbous claw slapped Korr's arm, then laughed as his relaxed triceps wobbled. The rest of the Warlords joined him, quick to find humour in the flimsiness of the human body compared to their concrete exteriors.

'I'm going to enjoy this,' Mog said. 'I'm sorry to take your flabby love from you, Bani.'

'I don't love him... I...' she stuttered, uncharacteristically shaky as Mog prodded at and boasted of Korr's end.

'I don't like liars, human.'

'Me neither,' Korr added.

'Shut it,' she growled.

'In fact I hate liars more than I hate Korr,' Mog said.

'And that's a lot,' Korr added again.

'I don't—'

'Speak the truth or join him!' Mog boomed.

Her ears thumped in the proceeding silence. They stung with heat and she rubbed them, trying to muffle her fears. She was so afraid. *Why?* she wondered, shaking with frustration. She would never say it, never admit her feelings when she was so happy already, chasing Korr across the galaxy. If she didn't say I love you, then that reality would exist forever; *right? But what if he doesn't escape?* Her heart beat tripled. The weight of her pursuit, her bloody career, suddenly became all too real and her vital organs drooped behind her rib cage. *What have I done?*

'Look at me, Vaern.'

Bani hadn't even felt the tears on her face until a cold gust blew through the chamber across her cheeks. That was the first time Korr had ever called her by her first name. She did as she was told and she saw the man who she had stabbed at for so long, the ever elusive Dredrick Korr. He was the same then as he was when she first stood over him with a blade to his throat, unable to make the cut.

Again she saw the human behind the stories; he was still that same man who had spared her when she did not deserve it. She was a woman who had killed so many, an unforgivable tyrant on par with the Rung'h Warlords themselves. Yet when Korr looked at her she became human too; tired in every sense of the word, sick of the pain she had forced upon herself and others. Stood before him in silence, she felt weak beneath the heavy load of her own darkness.

All of a sudden war, money, and power became an infinitesimal afterthought on the scale that measures what it is to simply be. In a universe where horridness creeps unchecked through its every crevice, to become one of its victims quickly upends your perspective.

Bani looked hard at Korr and said, 'I... Maybe...'

Korr smiled back. 'Good enough for me.'

Mog wasn't so convinced. 'You are done here, Bani,' he said.

She began to skulk away, her head bowed. It had been her plan all along, of course, but that niggling fear wriggled through her body. *What if he doesn't escape? Who will I chase? Who will let me chase them?* She made rushed, directionless prayers in silence, that Korr would slaughter the Warlords before she even left the High Chamber, and they would continue their violent dance across the stars forever. *Take it...* she told him in her head, loosening the binds that held Korr's sword to her back.

She too longed to unsheathe her Black Scimitar, but an old selfishness still lurked within and stayed her hand. As one cut from the same cloth that cloaked the Grim Reaper, risking her own life was too counter instinctive. *I'm so pathetic compared to you...* Her silent conclusion made Bani love Korr even more. It was a desperate love and she was certain that Korr knew. He knew that she was ashamed and afraid and that she wanted nothing more than to be held by him before it was too late; to become nothing. Through him, she would lose the malicious titles afforded to her and simply be. That was all she wanted. It was up to Korr now.

'Where are you going, Bani?' Mog asked.

His tone was clear, the horror had not ended yet. Although her exit had been an eternity within her mind, she stopped walking just a step past Korr.

'Finish the job you started,' Mog continued, 'the job you were paid to do. Finish him.'

She froze.

'Into the pit,' Mog boomed.

Bani mouthed, '*I can't.*' And trembled on the spot when Korr ushered her in front of him, putting himself between her and the pit. 'Look at me, Vaern,' he said again.

She looked for the final time, adoring the blemishes of his skin; the scars and tired eyes omitted from the story books. He was still bruised and battered from their own battle a few days ago. Just like then, there was nothing he could have done to stop her if she wanted to kill him, for nobody commands Death. But Death couldn't strike him down, he was too perfectly imperfect. No matter how horrid she was, he loved her, the only one who ever had.

Bani soaked in the rest of his body, her mind scrambling for another option, when she saw his free hands. He had escaped the chains. She really shouldn't have put it past him; he was the universe's greatest hero after all. A tiny clip, from the bow she had plastered to his head, twiddled between his thumbs. He was smiling and Bani believed with wonder expanded eyes that he really had dreamt up another epic escape and was going to take her with him. She had been a fool to doubt him. *Then when why is your smile wavering?* she thought. *Your smile never wavered before.* Korr clicked the shackles closed and shed his grin. Bani felt grey inside.

'It's okay, Vaern, do what you have to do. Then when I'm gone become the human I see in you. I am not strong enough to prop you up, not strong enough to save you. Your beauty has rendered me hollow. Only you can vanquish the weight of your sins now.'

'Don't you dare, you arsehole.'

She hated how serious he was being. *You've never been serious before.* Was this some kind of joke? Or another one of his ridiculous quips that she did not understand? Why would he ask this of her? If he loved her so much nothing else should matter but them escaping and living happily ever after. She felt sick at thought of such sentiment, but how she longed for it.

'This is the problem with being the universe's greatest hero,' he said. He was smiling again, but it was a sad, lonely smile. 'I've done enough good in this life, about time I took my talents to the next one. I leave this world to you.'

'You smug bastard! Live a life with me first, a real one. I'll die without you, I am *Death* without you!' She was breaking down. She threw her scimitar away and across the cold stone of the chamber in a terrifying tantrum, the runes on the blade shining and eliciting cracks of lightning as it spun into the shadows of the hall.

'I wish I could,' Korr said, but he was quivering. 'Oh, how I wish I could. Alas, I am more selfish than I appear. A life spent with you would not be enough, I want you for eternity.' Korr took a deep breath and then, through watery eyes, took on a more familiar grin. 'It should come as no surprise that you need to make amends for all the shit you've pulled.'

'Are you seriously lecturing me? Right now!?'

'I'll do as I please, especially if you only *maybe* love me. You do maybe love me, Vaern?'

There was no maybe about it. Her voice gave her away.

'Maybe.'

'Then do as I say. Earn the life that the innocence inside you deserves. Start with me, the swine who let a murderous, gorgeous, bounty hunter catch him; a fool who jeopardised thousands of lives in the process. Do it for me, I'll love you from the Otherside.'

She nodded and shook her head at the same time, face streaming. Her insides were pulling themselves apart. Then the sting of her choice came sharp and fast, as explosive as their relationship would have been had she not. With both palms, she shoved him into the pit. She gasped and clapped her hands over her mouth. Korr was smirking again, back to normal, over the moon that he had to convince Death to kill him. Then he was gone.

Bani stood alone a torn woman, the promise she had made to herself as she pushed Korr into the Rung'h nursery bouncing around her head. There was no doubt about it, she would earn the life the good in her deserved, and she would meet Dredrick Korr again, on better terms. She did not deserve him now, but she would. She locked her eyes on the doors, fixed on the prospect of a new life beyond them. The Rung'h could keep their pay.

She started around the pit but her footsteps sounded heavy. They clunked with every step and grew louder until she realised they were not hers. Mog was walking beside her. Before she could spit her fury at him, one of his mammoth claws latched around her throat, his hand so big that his thumb and index finger sent a crack veining through her jaw bone. Rather than foul words, Bani spat broken teeth from her mouth.

'Do you forget who we are, Bani?' he asked. 'We are the Rung'h and our contract is over, or was that fact lost to you during your lover's farewell speech? Pfft... He clearly thinks too highly of you; there can be no redemption for one so tainted by blood. But, if it's a place alongside our other trophies that you want...'

Mog lifted Bani off of the ground. She grasped his trunk-like forearm to avoid suffocation. Her eyes puffed, and with his three free hands Mog rubbed her cheeks dry and poked at her body.

'Do not cry, human. The tears will hamper your final words, and my enjoyment of your defeat.'

Even if she could speak, there was nothing to be said. Her toes hung over the deep black of the chamber's central pit and now her life as good as belonged to whatever mutants haunted the Queen's nursery. The door to her new life was no longer one of light, but circular darkness. She had failed. She had no final words for the Rung'h, just Korr. *Please, forgive me.*

She hawked up the last remnants of her broken mouth and plastered Mog's face with the gunk. Then her body left him. She watched the ceiling of the Magna Dortha, framed by the circle of the pit's rim, grow smaller and smaller as she fell weightlessly into the royal nursery. A second later her body bounced hard against its wet stone floor.

Her shattered ribs, which snapped around the crossguard of Korr's sword that was still strapped to her back, were an afterthought to the patter of invisible, rushing feet that filled her ears. Beyond her own limitations, she sat up, unable to breathe but forcing herself anyway. She couldn't see beyond the spotlight

271

that painted her as a bright bullseye for the Rung'h young to aim at.

Words and whispers dribbled incoherently in the darkness. She didn't know how many there were, nor what they looked like, but her ears painted a picture of locust like devourers of the flesh. She stretched and cracked her back, ready for her last fight, determined to take at least one more life with her. This time, it would be one that deserved it.

Her legs felt brittle as she stood. The pain in her back was too overwhelming to let her reach for Korr's sword, so she put up woozy fists. But as she wheeled about, unsure of where the Rung'h monsters would strike from first, she saw Korr. His legs lay in the same harsh spotlight that drenched Bani, the rest of his body hidden by the darkness.

She forgot her fight and charged over. Falling at his legs she wept into his thigh. Accompanied by cruel giggles, Korr's head rolled into the light, leaving a trail of blood and loose flesh along its path. Bani's eyes rolled with it until it balanced on the stump of his neck.

The mangled sorrow on his face crushed her spirit beyond repair. *No, no. He never makes faces like that. He smiles. Why isn't he smiling!?* She clutched onto Korr's trousers. She stood with them and felt the weightlessness of his legs. With her upper back bent like some snarling, primal beast, she walked back into the centre of the light, dragging Korr's legs with her, his entrails and half a spine lagging behind. She dropped them onto the floor and became truly empty; a shell of hate for all things. If, through his sacrifice, Korr had planned to make a hero of Bani, then he had overachieved as usual, this time to his detriment. The power building within her was wrought in a dangerous and unpredictable place, and it twisted his final words into something beyond horrifying. Oh, she would make amends for her vulgar life; she would cancel out every life thereafter, for such terror as the Rung'h would never rise again. Suffering would become obsolete, for there would be no one left to suffer.

She tilted her head back and saw the Magna Dortha's arched ceiling, and she hung there for a moment. As if awoken by some great disturbance, the slither of the animated Rung'h Queen surrounded the rim of the hole and its vile body blotted out the light. Donning the smile of her lover, Bani reached over her shoulder and wrapped her fingers around the hilt of his Sword of the West Nova. The splinters of her broken ribs ground together as she unsheathed it, but she did not grimace. Bani knew that the coming seconds would turn her into something far worse than Death because to be anything at all would not do. She would become Nothing, and she would cast that word over all things.

THE GREAT LIBRARY: PART 2

That final page turned slowly. After placing the book aside, Phillos looked over the pile of horror and wondered how he had stomached it all in one sitting. Such tragedy, such grief and pain, he had experienced nothing of the sort yet understood every ounce. He wanted to weep but was unsure if the stories had even been real.

'Where am I?' a voice opposite him asked, one that rang like the bells of heaven.

Phillos jumped. He had felt a presence while reading the books but was so uncontrollably drawn by them he could not stand to notice beyond that.

This new intruder of the Great Library was made of solid gold and stood naked in the centre of the room. He was a human man, although outwardly sexless, and leaner than any human could be. His muscles were tense, twitching beneath their own limitless power. He looked himself over, stroking the bumps and definitions of his body.

Whenever his hand grazed his skin the sound of knives upon metal sang. It muted when his fingers rested on a second spine, growing from his upper back and into the top of his bald head. Satisfied with the shape of himself, he relaxed, and asked Phillos again, 'Where am I?'

'Why, the Great Library, Sir,' Phillos replied, in a welcoming tone, as though he were greeting some great king.

The golden man in the centre of the room cocked his head. It sounded like bending iron. 'How long do we have?' he asked.

'Until what?'

'The world ends.'

'I... I'm not sure,' Phillos said, unsure of the question's implications. Then he took a moment to mull the question. 'Not until I die, I suppose. Then there's no one left.' Phillos had never said that reality out loud. He deflated in his transport. 'Or so I thought until you came along. But then I don't actually know who or what you are? My imagination, perhaps? Are you with the other metal men?'

'Many would call me a God.'

Phillos found it easy to believe. From ghostly visions to divine apparitions, this was a bizarre day for the once sheltered Librarian. 'And are you?'

'I do not cling to titles. There is one who sits above all things, the one we call Creator. I am not him. He has not walked this world in countless ages past. Thus a mortal's relativity is skewed. I am more of an admirer.'

Books floated off the shelves and orbited about the golden being. His hands lightly conducted their movements, and whenever one passed by his face, the pages turned rapidly. His eyes, as metallic as the rest of him, lit up; he was hardly interested in Phillos at all.

Strangeness was at work here, so strange the Librarian couldn't digest it, especially after the stomach-churning words he had read. He could have been dreaming; he certainly was not feeling himself. One moment he was alone, the next in the presence of a God. As unnatural as it was for him, all he could do was talk.

'An admirer of what?'

'The universe.'

Phillos glanced back over the pile of books. 'After what I've read, no one should want to see this place up close.'

'Because?' the God asked, finally looking at him.

'I presume you know about these stories, and what happens in them? Your appearance coincided with me reading them after all. Why would you admire that?'

'*You* read the stories?

'I did.'

The God looked him up and down, then rolled his eyes in bare acceptance. 'Would you rather I destroyed everything?'

A book began floating away from him, weakly flapping towards the door. The God held out his hand and, from pages to cover, it glowed bright and turned to ash. Phillos felt the heat against his skin.

'No,' Phillos said, quickly. 'Not like that. But... But couldn't you, as a God, have just destroyed the bad people? Destroyed the very premise of evil?'

'Good does not exist without evil. Balance is everything, and physics is a cruel mistress. Some of her tenants bear the brunt of reality worse than others.'

'Then destroy it all.'

'Pardon?'

'Destroy it. I would gladly give my life to stop the suffering of others.'

The God smirked and said, 'Like you've had much of a life.'

The insult cut deep. Compared to the rest of his species Phillos would have been deemed an anarchist. Abandoning his duty to follow footsteps was unheard of. 'How dare you!' he said. He slapped his hands over his mouth. He did not want to offend, did not want to face the brunt of the consequence.

'I have seen the great adventurers of this universe suffer immense trials to achieve happiness, to escape its hells. Those range of emotions are the very essence of life. You have done nothing, understand nothing, and would see joy cast out with suffering both the same?'

The God looked down his nose at Phillos. He was big, impossibly big. So large the stars couldn't contain him, so tiny the eye couldn't see. He was exactly the size he needed to be, and although in that moment he was as tall as a man, his true self dwarfed the cosmos. Phillos quivered, and he felt the same unfamiliar invasiveness that he had felt hours before.

'You mustn't raise your voice like that here,' he said, falling back into instinct, hoping it would unleash normality back into his world. 'I don't know where you came from, but insulting members of staff will not be tolerated and your membership revo—'

'Regardless, I suppose I should thank you,' said the God, ignoring the rant. The floating books placed themselves back on the shelves.

'You're welcome?'

'By reading these ten tales you have summoned me. Just in time too.' The God gazed up at the old Library, like an architect faced with irrevocable damage and the task to fix it.

Phillos had been thrown. 'Well, if you're going to stay here there are rules and—'

The God waved a hand and Phillos was silent.

'Rules are beneath me. There is nothing here to look forward to. I must go back, stop what has started. Save the world from ending this way. From ending at all.'

'Save it? It's over, this is it,' Phillos said, losing patience with the insults.

'I love this world!' the God roared.

Phillos shrunk as a far off storm shook the Great Library. He whimpered like a puppy who did not know what he had done or said to cause such a cataclysmic outburst.

'I will not let creation end this way!' the golden one continued. 'The stories you have read are my purpose, and I was compelled here to address them. They are the universe's first act; I will not see the story conclude in war and disease. It will go on.'

'These stories are true? But if that's so you'll know they ended already, in heartbreak and pain; Samson, the Nox soldiers, Korr and Bani, the Bullet Boy, all of them, ended. Nearly all of them suffered at the hands of *your* kind.'

'*My* kind? Yes, my kind. Those from my side of the universal coin. Do you not understand that is why I am here? To repair what they have destroyed. Immortals, demons, Gods, whatever you call us, we are an envious species. We lust after the fruits of this world, but only one of us can create, only one, and he does not share that power. So we slither from the Otherside, to bask in the real. Of course, such a transition comes at a price. Where we were once beings of glory, in this world we are disjointed nightmares, forced to feed on that beyond food, bound by the rules of this universe and the next. We are so jealous of this world, so inspired and captivated, yet we can never truly understand it. Any form we take here refuses to sit well in the stomachs of mortals.'

'But you,' Phillos said, 'you do not look so terrible.'

'And yet you tremble before me.'

Phillos shuddered as the God glared. The eyes of this golden man did not belong.

The God continued. 'Only those most shameful creatures made the journey; be grateful that you stand before me and not them. As for those whose pain lives forever within those books, fear not, their stories are just beginning. Yours, however, is at an end.'

Phillos' face bulged and dropped. He edged towards the door, slowly, trying his best to keep his platform silent. The hostility was clear, he needed out.

'So that's it?' Phillos said. 'You go back, change history, and this reality ceases to exist?'

'If it's deletion you fear then allow me to reassure you: I've no doubt you will rise again, in a similar but different form. You have been too integral for fate to just cast aside. You might even live a life worth living.'

'But no! I don't want to sacrifice myself just so suffering can continue! Even if you do destroy these other demons, what about the mortals? War will go on just the same. Disease and murder are not an exclusively spiritual thing.'

'Stop.'

Phillos' transport stalled. The Librarian tugged on the analogue stick but it broke off in his hand.

'This universe is a short one, Phillos,' the God said.

'You don't know me. Don't say my name.'

'It may reach endlessly but it is short. It is confined to those who exist within it, and they only ever experience the minutest fraction. The universe is only as large and long as a solitary life living within it. Some live happily, some live in sorrow, most don't truly live at all. But I will not let it fade into nothing, as it already has. *Nothing* is the death of hope.'

'But you want the entire spectrum to remain, the good and the evil.'

'I want the world to live, to embrace the restraints of life and conquer them, to be rewarded with its riches, riches I can never know. Trust me when I say immortality is a far more empty existence, even than yours. This short universe is the ideal, and I will do what I can to restore it.'

'And what of me?'

'As I said: Your story ends here.'

Phillos remembered the burning book and feared that he would be next.

'Before, you mentioned ten stories?' Phillos said. 'I only read nine.' The Librarian pulled a switch that released the suction holding his flab in place around the ring of the hovercraft. Judging by how those other stories went, he didn't want to stick around.

The God craned his neck. 'You are living the tenth.'

'Then my story continues,' Phillos said, refusing to accept that this was it.

'It continues and ends here. Your purpose was to summon me, and the ritual that has led to my presence here concludes with the trading of your soul for mine. I am but a guest in your world without it. Unjust? I know. I too am sickened to be bound by the same sustenance as my brothers.'

'You're a monster. The same as all the others! You care about the whole but not the singular. Not *me*. What's the point?'

'What is your point, your purpose then? That I should spare it for all existence?'

'The point is I have work to do! Managing the Great Library by yourself is no easy task, you know.'

'A moot task. Sacrifices must be made.'

He waved a hand and two more humanoid shapes joined them in the Library. They were shorter than the God, their metallic frames without the same shimmer. Their heads looked spongy and soft and deformed. Phillos had met them before and was disheartened to see there were two rather than one.

'They made sacrifices,' the God said, 'mutilated themselves in order to cross over, so that they might lead you to this lower Library and awaken me; difficult to read the stories themselves without faces. Once so beautiful, now hideous, all because it was the right thing to do. I'm thankful for what you have done, but not having lived a real life, this universe will not miss you. It did not even see you. I'm sorry.'

'You're not sorry.'

Phillos pushed his chubby self out of the hovercraft using all four of his arms. His globbiness splatted against the marble floor. Glowing pink, he pushed the sharp sting to the back of his mind and began dragging himself into the corridor. His belly squeaked and burned against it, and he moved so slowly that the God and his two followers had barely taken a few casual steps before overtaking him.

'Do not take this the wrong way,' the God said, 'I am giving your life purpose. You've experienced more emotion these past few hours than you had your entire life.'

Phillos replied between exhausted moans, 'Everything you've said... Everything you've said is wrong. I will not die. I have work to do.'

'I know you disagree, but I am the one with the power, so the decision lies with me. The world will live on.'

Phillos watched the shimmering figure of the God waltz away into the depths of the Library, without a care, without turning back. Four cold hands plunged into Phillos' spine and the Librarian felt, all of a sudden, remarkably empty for someone who apparently *hadn't lived a real life*.

THE AUTHOR

Joshua Radburn is an independent author of Horror, Science Fiction, and Fantasy. He studied Computer Animation Arts at Bournemouth University, and has had middling stints as a graphic designer, teacher, and personal trainer. He lives in Berkhamsted, Hertfordshire, with his wife and daughter.

With nowhere else to go, his wife and daughter graciously suffer the intrinsic quirks found in those who struggle with the monotony of day to day life, as the author pursues the intangible riches of creation . . .

To keep informed of his frantic attempts to escape reality, you can sign up to his non-invasive mailing list at *joshuaradburnauthor.com*, or interact with Josh on:

Twitter (@AuthorJDRadburn)
Instagram (@theblondjosh)
Facbook (AuthorJoshuaRadburn)